LARCUM MUDGE

LARCUM MUDGE

BY

PHILIP K ALLAN

Larcum Mudge by Philip K Allan

ISBN-13: 9798638972721

Cover design by Christine Horner
Edited by Dr Catherine Hanley

Dedication

To my mother, who never got to read her son's novels

Acknowledgements

Success as an author requires the support of many. My books start with my passion for the age of sail, which was first awakened when I discovered the works of C S Forester as a child, and later when I graduated to the novels of Patrick O'Brian. That interest was given some academic rigor when I studied the 18th century navy under Patricia Crimmin as part of my history degree at London University.

Many years later, I decided to leave my career in the motor industry to see if I could survive as a writer. I received the unconditional support and cheerful encouragement of my darling wife and two wonderful daughters. I first test my work to see if I have hit the mark with my family, and especially my wife Jan, whose input is invaluable.

One of the pleasures of my new career is the generous support and encouragement I continue to receive from my fellow writers. In theory we are in competition, but you would never know it. When I have needed help, advice and support, I have received it from David Donachie, Bernard Cornwell, Marc Liebman, Jeffrey K Walker, Helen Hollick and Ian Drury. I have received particular help from my friends Peter Northern, Alaric Bond, creator of the Fighting Sail series of books and Chris Durbin, author of the Carlisle & Holbrooke Naval Adventures.

This book is my first venture into self-publishing, something I told myself I would never do. It has only been made possible with the help of Dr Catherine Hanley's excellent editing, and Christine Horner's splendid cover design. Whether this is the first of many, or only a brief foray, I will always be grateful to Michael James, and the team at Penmore Press, for having the faith in me to publish my first seven novels.

Cast of Main Characters

The Crew of the Frigate *Griffin*

Alexander Clay – Captain RN

George Taylor – First lieutenant
John Blake – Second lieutenant
Edward Preston – Third lieutenant
Thomas Macpherson – Lieutenant of marines

Jacob Armstrong – Sailing master
Richard Corbett – Surgeon
Charles Faulkner – Purser

Nathaniel Hutchinson – Boatswain
Josh Andrews – Boatswain's mate, who formerly served on the *Peregrine*

Able Sedgwick – Captain's coxswain

Sean O'Malley – Able seaman
Adam Trevan – Able seaman
Larcum Mudge – Able seaman
Samuel Evans – Seaman

In Antigua

Sir George Montague – Rear admiral commanding in the

Leeward Islands
John Sutton – Commander of the sloop of war *Echo*.
Married to Clay's sister Betsey
Stephen Camelford – Commander of the sloop of war *Daring*

In Lower Staverton

Lydia Clay – Wife of Alexander Clay
Francis Clay – Their son

Others

John Jervis, Earl St Vincent – First Lord of the Admiralty
Jack Broadbent – A mutineer
John 'Tombstone' Graves – A mutineer

Contents

Philip K Allan

Prologue

It was a warm night in the Mona Passage, with a gentle breeze blowing in from the Atlantic. Off to one side lay the island of Hispaniola, a presence crouching across the horizon. The moon hung in the clear sky, its light frosting the rigging and topsails of the Royal Navy sloop *Peregrine* as she slipped through the dark water, leaving swirls of phosphorescence behind her. The windows of her stern cabin were aglow with lamplight, where her captain caroused with some of his officers. On the deck above, the officer of the watch stood beside the quartermaster, their faces lit by the faint glow from the compass binnacle. Farther forward the ship seemed strangely quiet. The planking on her forecastle was divided between silver triangles of moonlight, and deeper patches of shade in which most of her crew had gathered in silence.

'Lay aside your arms, and drink your fill of knock-me-down, lads,' urged John Graves, a hulking seaman with a long, puckered scar across his face. 'You'll be wanting some Dutch courage, presently.'

He handed the first of the earthenware jars to one of the waiting sailors. The night filled with the clink and rattle of muskets and cutlasses being placed on the deck, followed by the gentle popping of cork stoppers.

The lean face and thick sideburns of Jack Broadbent appeared from beneath the shade of his hat as he tilted his head back. The others watched him drink his fill, his Adam's apple working. 'Ah! That be a nice drop of grog, Tombstone,' he commented at last, wiping his mouth on his shirt sleeve and passing the heavy container on to the next man. 'Better than the gut-rot that arse of a purser serves. Thank'ee kindly.'

'How did you come by it?' asked one of the other sailors.

'You after turning your nose up at a mug of rum, Seamus O'Connell?' queried Graves, to quiet laughter. 'That's a bleeding first. If you has to know, I took it from the wardroom pantry.'

'Might have known they'd have the good stuff,' spluttered another of the crew, rum dripping from his chin. 'Strange to tell, but it being lifted do give it a better savour.'

'Oh, I have been a naughty boy this night,' chuckled Graves, as he handed out another jar. 'Stealing from the Grunters, on top of breaking into the arms chest.'

'Both of them be hanging matters, Tombstone,' cautioned another voice, a silver-haired veteran with a pigtail that reached his waist.

'There'll be no more call for hanging aboard the *Peregrine* after tonight, Old Ben,' explained Graves. 'Nor any flogging neither. We've had our fill of the cat, ain't we lads? Now it's that bastard Daniels's turn, may he burn in hell for what he's done.'

'Hear him!' rumbled the sailors, as the drink started to take hold.

'I ain't so sure about this,' said a younger sailor, the jar of rum untouched on the deck before him.

'There be no shame in feeling shy afore such deeds as we be minded to do,' said Graves. 'But grog will serve in place of courage, so just you drink up.'

'What did Daniels give you them two dozen for last week, lad?' asked O'Connell.

'Leaving a gasket untied on the mizzen topsail,' he

replied. 'I were that flustered, I clean forgot.'

'One line untied, no harm done, and I dare say you only forgot 'cause you didn't want to cop it for being last man down ag'in?' said Graves.

'Aye, ain't that the truth of it,' said the youngster. 'Maybe I will have a drop of that rum.'

'Floggings for trifles, day after day,' continued Graves, his voice rasping with anger. 'Two good men dead after falling from aloft in their haste to avoid the lash. An' what does that devil of a captain do? Has 'em pitched into the sea for the sharks to feast on, without so much as a Christian word spoke over them.'

'I'd like to toss Daniels to the fecking sharks, so I would,' growled O'Connell.

'So you shall, Seamus, and here be my hand upon it,' said Graves, before turning to the others. 'Life on board ain't going to change any, lest we make it so, lads. Which of us on this cursed ship ain't been flogged by Daniels on a whim? An' which of us will he spare tomorrow?'

'None, and that's the bleeding truth,' said another voice.

'What of the Lobsters, Tombstone?' asked the tall figure of Broadbent, who stood back from the others, leaning against the foremast. 'Them is trained in proper soldiering, an' all.'

Graves smiled at this. 'Don't you go a fretting over them, any. Their Grunter's below, dying of the Yellow Jack, and that fool of a corporal couldn't find a tit in a whorehouse. With no direction, they'll be meek as lambs. Most of them'll be with us, and the rest shan't lift a finger.'

'What happens once the ship be ours?' queried a voice. 'Ain't the navy sure to track us down?'

'They can hang me, if they chose, so long as I can throttle Daniels first,' snarled another. 'I've had my fill of his ways.'

'You'll have to beat me to him, Josh!' exclaimed another voice.

Graves glanced back towards the quarterdeck, and held up his hands to quieten the crowd. 'None of us need swing for this, if we plays matters right,' he urged. 'Look around you, lads! Ain't no one to mark what we do this night, save ourselves. Once the ship be ours, we shall vanish into the heart of the Caribee, like summer mist. It'll be the hurricano season afore long. Those arses will just reckon we must have foundered.' Sailors muttered their approval at this, others banged the deck, the volume of sound rising as the rum took hold.

'Steady, lads', urged their leader. 'Keep the noise down.'

'But where shall we go an' bleeding hide, Tombstone?' asked another of the sailors. 'When it comes on to blow, like.'

'Over yonder be the Frogs on Guadeloupe,' said Graves, pointing towards the east. 'After the barky be ours, we shall trade it to them. Nice sloop like this'll earn us a hatful of chink each. Then we all changes our names and swears to never mention the *Peregrine* or what we done again. If every man here holds his tongue, we'll be safe enough.'

'And then where shall we fecking go?' asked O'Connell.

'We be sailors, ain't we?' said Graves. 'Frog privateers in Guadeloupe will take any jack as can hand, reef an' steer. No end of work with the Yanks, an' all.'

'That be true, lads,' agreed Broadbent, who continued

to listen to the exchange from the edge of the group. 'I was pressed off a New Bedford whaler. They be always short of hands, with no master too fussed 'bout where you hails from.'

'An' what of the navy, Tombstone?' asked Old Ben. 'What will they do when they gets to hear of this? They got a proper long reach.'

Graves pulled off his hat and leant close to the others. His face was stone-hard in the moonlight, the eyes fierce above his scar. 'It's like I said. Every man changes his name, and holds his tongue,' he said. 'If we all does that, how will tidings reach them?'

'What of the loyal hands, or the other fecking Grunters?' asked O'Connell. 'They'll talk, readily enough.'

'None so silent as they what cannot speak. Them as ain't with us, can't see the dawn.' He held out his hand, palm down. 'Swear it!'

'But some of them midshipmen be no more than nippers,' protested Old Ben.

'You want to spend another day serving under that bastard?' asked Graves. 'Coz I bleeding don't!'

Graves glared around the forecastle, and one by one the men placed their hands in the ring. After a long pause, Old Ben added his, which left only Broadbent, still leaning against the foremast, the expression on his face lost beneath the shade of his hat.

'You with us, Jack?' growled O'Connell. 'Or you going to stand with that fecker Daniels?'

'I'll be the first to strike that bastard down, right enough,' said the sailor. 'But I ain't going to kill no nipper.'

'Too damned high and mighty for dirty work, is it?' said Graves, spitting to one side and fingering the hilt of his cutlass.

O'Connell held his arm, and bent across to whisper in his ear. 'We needs him, Tombstone,' he murmured. 'The lads look up to him. We've enough fecking hot-heads soaked in grog to do the slaughtering.'

Graves considered this, while continuing to glare at Broadbent. Then he shrugged his shoulders. 'You play me false, and I'll strike you dead with my own bleeding hands, Jack Broadbent,' he threatened. 'The rest of you keep at the grog. It'll give you heart for what's to come.'

Another half hour of steady drinking and the men on the forecastle were all fighting drunk. From the stern cabin a burst of laughter accompanied the crash of a chair being knocked over.

'Them Grunters sound proper pissed, an all,' commented O'Connell. 'They've no notion of what we're about.'

'Ain't that the truth,' agreed Graves, a smile spreading across his face. 'This is going to be a deal easier than I thought. On your feet, lads, and let's be at them! Now be our time!'

Chapter 1
Recruiting

Captain Alexander Clay stood in the tight little basement room and looked around with distaste. The space would have been uncomfortable for him at the best of times. Even with his head stooped, his curly chestnut hair brushed the beams that ran across the ceiling. All the benches and shelves about him were piled high with stacks of printed paper, demijohns of dark liquid and boxes of assorted letter blocks. The walls were smeared with ink, as were most of the flat surfaces, and the atmosphere was damp and musty. Looking through the grimy window, he found he was at eye level with the pavement outside. The boots and shoes of passers-by clattered past; the number of feet multiplied by each little diamond-shaped pane of glass.

He had declined the stained chair that Mr Rashford had offered him, and instead stood holding his Royal Navy uniform coat close, so as to avoid it collecting any ink from the furniture. While he waited, he looked over some examples of the printer's work stacked ready to be collected. The nearest pile was of song sheets. *The Rambling Sailor – A Ballad of the Sea* was picked out in copperplate letters across the top. Intrigued, he read on.

Larcum Mudge

I am a sailor stout and bold,
Long time I've ploughed the ocean;
I've fought for king and country too,
Won honour and promotion.

'Ain't rambling the word,' muttered Clay, eyeing the multitude of verses that followed the first, before moving on to glance over some of the other stacks. There were political pamphlets, deploring the price of grain or the intrusion of the new census; flyers announcing various events, from a local fair to an Abolitionist meeting; and bills advertising all manner of products. There were also a depressing number of naval recruitment posters, just like the one that he had commissioned.

'Here we are, Captain,' announced Rashford, bustling in, 'and still wet from the press.' He spread out the sheet on the only empty space in the room, then stepped back, wiping his hands on his filthy apron and pushing his stained periwig a little straighter. Clay leant over the desk and examined the poster. The print quality was poor and some of the letters had smudged, but the large bold type was certainly legible.

GOD SAVE THE KING!

it began.

The mighty GRIFFIN, of 38 GUNS, currently lying at PLYMOUTH, is a new and uncommonly fine FRIGATE, returned triumphant from LORD NELSON'S most famous VICTORY over the PERFIDIOUS DANES before COPENHAGEN! Captain ALEXANDER CLAY, that famous SCOURGE of BONEY, commands her!

She awaits fresh ADVENTURE, as soon as some more GOOD HANDS are on board! None need apply but STOUT HEARTS, wishing for PRIZE MONEY by the HATFUL, able to rouse about the cannon, and carry an hundred weight of PEWTER, without stopping, at least three miles.

In the place where this notice is displayed may be found an officer of the GRIFFIN, with a BOUNTY for any men of SPIRIT who thirst for GLORY!

S. Rashford, Printer, Wardour Street, Plymouth.

It was well crafted, if rather deceitful, thought Clay to himself. That reference to carrying pewter, naval slang for silver bullion, hinted at a voyage after Spanish treasure, even though Clay had yet to learn where his ship might be sent next. There was also no mention of the casualties the *Griffin* had suffered at Copenhagen, leaving him so under-manned that he was having to send his officers out into the countryside to recruit volunteers, armed with this very poster. His sleep was still haunted by images of the waves of Danish boarders who had clawed their way onto his frigate, and the desperate and bloody hand-to-hand fight that had followed.

'Will it work, I wonder,' mused Clay, as he read through the wording one more time. He settled his pale grey eyes on the printer.

'Oh, for certain it will, sir!' said Rashford, with a burst of enthusiasm. 'We do no end of such sheets in these times, what with the shortage of good sailors. Most flyers answer well enough, especially those for frigates. I don't doubt you'll find enough prime hands. It's captains trying to man ships of the line for the blockade that struggle. After so many years of war, the press gangs have run dry. Gaol bait and ne'er-do-wells is all they can generally find, God help them. Not that I don't appreciate the work, but I do sometimes think that peace can't come soon enough.'

'It takes two to dance a reel, Mr Rashford,' said Clay. 'The French have to be willing to play their part.' He returned to the poster and came to a decision. 'Kindly strike me off a gross, as soon as may be convenient.'

'It shall be done this very morn, Captain,' said the printer, 'the moment I have completed an urgent commission for the port admiral. His messenger has just now brought it across. Details of some mutineers who are being hunted.'

'Mutineers?' queried Clay. 'From a king's ship? I have not heard of any such incident.'

'If it's of interest, I have the particulars here,' said Rashford, plunging a hand deep into the pocket of his apron and dredging out a sheet of paper. He next produced a pair of spectacles, barely cleaner than the window, and hooked them over his ears. 'They are sought from a man-of-war by the name of *Peregrine* for rebellion and murder. Goodness! The Admiralty are not stinting in the matter of the reward on offer. The main part is a list of the malefactors, headed by one called John Graves, and another by the name of Seamus O'Connell. Ha! I might have known that a papist would be at the root of such mischief. Please make free to examine the message, if you care to.' He held out the ink-smudged paper.

'My thanks, but no,' said Clay. 'I had heard tell of the *Peregrine*, but I thought her reported lost with all hands in a storm last year. Somewhere in the Leeward Islands, if I remember rightly.'

'I am sure you understand such matters best, Captain,

but the ship's name is set out quite plain,' said Rashford, tapping the note.

'Doubtless all will be made clear,' said Clay, putting on his hat. 'Kindly have those posters sent across to my ship. Ask for Mr Taylor, my first lieutenant, who will attend to them. I must go to the George directly, or I small miss the London coach.'

'Ah, orders for you waiting at the Admiralty, I don't doubt, now that your ship is out of the dockyard. They have done a tolerable job at repairing her bow,' said the printer.

Clay looked at him aghast. 'How in all creation do you …' he spluttered.

'Oh, take no notice of me, sir,' chuckled Rashford. 'This is Plymouth, after all. The affairs of the navy are our business. Half the town supply it and the rest serve in it.'

'Is that so?' sniffed Clay. 'Well, I bid you a good day, Mr Rashford. I must go and collect those orders you speak of, unless, perchance, you know their content already, and can save me the trouble of my journey?'

'Ha ha, very witty,' laughed the printer, 'although I should have your purser lay in some warm-weather slops, if I were you.' He touched the side of his nose, leaving a fresh smudge of ink. 'Have a prosperous voyage, Captain.' Rashford held out a filthy hand, and after a moment of hesitation, Clay took it.

*****

'Earl St Vincent is ready to see you, sir,' said the elderly clerk, bobbing his wigged head at the mention of the First Lord of the Admiralty's name. 'Perhaps you would be good enough to follow me?' Clay placed his glass of madeira down on the table beside his chair and rose to his feet.

'Thank you, Higgins,' he replied. He followed the older man down a long, panelled corridor, lined with the portraits of previous First Lords. Eyes stared down at him from both sides, seeming to follow him as he walked. Some were figures from an earlier age, their faces framed by cascades of curling hair, while others he recognised from his own career. There was Lord Keppel, his sunken cheeks hinting at the empty gums they concealed, every tooth lost to the scurvy he contracted as a midshipman. Next to him was Lord Howe, his honest blue eyes set deep beside his prominent nose. Last of all was Earl Spencer, dressed in the very height of fashion, just as Clay remembered him from his last visit to the Admiralty the previous year. Now there was a new incumbent in the office.

'How do you find labouring under his lordship?' asked Clay.

'Labouring is the very word, sir,' said the clerk. 'In truth, his lordship does seem in a perishing hurry to change all that his predecessor set in train.'

'I daresay there was much that need changing,' suggested Clay. 'Some of the naval contractors' practices would make a highwayman blush.'

'Aye, that may be so, sir,' conceded Higgins. 'But it goes far beyond that, as you will see for yourself, presently.' He knocked on the large double door, and without waiting for an answer, held it open for Clay, who walked into an office that had been transformed from his last visit.

Gone was the thick pile carpet underfoot, stripped away to reveal oak floorboards that looked to have been scrubbed that morning. Gone too were the gilt framed landscapes that had lined the walls of the room in Earl

Spencer's time. In their place were large maps painted on sheets of canvas showing the various oceans of the world. Behind the desk sat the brooding frame of Admiral John Jervis, Earl St Vincent, even stouter than when Clay had last seen him. His square, jowly face was as mirthless as he remembered. The strands of grey curly hair that framed it were thinner than before, but the eyes that watched Clay's approach were the same intense, china blue.

'Don't you approve of my taste in furnishings, Captain?' demanded the admiral.

'Eh, it is not really my place to voice approval or otherwise, my lord,' said Clay. 'But I confess I was a trifle taken aback by the changes since your predecessor's time.'

'That coxcomb Spencer?' snorted St Vincent. 'Aye, he left very little behind him that has met with my approval.' He stood up and gripped Clay's hand. 'It is good to meet with another fighting man, among all these scraping clerks and bowing flunkies. Pray be seated.'

'Thank you, my lord,' said Clay. 'Do I collect you are minded to reform the service?'

'Not the sailing part, but matters ashore,' explained the First Lord. 'We are at war, yet what do I find? Criminal sloth and corruption in every place I care to look. Emoluments here, perquisites there. I tell you, Captain, left unchecked, the rogues would swallow up all the means of the country, to the ruin of us all.'

'I am pleased to find the navy in such capable hands, my lord.'

'This a fighting service, Captain,' said the First Lord. 'A fact that seems to have been forgot in this building. If oak underfoot is good enough for our ships, then it will serve for me. Do you know that Spencer even had a mirror concealed in that alcove there, so he could check upon his countenance like some damned harlot, the popinjay!'

Clay looked towards the place beside the desk. He remembered the oval mirror that had hung there. In its place was a long glass barometer and a brass tell-tale disc with an arrow to relay the wind direction from the weathervane on the Admiralty roof. When he returned his attention to St Vincent, he saw those appraising blue eyes were on him again.

'I see you are a senior post captain now,' he said, his gaze resting on the second epaulette that lay on Clay's left shoulder. 'How old are you?'

'I shall be three and thirty presently, my lord.'

'You have done well, to have obtained such a rank at your age, without the benefits of preferment,' said St Vincent. 'War is a good time for finding the able and exposing the indifferent.'

'And in which camp would you place me, my lord?'

'The able, for the present,' said the admiral, making the compliment sound like a threat. 'Which is why I have sent for you. Is that *Griffin* of yours repaired?'

'Just returned from the dockyard,' said Clay. 'A week or so of work will have her ready for sea.'

'Good, because I have chosen you for a particular service. I had thought that we had dealt with the blight of mutiny back in ninety-seven, but I was wrong. It would seem that the crew of one of our ships has forgotten their duty to their king and risen in bloody rebellion.' He brought a fist the size of a modest ham down on the desk, causing his writing stand to jolt.

'Would that be the crew of the *Peregrine*, my lord?' asked Clay. 'There were posters seeking them when I left Plymouth.'

'Quite so,' confirmed St. Vincent, blotting up a little spilt ink. 'She was on patrol off Hispaniola last July but failed to return to Antigua. Sir George Montague, who commands the Leeward Island squadron – you know him, of course?'

'I served under Sir George two years back, in the Indian Ocean, my lord.'

'So you did,' said the admiral. 'He was unable to institute an immediate search, on account of poor weather. A damned savage hurricane passed through the Leeward Islands the following month. When it had gone, there was no trace of the *Peregrine*. Montague assumed she had foundered, and reported the same. There the matter might have rested, but the ill deeds of the wicked always come to the surface in time, Captain.'

St Vincent pulled a page of notes towards him and consulted them. 'The *Cyclops* captured a French privateer off Cork last month,' he continued. 'Captain Fyffe grew suspicious concerning four of the crew, who were plainly not Frenchmen. Fyffe is a shrewd cove, so he questioned them apart. They all confessed to being Royal Navy deserters, sharp enough, but none of their stories bore much scrutiny. One claimed to have run from the frigate *Thames*, for example, but couldn't name her officers correctly. The privateer had papers signed by the governor of Guadeloupe, yet two of them swore blind that they had never been near the Caribbean. Captain Fyffe threatened to string the deceitful vermin up, and when the first of them felt the hemp about his throat, he resolved to tell all.'

The First Sea Lord rose to his feet and walked across to the window. It opened onto the courtyard below, where clerks and naval officers passed to and fro. 'It is a truly dreadful tale, Captain,' he continued, towards the glass. 'The hands had become enraged from a combination of stolen rum and imagined grievances. First Captain Daniels was murdered. Then they searched through the ship for the officers, butchering them as they went, and tossing their bodies into the water. None were spared, not even the midshipmen, the youngest of whom was but fourteen. He was found cowering beneath a table. Even Lieutenant MacDonald of the marines, who was certain to die in any event from the Yellow Jack, was dragged up from the sick berth and killed.'

'Were there no loyal hands, my lord?' asked Clay.

'If there were, they were too frit to oppose the rebellion,' said St Vincent, returning to his desk. 'The mutineers made it plain that none who stood against them would survive the night. Those who led them on were damned shrewd. When the *Peregrine* was in their possession, they sailed south into open water and waited for the start of the season of hurricanes. Once they were certain our cruisers would have been obliged to withdraw, they headed to Guadeloupe. Of course, the damned Frogs welcomed them as brothers, agreed to purchase the ship, and not to crow about our loss.'

'So does the *Peregrine* remain in their hands then, my lord?' asked Clay.

'I believe so, Captain, although doubtless they will have changed her appearance and name. I have found a steady cove who served on her long before all of this, whom I shall transfer to the *Griffin*. He is a boatswain's mate by the name of Andrews, who was six years aboard, so he should recognise her. I take it you are still short-handed?'

'We suffered badly at Copenhagen, but I have my officers out seeking volunteers, and I have hope that the press will supply the rest, my lord,' explained Clay. 'What is it that you would have me do – track down the mutineers?'

'You can leave them to me,' growled the First Lord. 'Now I am aware what they are about, they will not long escape vengeance. Every agent and officer in our employ will be hunting for them. The wages of Judas will tease them out, I make no doubt. No, it is the stain of the ship itself that I need you to expunge. While it remains in French hands, it will be a constant affront to the dignity of our king.'

'I believe I understand, my lord. What are my orders to be?'

'Complete your preparations for the *Griffin* to depart by the end of the month,' said St Vincent. 'You will come under the command of Sir George in Antigua. Is your brother-in-law not serving there?'

'Captain Sutton? Yes, he commands the *Echo*. It shall be good to see him once more.'

'I doubt you will have much occasion for fraternising,' rumbled the First Lord. 'Peace is coming, Clay. The government is broke, the land tax can go no higher, and the last harvest was very indifferent. Addington is minded to ask for a truce, and from what I hear, Boney wants the same. I need that ship recaptured or destroyed while we are yet at war. Go and wipe that stain on our honour clean.'

*****

A lively crowd was milling through West Street in Tavistock. It was market day, and the warm Devon sunshine had done much to empty the surrounding villages and crofts. Shepherds had driven their spring lambs down from the purple hills of Dartmoor that loomed above the town. Tradesmen and entertainers had been arriving up the Plymouth road since long before dawn. Both sides of the street were lined with booths and trestles, all laden with wares. One stall had a display of buttons and coloured ribbons, the next a collection of farming implements. A little farther along the road a queue had formed beside the tented enclosure where Mistress Certainty promised to use her fortune-telling powers to predict the weather to farmers, the sex of the unborn to wives, and the faithfulness of lovers to maidens.

Halfway along West Street was the Queen's Head tavern. In front of the building stood a Royal Marine officer with dark hair and magnificent black sideburns, contemplating a poster that had been pasted on the wall beside the entrance. Behind Lieutenant Thomas Macpherson's back, his scarlet tunic and trim figure were attracting admiring glances from the passing milkmaids and serving wenches. Standing close beside him was a respectful group of four men. Their shirts were richly decorated, and they all wore the high-waisted trousers and short jackets of sailors. On their heads were wide-brimmed hats, each crown encircled by a band of dark material with the word *Griffin* painted on it.

'Are we certain this wee flyer will be seen from yon thoroughfare?' mused Macpherson, in his gentle Highland drawl. He eyed the narrow gap that had been left in the row of stalls in front of the inn.

'If your honour is worried, like, we could take our ease out here, sir,' suggested Sean O'Malley, a wiry Irish sailor with curly dark hair. 'Some jacks in shore-going rig in this dump will be certain to cause a stir. Half the colleens have been giving me the eye this last hour or more.'

'Regrettably there is not much call for your female admirers in the navy, O'Malley, but having you four out in front of the alehouse is a worthy suggestion,' said the marine.

'Very well, Sedgwick, you're in charge. Bring any suitable volunteers through to me in the snug.'

'Aye aye, sir,' said a heavily built, handsome man with dark hair and eyes, and an air of authority about him. Once Macpherson had gone inside, the sailors brought up chairs and sat back in the sunshine.

'Ain't this the life,' said O'Malley, placing his hands behind his head and rocking backwards. 'It beats scrubbing decks afore dawn, with Harrison breathing down our fecking necks, to be sure. You lads can owe me for suggesting it.'

The others settled in a row along the sunlit wall beneath the poster, and tilted their hats over their eyes against the light as they watched the market crowd drift by. One figure soon detached himself from the mass and approached to read the poster. This appeared to be a troublesome task for him. He leant across and ran a large, none-too-clean finger beneath each word, his lips mouthing them as he did so. He was a solid-looking young man, in his late teens with wild, straw-coloured hair and the start of a little golden fluff where a beard would one day grow. His leggings and smock marked him out as a farm labourer. He reached the end of the poster and turned to the sailors.

'You be recruitin' for thar navy, like?' he asked, his accent pure Devon. One of the seamen, who had a long blond pigtail and clear blue eyes, rose to his feet, removed the clay pipe he had been smoking and held his hand out. 'That we are,' he replied. 'My name be Adam Trevan, and I be a sailor aboard the *Griffin*.'

'Oh, you be Cornish!,' exclaimed the labourer.

'Aye, there be a few of us as is jacks,' confirmed Trevan. 'A good few from Devon, an' all. You been to sea, like?'

'Oh lord, no!' exclaimed the potential recruit. 'Watering the cattle in thar Tavy and taking a plunge in Farmer Guthridge's duck pond be the most water I've come by. No, I ain't never set eyes on it, although I hear tell it be mighty large.'

'Only a touch bigger than you're accustomed to,' conceded O'Malley, joining the conversation. 'But a man as has endured Guthridge's pool will have nothing to fear from the fecking ocean.'

'Ain't the navy burdensome?' continued the local. 'With floggin' and storms an' the like?'

'Burdensome?' queried the Irishman. 'Will yer look at the fine specimens of manhood afore yous?' He jerked a thumb towards the fourth sailor, a colossus, six foot six tall and built like the prize-fighter he had once been. 'Feast your eyes on your man Sam Evans there, standing as tall as a fecking elm. Goliath ain't in it! Would you believe that he was shorter than me not six year ago, when he left the slums of London town to go to sea.'

'He do seem uncommon large,' agreed the potential recruit.

'Come close, and I'll tell you his secret,' whispered O'Malley, drawing the youngster to him with an arm around his shoulder. 'He gives me his grog every day and downs a draft of seawater in its place.'

'Do he now?' marvelled the labourer, running a hand over his chin. 'I'd like to be so lofty.'

Sedgwick disentangled O'Malley's arm from around the youngster, and took him to one side.

'Don't you a go heeding Sean, overly,' he advised. 'He's after making game of you. Nor what be marked down on recruiting posts, neither. I'm Able Sedgwick, coxswain to our captain, and I'll tell you how it is, straight. Our *Griffin*'s a happy enough ship, and if you works hard and follows the rules, you'll do fine. The pay's fair, and we does alright for prize money and vittles. It don't signify if you ain't been to sea. Sam there was a proper lubber when he joined, and I'm a run slave from Barbados. We ain't done so bad.'

'Ah, that'll explain you looking like a Moor,' said the man.

'You'll encounter stranger folk than me on the lower deck, lad,' continued Sedgwick. 'Including some as is proper Moors. Now, just you attend to the stuff as ain't so fine. Listen with care, for once I take you to make your pledge before Mr Macpherson, that'll be that. You can only leave the ship when the Grunters let you; if you're slack you'll be started with a rope's end; the captain can flog you if he be so minded; and you'll be away from home for months, maybe years at a time. All of that, and the odd battle to be fought, an' all.'

'Away for months, be it?' enthused the labourer. 'Thar sounds grand! I could proper use getting clear of these parts.'

'What you been an' done, lad?' asked Trevan.

'I ain't in no trouble with the law,' said the youngster. 'It just be Grace in the dairy. She be getting proper heavy now, an' says as how she's after telling her Pa it was me what done it. He ain't the sort you want to cross, so I reckon I'll chance it. Where be this Macpherson bloke?'

'Is this wench's Pa to be dreaded above a Frog broadside?' queried Evans. The new recruit nodded. 'Bleeding hell, he must be a brute. Welcome on board.'

Sedgwick took the young man inside the Queen's Head, while the other sailors settled back in their chairs to discuss the new shipmate.

'Where would the fecking navy be without fools to

recruit,' chuckled O'Malley. 'Your man works on a farm, for the love of God! You'd think he'd know how fornication works.'

'Oh aye, listen to Parson O'Malley, will you,' commented Evans. 'I didn't see you showing much bleeding restraint last bawdy house we was in.'

'If you ask me, I reckon he should be standing by this lass,' said Trevan, shaking his head. 'How would my Molly have fared, if I'd left her to the parish in such a fashion?'

'I see the navy be still fond of hoodwinking ploughboys with tales of glory,' said a voice. They turned to see a tall, spare man regarding them. He had been lolling unnoticed against the tavern wall, listening to their talk. He was dressed as a sailor who had prospered. A moleskin waistcoat lay behind his short jacket, his pigtail was secured by a velvet ribbon, and a hoop of gold glistened in one ear.

'We be happy to take experienced hands, an' all,' said Trevan. 'Although how the press ain't swept you up afore now be a proper marvel.'

'I prefers to volunteer and chose where I'll serve,' replied the man. He looked at the poster for a moment, and then shrugged his shoulders. 'Sorry lads, but I ain't got me letters. What ship be you from?'

'The *Griffin*, thirty-eight gun frigate,' said O'Malley. 'She be less than a year old, nice an' dry in a blow. Captain Alexander Clay has her at present.'

'Is he blessed with good fortune in the matter of prize money?' asked the man.

'Lucky bugger, for sure,' confirmed Evans. 'A proper deep one in battle, an' all. Ain't we followed him these last six years? This be the fourth ship we served with him.'

'So he ain't one of them tartars?' asked the man.

'Flogging on a whim, and the like?'

'Very fair is Pipe, for a fecking Englishman,' said O'Malley. 'Last commission there can't have been above a half dozen floggings, an' all was merited.'

'Where you been serving, like?' asked Trevan. 'You done alright from the look of you, what with your plush weskit an' all.'

'I been away on a Yankee whaler these past few years,' said the man. 'I done alright for myself, but that be a tough calling. Years away, fighting to subdue beasts, an' then rendering them down for their oil.'

'That be the truth,' said the Cornishman. 'I were two year on the old *Emilia* during the peace. So you going to trade battling fish for milling with Frogs? They be paying a bounty for them as volunteer.'

'Aye, that I do,' said the sailor. 'I reckon I shall try the navy, for a change.' He held out a hand calloused by years at sea. 'As we're to be shipmates now, the name is Mudge. Larcum Mudge.'

'Larcum Mudge?' queried Evans. 'What bleeding manner of name is that?'

'A right good one, I think you'll find, mate.'

Chapter 2
Prize

Clay stretched out his long legs inside the phaeton and wondered how long the journey would last. Through the window the lush green of Devon slowly rattled past, as it had done for the last two hours or more. They were clattering along a raised section of turnpike, cut into the hillside above the bank of a river. Willow trees hunched over the water and further back, on a rise in the ground, a small village was clustered around the stone spire of its church. Between river and village was a spread of water meadows, speckled with wild flowers and dotted with grazing brown and white cattle. Clay pondered the animals, and his mind turned towards casks of salt beef. I wonder if the victualling yard have replaced the last batch yet, he thought. Faulkner, his purser, had done well to realise they were being palmed off with meat that had been a good two years in the barrel. Space would need to be found for their replacements. Somewhere abaft the main mast would be best, if the trim of the ship was not to be sadly compromised.

'Alexander, I do not believe you have attended to what I have been saying this last quarter hour or more,' chided his wife, from the seat beside him.

'Your pardon Lydia, my dear,' he said, with a start. 'In truth, my thoughts had drifted a little, towards the matter of my ship's provisions.' He pointed at the cattle by way of justification. 'But I yet had an ear for you, my darling. Were you not telling me that you have placed a bundle of my sister's letters in the smaller chest, to deliver to her husband when I see him in Antigua? Goodness, but it will be good to see John again!' He favoured her with his most winning smile, but her blue eyes were hard as flint.

'No, I had completed my remarks on that matter shortly after we left Tiverton,' she said, folding her arms. Clay looked away in the hope of inspiration. On the driving seat in front of him was the broad back of his coxswain, handling the carriage's two horses with the accomplished ease with which he did most things. My son is going to miss Sedgwick, he thought. The sailor had returned from helping Lieutenant Macpherson a week ago and had proved an instant hit with the toddler. There had been tears from the boy when they had left Lower Staverton that morning, and Clay suspected they were not all on account of his parents' departure.

'You were speaking of Master Francis, were you not, my dear,' he guessed. 'And that lovely toy boat that Sedgwick carved for him.'

'I was not,' said Lydia. The corners of her generous mouth twitched a little as she tried to remain stern, a hard task when her son was under discussion.

'Then you must have been talking of his sister,' said Clay, cupping a hand over her belly, which was just starting to swell with the new life inside her.

'Alex!' said Lydia, scandalised at such talk, although she did nothing to remove his hand. He slipped his other arm around behind her and drew her to him.

'I beg your pardon, my dear,' he said. 'You have exposed me as the truant that I am, but you have my full attention now.' He kissed her on the mouth, and after a moment of resistance she melted against him.

'Oh Alex, I will so miss you,' she murmured, and he crushed her against him. After a few more miles she pushed him gently away. 'You must let me reorder my bonnet, before we reach the next post-house.' She looked at her reflection in the window, and prodded some of the streams of dark, glossy hair that had escaped back into place, while continuing to talk. 'What I was actually saying was that I have had a letter from my aunt.'

'Have you indeed,' said Clay. 'And how is Lady Ashton finding Bath?'

'Very agreeable, I thank you,' said Lydia. 'She is enjoying the society there, and reports that all the talk in the Assembly Rooms and salons is of peace with France. Isn't it wonderful? At last Betsey and I will have you and John back for more than a few weeks here and there.'

'That will be marvellous,' said Clay, patting her hand. 'Earl St Vincent did say as much when I saw him. But it is by no means certain yet, and even if it comes, I do wonder how long it will last. Boney doesn't strike me as the sort who will be content with his current size in hats.'

'But what I fail to comprehend is that if peace is to be declared so soon, why are you being dispatched to the Caribbean?' asked Lydia. 'Surely you will have to come home again as soon as you have arrived?'

'Well, as for that, a negotiated peace may well take a deal longer to arrange than you suppose,' said Clay. 'Consider how extended the conflict has been. We shall have to return some of the places we have captured, they will need to withdraw from others they hold. In the meantime, we must continue to press our enemy hard. The more we can achieve in the last few months of war, the stronger will be the government's negotiating hand.'

'I dare say that is true, but please don't go risking your neck in a war that has run its course, Alex,' said Lydia, her eyes welling up. 'You have responsibilities to those who await your return.'

'I have been given one more task to perform, and then, God willing, I shall return to you all,' he promised, taking her in his arms once more. They kissed again, with long, lingering passion as the miles rolled by.

It was only the sound of Sedgwick clearing his throat that brought them back into the present. 'I had thought to change these here cobs at the King's Head, sir,' he said, over his shoulder. 'But they be running so well they've served us right through to Plymouth.'

'Thank you, Sedgwick,' said Clay, noticing for the first time that the trees and fields were increasingly masked by houses. 'I fear your bonnet has become sadly disordered once more, my dear, but we have a little time for you to regain your composure.'

'Shall I go directly to the inn, sir?' asked Sedgwick. 'Or do you want the Hard, so as to get out to the *Griffin*?'

Lydia looked at him, her eyes bright, but her face calm. 'Go directly to your ship, Alex,' she said. 'It was good of you to delay leaving home as long as you did. There will be much for you to attend to, if you are to make your tide tomorrow. Sedgwick can see me to the Dolphin.'

'Are you certain?' he asked. 'I am sure Mr Taylor will have all the preparations in hand.'

'Duty before pleasure, isn't that how you would have it?' she replied with a smile. 'When you can, come to me. I shall be waiting.'

*****

Larcum Mudge

His Majesty's frigate *Griffin* left her moorings the following afternoon, just as the tide began to flood out into the Channel. She slipped down Plymouth Sound and out into the sunlit sea. It was a warm day, with the promise of a fine evening to follow. Only a few idlers joined the families of those on board to note her departure. Magnificent as the *Griffin* looked, so many ships had left the port over the last decade of war that one more made little stir. Lydia watched from the upper parlour of the Dolphin. She had wanted to go out onto the Hoe to see the frigate leave, but the landlady of the inn had been horrified at the thought. 'In your condition, madam!' she had exclaimed, her mobcap trembling with indignation. 'Why, it would be perilous for you up there.'

'I suppose I could take your ostler with me, if you're concerned,' said Lydia. 'He seems a solid lad, and he has a cudgel.'

'Lord, it ain't footpads as worry me, madam, but the air! Think of your child, exposed to all manner of chills and noxious miasmas! The view from your private parlour be every bit as good, and with a nice fire of sea coal, you'll be safe as can be.'

Lydia had thought of sharing with her that she still rode side-saddle most mornings, with little apparent ill effect, but decided it was best not to prompt a fresh torrent of protest. She felt empty of fight, as she faced yet another departure of her husband to the vagaries of war. She thought of their wedding - had it really been four years ago? Yet they had only spent a fraction of that time together. Long months alone, with barely any word from him. Now she was alone again, standing in the bay window of the parlour, gripping the curtain tight in one hand.

'Let him come home unharmed, and let this be the final furlong,' she whispered to herself in quiet prayer, as the frigate rounded Rame Head and vanished from her sight.

*****

A few weeks later, George Taylor, the *Griffin*'s grey-haired first lieutenant stood beside her wheel, balancing easily to the rise and fall of the deck beneath his feet. He looked around him, and was content with what he saw. The sky overhead was largely cloudless, the sun was warm and the broad ocean stretched out in a carpet of deep blue in every direction. The frigate had sailed sufficiently southward to have picked up the north-east trade winds, and was travelling westwards towards the Caribbean, her pyramids of white canvas spread wide to catch the keen air. She drove hard into each roller, her rebuilt bow butting the sea aside in wings of white foam.

'She makes good progress, does she not, sir,' said Edward Preston, the *Griffin*'s third lieutenant, who was officer of the watch. He was a handsome young man, with dark hair and eyes and a friendly looking face. With his right hand he gripped the top of the binnacle against the heel of the deck. His left sleeve was flat and empty, and was pinned across the front of his coat.

'She does,' agreed Taylor. 'We have a ship we can be proud of, Mr Preston.'

'Indeed so, sir. I wonder if I shall ever command such a frigate?'

'Would you like to, Edward?'

'Oh, above all things, sir,' enthused the younger man. 'Did you not ever wish for such a position?'

'I daresay I did, when I was a keen young officer of your age,' he said. 'I captained Whitby colliers, of course, during the peace after the American War. But now it is a little late for me, which is probably for the best.'

'Really, sir?' queried Preston. 'But you regulate the affairs of the ship so well.'

'That is kind of you to say. In truth, managing a large frigate like the *Griffin*, with two hundred and fifty souls on board, doesn't trouble me. Oak and iron, rope and sail, pitch and tar; all of these I understand well. It is the rest that would have me awake at nights.'

'What else is there, sir?'

'Have you not marked those slim packages of orders that arrived on board just before we depart?' said Taylor. 'The burdens they bring are legion. No, I am content to leave them to the captain, and concern myself with seeing that we are ready for whatever lies away yonder.' He gazed towards the silver horizon ahead, then over the side. 'How fast do you suppose we are proceeding?' he asked.

'We were doing eight knots by the last heave of the log, but I fancy we may be a touch more swift now, sir,' he reported, looking aloft at the ship's commissioning pennant as it streamed out from the masthead. 'If it should blow much stronger, we may need to reef the topgallants.'

'Perhaps so,' said Taylor. 'And what do you make of our new hands?'

'Better, ever since the clodhoppers Mr Blake recruited have stopped puking over the rail, sir,' grinned Preston. 'The endless sail drill we have put them through is starting to answer, and I live in hope a few may one day make sailors.'

'They are not all bumpkins, mind,' said the older man. He indicated where a tall, spare man stood among the afterguard, chatting with Evans. 'What do you make of that fellow?'

'Mudge?' said Preston, following his gaze. 'I would say he is a most valuable recruit, sir. I thought that we should rate him able, and trial him as a top man. Mr Hutchinson agrees. He holds his long splicing to be almost a match for his own.'

'High praise indeed from the boatswain,' said Taylor. 'I will make the suggestion to the captain.'

Both men turned from their appraisal of the new recruit as a lean young man with thinning sandy hair came up the companionway ladder and crossed the deck to join them. Clamped beneath his arm was a leather folder.

'Were your ears aflame, John?' asked Preston, with a smile for his fellow lieutenant. 'We were just discussing if any of the peasants you rounded up for us will ever bring a little credit on the ship.'

'Volunteers was what I was commissioned to scour Devonshire for, and volunteers was what I procured,' he protested. 'No one said that they should be sailors.'

'Are you planning on doing some sketching, Mr Blake?' asked Taylor, pointing at the leather folder. 'You may find it a little breezy up on the quarterdeck.'

'Not on this occasion, sir,' replied Blake. 'Although I do plan to do some painting this commission. The light in the Caribbean is so agreeable. No, I have the latest watch bill here. I was hoping to exercise some of the newer hands on the great guns this morning, if you gentlemen are done with driving them up and down the masts every other watch?'

'Sail drill is very important, Mr Blake,' said the first lieutenant. 'If we should meet dirty weather with half the crew unsure of their duties, their knowing how to handle the great guns will not aid us any.'

'With respect, nor will being able to strike our topmasts in a blow serve us any in a fight, sir,' said Blake.

'I might have known your precious guns would be behind your visit, John,' commented Preston. 'I sometime wonder if you prize them as you do wine or even women.'

'Wine and women!' scoffed Blake. 'Gunnery is far more important than either!'

'You have me convinced,' laughed Taylor, returning the watch list. 'You may exercise them until eight bells, but go steady until they all understand their parts, I pray. I don't want Mr Corbett complaining to me that you have filled his sick berth with crushed feet and hands.'

'Aye aye, sir,' said Blake, touching his hat. He drew a list of names from the folder and handed it across to the midshipman of the watch. 'Mr Russell, kindly take this list to the boatswain, with my compliments, and ask him to have all those named join me down on the main deck.'

A little while later the sound of Blake's voice, full of enthusiasm, came drifting up from beneath their feet, as he and his assistants started on the process of turning a collection of ploughboys, shepherds and labourers into Royal Navy gunners.

'And what of you, Mr Preston?' asked Taylor. 'I have yet to ask you about your trip home?'

'Yorkshire in the springtime is always pleasant, sir,' the officer replied.

'I dare say it is,' said the older man. 'But pray do not make sport of me. Did you not find time to enjoy the society of Miss Hockley at all?'

'I did indeed,' smiled the young man. 'We renewed our understanding, but we will not be wed quite yet. With all this talk of peace, we thought to wait until we have the leisure to be married in a proper fashion, rather than in haste during my two weeks of leave.'

'Very wise,' said Taylor. 'Let us hope the peace comes soon, then. I daresay you can barely recall not being at war, Mr Preston?'

'I was fifteen when it began, and just newly come to sea,' recalled the lieutenant. 'It will be strange not to be serving in the navy, but Sarah's father has promised me one of his trading brigs when we are married, so I shall not be quitting the sea just yet. What will you do, sir?'

'I fear I am a little old to return to the merchant service, Edward,' said Taylor. 'But I have some prize money put aside, enough to buy myself a little cottage and perhaps some land. With my half pay I dare say I will be able to live, in a modest way.'

The two officers were quiet for a moment, both lost in thoughts of what their respective futures might hold, while beneath their feet the frigate bounded across the ocean, rushing them ever forwards.

*****

'Sail ho!' bellowed the lookout, a few days later.

The officer of the watch was now Jacob Armstrong, the *Griffin*'s stout sailing master. He stepped to one side of the quarterdeck to give himself an uninterrupted view of the masthead. He inflated his considerable lungs, cupped one hand beside his mouth, and used the other to keep his hat and periwig in place as he angled his head back.

'Where away, Pedersen?' he roared, in an accent still heavy with the New England of his birth.

Larcum Mudge

'Two points off the larboard bow, sir,' replied the sailor. 'Topgallants just lifting over the horizon.'

'What do you make of her?'

'Small brig, I should say, sir,' replied the lookout. 'She looks to have hauled her wind, and is going about.'

'They don't care for the look of us, eh,' muttered Armstrong. He turned to one of the midshipmen standing by the wheel. 'My compliments to the captain, Mr Todd, and kindly tell him that there is a sail in sight.'

'Aye aye, sir,' said the youngster, touching his hat before scampering over to the ladderway. A few minutes later he returned with the tall figure of his captain on his heels.

'Is she in sight from the deck, Mr Armstrong?' he asked, pulling a telescope from its place beside the binnacle.

'Not yet, sir,' replied the sailing master. 'She was on a converging course, but turned away when she laid eyes on us.'

'I daresay that may mean very little,' mused Clay. 'Any trading brig would be warry of a strange sail, but it may signify something.' He passed the telescope across to the midshipman. 'Up you go, Mr Todd, and tell us what they are about, if you please.'

'Aye aye, sir,' replied the youngster, running for the mainmast shrouds.

'If she were one of ours, would you not have expected her to be in a convoy, sir?' asked the American.

'I would indeed, Mr Armstrong,' confirmed his captain. 'Which is why we must investigate. Kindly put us on a course to close with her, and have those reefs shaken out of the topgallants.'

With her towering masts and sleek hull, the *Griffin* would always have had the beating of a heavily laden brig. The keen trade wind was still blowing, and she rapidly began to overhaul the strange sail. Before long a little square of white was visible from the deck, rising above the horizon. It grew quickly as the frigate dashed across the sea towards her.

'Chase is setting more sail, sir!' reported Todd from the masthead.

'Is it me, Mr Armstrong, or is she setting that fore course in a very indifferent fashion,' Clay observed. Both men focused on the big white sail that had appeared, billowing and flapping in the wind.

'Like Old Mistress Allerton's washing,' muttered the American, once the sail was finally sheeted home. 'That was poorly done, even for the crew of a merchant ship, sir.'

'British colours, sir!' supplemented Todd from the masthead.

'Mr Russell, would you kindly make the private recognition signal for a merchantman,' ordered his captain.

'Aye aye, sir,' said the midshipman, making his way over to the flag locker.

'Deck there!' came Todd's cry once more. 'Her sails look damaged to me, sir. The foretopsail has a couple of rents in it.'

'So it does,' confirmed Armstrong.

Clay looked towards the sail for a moment longer, then closed his telescope. 'Has she responded to our signal yet, Mr Russell?' he asked.

'Not yet, sir,' said the youngster. 'I can see some men trying to work the mizzen halliard, but they seem to be struggling.'

'For sure they are,' snorted Clay. 'Struggling to know what flags to run up, I'll warrant.'

The brig was no more than a few miles off the bow, but continued to sail away from them. Through his telescope

Clay could see more detail now. The ship sat heavy in the sea, her hold full of cargo. The rents in her topsails appeared as pale blue discs, where the sky beyond was visible. They must be shot holes, and he fancied that some of the rigging looked to have been spliced, thickened in places like the joints on a finger. The group of men clustered around the signal halliard finally began attaching flags to the line, and hauling them aloft.

'Chase is signalling, sir,' announced Russell. 'Now that is odd!'

'Is it not the correct response?' asked Clay.

'I am not sure what to make of it, in truth, sir. It has the correct flags, but the order is wrong.'

'Incompetent lubbers, sir?' suggested the American.

'Or someone under duress required to make the signal, and using the opportunity to send a message of a different character,' said Clay. 'The laboured manner in which they made sail speaks to me of a prize crew, unfamiliar with their capture. That would also explain the damage aloft. Kindly have the watch below turned up, Mr Armstrong. I'll have the forward section of guns on the larboard side manned and run out, if you please, and one of the cutters ready to launch. You had best arm the crew.'

'Aye aye, sir, said Armstrong, turning away to issue the instructions.

'Mr Russell, signal to the chase to haul her wind,' ordered Clay.

'Aye aye, sir.'

The squeal of boatswain's pipes echoed through the lower deck, and the watch below came boiling up the ladderways. Lieutenant Blake strode out onto the main deck beneath Clay's feet, his delight obvious at the prospect of his beloved guns seeing action. Taylor came running up onto the quarterdeck to join his captain, shrugging on his coat and tweaking his neckcloth straight as he came. On the forecastle Hutchinson bellowed instructions to the men rigging the tackles for the cutter, while by the entry port her crew were being issued with cutlasses and pistols by Arkwright, the frigate's armourer.

Midshipman Todd had made his way down from the masthead in order to take command of the boat. He collected a cutlass from Arkwright and stood beside a tall, gaunt sailor with a hooked nose who was checking the priming on his pistol, prior to stuffing it into the waistband of his trousers. Clay watched him for a moment. That must be the new recruit with the curious name that Taylor wants to promote, he thought to himself. He certainly seemed assured enough, as he waited patiently among his fellow shipmates. Clay returned his attention to the brig, which was just off the frigate's bow. She was so close that Clay could see the detail of her battered stern. There was a row of four large window lights beneath a decorative arc of carved wood, picked out in blue and white paint. Below the windows, on her counter, was the ship's name in bold white letters, *Margaret Harmony*.

'Why has the chase not heaved to, Mr Russell?' he demanded. 'Did she not acknowledge your order?'

'She has not done so yet, sir,' said the midshipman.

'Then let us send her a signal that she may find easier to follow,' said Clay, stepping forward to the rail. 'Mr Blake!'

'Yes sir,' said the officer, looking up at him.

'Give her a gun, if you please,' he ordered.

The *Griffin*'s foremost cannon banged out, sending a cloud of smoke billowing away across the sea. A fountain of water rose up, just ahead of the chase, and moments later she turned into the wind, her sails volleying in the keen breeze. The frigate followed her in the turn, coming up just to windward of her, and then backed her topsails so as to keep the brig covered by a half dozen of her big eighteen-pounders.

'Cutter away!' yelled Clay, over the sound of flapping canvas. 'Mr Todd, kindly take possession of her, and then come back and report what you find. Send me her master across, if you can locate him.'

'Aye aye, sir,' said the youngster, touching his hat, and then he followed his crew down the side and into the cutter. Soon the boat reappeared, rising and falling in the long blue swell as she rowed across to the little brig.

*****

'Clap on in the bow, there Davis,' ordered Todd, as the cutter came alongside the wallowing ship. 'You and O'Brien stay with the boat; the rest follow me.'

The fourteen-year old's unbroken voice had risen to a falsetto with excitement, leading some of his crew to raise an eyebrow to each other, but there was no denying their young leader's enthusiasm for his task. He got to his feet, settled his hat a little more firmly on his mass of blond curls, and made his way unsteadily down the rocking boat.

'Your pardon, Jones, was that your hand?' said the midshipman, as one of the oarsmen yelped with pain.

'No matter, sir,' grunted the sailor, 'for I have another.'

Todd arrived at the gunnel and stared thoughtfully at the wall of battered oak before him. The side of the brig was not particularly high, especially when compared with that of the hulking *Griffin*, but there the comparison ended. The well-maintained flight of steps that ran up the frigate's side were here replaced by a few broken remnants, all slimy with weed, and there was no trace of the *Griffin*'s convenient hand ropes. To add to his discomfort, the height of the climb was swelling and shrinking by a good four feet with each fresh Atlantic roller that passed beneath the boat. But he was a good officer who knew his duty. With a flash of silver, he drew out the cutlass, and steeled himself to make the leap.

'Goldilocks be in for a dunking, if you don't help him, Larcum,' he heard one sailor mutter to another behind him.

A moment later Todd felt the firm hand of the nearest oarsman steading him. 'Beggin' yer pardon, sir, but I'd be stowing that blade for the present,' said Mudge. 'You'll be needing both fins for that there climb. That be better. Now, best to wait for the rise. Steady and … jump!'

As the swell pushed the cutter upwards, Todd launched himself. His right foot slithered down the wet side, but his left found a solid hold. For a moment the heavy cutlass scabbard threatened to dislodge him as it clattered about his legs, but with a final, breathless scramble he reached the entry port and stumbled onto the deck of the brig.

The planking was filthy when compared with the scrubbed oak he was used to, and open boxes and sacks littered the space. A dozen men of various races, all heavily armed, eyed the new arrival with hostility. With the next passing wave, the hawkish face of Mudge appeared behind him in the entry port, and quickly advanced to his side.

'Who is in charge here?' demanded the youngster. No one reacted to him.

'I reckon it be that fat arse what needs a shave, stood by the wheel, sir,' suggested Mudge, pointing his pistol towards a large man in a long coat and sea boots. Seeing the weapon reminded Todd to draw his own sword. 'Shall I be lowering a line to help fetch the others up to join us, sir?' continued the sailor.

'If you please, Mudge,' said Todd, advancing on the man, who was at least twice his size. 'You are a French prize crew, are you not?'

'Of course,' growled the sailor. 'Except for that pig there, who sends the wrong signal.' He indicated a silver-haired man who was sitting by the stern rail.

The latter rose to his feet and came across. 'By God, but I am pleased to see you, young man,' he enthused, wringing Todd's hand. 'My name is Slocum, Harold Slocum, master of the *Margaret Harmony*.'

'Pleased to meet you, Captain,' said Todd. 'How did you come to lose your ship?'

'We were two days out of Antigua with a cargo of rum and sugar, heading to the rendezvous for the convoy home,' said Slocum. 'Then out of the night comes this armed sloop, full of yelling men, and boards us like damned pirates! Not so much as a trace of the navy, I might add.'

'We not pirates!' said the sailor, wagging his finger at Slocum. 'We French privateersmen, from Guadeloupe. I have papers to prove.'

'French!' exclaimed Slocum. 'Not above a bare half of them! The rest were dagos, blacks and all manner of ne'er-do-wells.'

'You must surrender, sir,' Todd demanded, pointing towards the *Griffin*. The man by the wheel glanced at the British frigate, with its line of cannon, manned and ready. He shrugged, unbuckled the cutlass belt from around his waist and pulled a heavy pistol from deep in his pocket.

'She is yours, monsieur,' he conceded, dumping his weapons into the youngster's arms.

'Best let me be having all that gear, like, sir,' said Mudge from behind his shoulder, relieving his diminutive superior of his burden. Behind Mudge the rest of the cutter's crew had formed up, a solid crowd of armed seamen.

'Waite, go with Captain Slocum here and release his crew,' Todd ordered. 'Then I shall require you to go across with me to be interviewed by my captain,' he added to Slocum.

'Happy to oblige, young man,' said the ship's master.

'Jones, man the wheel,' continued Todd. 'The rest of you, disarm these Frogs, and put them under the forecastle.'

'Right, you come with me,' said Larcum, to the leader of the privateers, pulling him along by the arm.

Todd went to the wheel next, and after a brief search found a battered brass speaking trumpet in the locker under the binnacle.

'Best let Pipe know what is happening,' he muttered to himself as he crossed to the rail facing the *Griffin*. He inflated his lungs to hail his captain, but got no further. Suddenly there was a flash from forward and the sound of a shot rang out. He spun round to see a cloud of gun smoke dispersing in the wind. The body of one of the privateersmen lay on the deck, while the others had backed away, hands held aloft.

'What the hell is going on?' he demanded, running up.

'It be Mudge, sir,' reported one of the boat crew. 'He's only gone an' shot one of the buggers.'

'He pulled a knife on me, the bastard, sir,' said the sailor, standing over the body.

'We'd best get him back to the *Griffin* for Mr Corbett to look at,' said Todd.

'Not sure as the sawbones can help him any, sir,' commented one of the other seamen. 'Him's got a bullet in his head.'

Larcum Mudge

Todd looked at the crumpled figure of the dead privateer. He was lying face down in a spreading pool of blood, with a long pigtail twisted out on the deck beside him. The sleeve of his shirt had fallen back from his heavily tattooed forearm. The youngster bent down to examine some of them.

'*Dread Nought*,' he read, 'and a fouled anchor. This man is a damned deserter!'

'Aye, perhaps that be why he wanted to stick me,' said Mudge. Todd looked up at the sailor, but could read nothing in the man's dark eyes.

Chapter 3
English Harbour

The lower deck of the *Griffin* was bustling and noisy later that evening, as the men awaited their dinner. Along both sides of the space were rows of mess tables, each one surrounded by half a dozen hands. The gloom this deep in the ship was dispersed a little by the bright evening sunshine that filtered down through the gratings, supplemented by the glow of the horn lanterns that swung above each table. The excitement of the chase and capture earlier that day had given the crew of the frigate plenty to discuss, not least the prize money they had gained from the encounter.

'That *Maggie Harpy* is a tired old ship, for sure, as will not fetch us much, but what of the fecking cargo!' enthused O'Malley to his fellow messmates. 'Tons of best sugar, and grog to boot. That'll fetch us a pretty penny, what with the war an' all.'

'It will, so long as she gets condemned afore the peace,' cautioned Sedgwick. 'Price of sugar will fall swiftly enough after that.'

'Aye, I suppose that'll be right,' said O'Malley. 'Any excuse for them thieving feckers to cheat honest tars.'

'How do you work this stuff out, Able?' queried Mudge, the newest member of the mess. 'I ain't never heard of no negros as had learning and stuff.'

'Maybe you ain't been mixing with the right sort,' said

the coxswain, with a hard look in his eye. 'As for sugar, I've cut enough cane in my time to know of what I speak, Larcum.'

'I suppose you have,' agreed Mudge. 'An' copped a flogging or two whenever you slacked, from the look of that back of yours.'

'Just like the fecking navy,' said O'Malley.

'A deal worse, in truth, for you didn't need to err to be punished,' said Sedgwick. 'As for the price falling, that just stands to reason. Once peace comes, all them big Frog and Don islands will be free to sell the stuff, hand over fist.'

'Aye, that do make sense,' said Mudge. 'But only after you been an' said it, like.'

'Proper scholar is our Able,' said Evans, basking in the reflected pride of association. 'He's been an' writ a bleeding book an' the like.'

'That right?' said the Mudge. 'So how come you still be on the lower deck then. Captain's coxswain be a proper position, I grant you, but with your letters an' all, don't you fancy being a Grunter?'

'Pipe offered to make me be a master's mate, or a snotty, but I be happy where I is,' said Sedgwick. 'Look around you. Turks, Dagoes, Negros, Lascars, Chinese, even Irish,' he added with a wink to the others. 'No one down here cares where I be from. I ain't so sure as Grunters and toffs will be so welcoming to the likes of me.'

'Not just them folk, it seems,' said Mudge. 'I reckon I've just been every part as unjust as any of them types, rattling on about negros with no learning. Sad to say, I thought you were naught but a savage when I first clapped eyes on you, but I own now that I got you all wrong, Able Sedgwick. An' there be my hand to say how sorry I be.'

'Well then, isn't this is the touching scene, to be sure,'

said O'Malley, once the two sailors had shaken hands. 'Now we're all fecking lovers again, where are our vittles?'

'It be a coming, Sean,' said Trevan, arriving at the end of the table with several tubs of steaming food. 'Pork and pease today, lads, what with it being a Thursday.'

'Ladle it on then, Adam,' urged Evans, holding out his square wooden plate. 'I could eat a bleeding horse.'

'I dare say you'll be hungry an' all, Larcum,' said O'Malley. 'They do say killing gives a man a fecking appetite.'

'I ain't sure about that,' said the sailor. 'I do feel proper raw over him, lads. Turned out he be one of ours as had joined the Frogs.'

'Got what he bleeding deserved, then, didn't he?' said Evans, through a mouthful of food. 'Filthy turncoat! If you hadn't stuck a ball in his nut, he'd have been hanged. You probably did him a kindness.' There was nodding agreement at this from the others, more concerned with eating than talking. The exception was Sedgwick, who toyed with his food.

'But what were he doing on a Frog privateer?' he asked, laying aside his spoon.

'How do you mean, Able,' said Mudge.

'Ain't it strange for a deserter to choose such a calling?' said the coxswain. 'You'd be certain to cross paths with the navy afore long. I heard he even had tattoos and a pigtail to mark him as a man-of-war's man. It don't make no sense, to my way of thinking.'

'Desperate fecker, then,' said O'Malley. 'To chance such hazards?'

'Maybe, so,' mused Sedgwick. 'An' what drove him to that pass, I wonder?'

Larcum Mudge

O'Malley looked about him to check that they were not being overheard, and then gestured to the others to come close.

'You'll recall how that old gossip Harte an' I share a twist of backy, hard by the galley of an evening?'

'You an' Pipe's steward?' said Mudge. 'That be bleeding handy!'

'Too fecking right!' enthused the Irishman. 'So, he was after polishing the lamp in Pipe's sleeping quarters the other day, an' his ear chanced to stray close to the bulkhead, so it did.' The other sailors chuckled at this, and leant a little closer.

'Now, he did make me swear not to tell a soul, on the grave of my mother,' cautioned O'Malley, with a solemnly raised finger. 'But as I've no fecking notion where that might be, I am sure it will do no harm if I tells you lads. He was after telling Old Man Taylor that we're to hunt the Caribee for that sloop what fecking mutinied last year.'

'The one in all them bleeding posters as were going up in Plymouth?' queried Evans. 'The *Pelican*? Or were it the *Pigeon*?'

'The *Peregrine*?' offered Mudge.

'Aye, that were it!' confirmed the Londoner. 'I knew it were some manner of fowl.'

'Listen up, now,' continued O'Malley, 'Might this here turncoat as Larcum shot be one of them feckers?'

'What made you say …' began Mudge.

'Easy lads,' hissed O'Malley, urging caution. He motioned to a group of younger sailors who were coming in their direction, as if summoned by the indiscretion. 'Not a word! Harte told me all that on the fecking quiet!'

The sailors arrived in a shuffling group at the end of the table. 'Evening shipmates,' said their leader.

'An' what is the fecking meaning of this, Peter Hobbs?' demanded O'Malley. 'Sneaking up on folk all underhand like, to earwig on the talk of your betters.'

'I didn't mean nothing by it, Sean,' said the young man. 'Nor did I hear aught.'

'Of course not,' said the Irishman, hastily. 'What with there being nothing of import to fecking hear … about mutineers … an' retaking ships, and the like.' There was a pause while the new arrivals absorbed this. Sedgwick clapped his bowed forehead into his open hand.

'You be talking about how we be off to recapture that there *Peregrine* from them Frogs?' queried one of the others.

'How … how … how do you feckers know that?' spluttered O'Malley.

'You know Josh Andrews, that new boatswain's mate as joined just afore we left Plymouth,' said Hobbs, jerking a thumb towards where the petty officers messed. 'He were saying how he served on her a few years back, an' how he's come on board to help smoke her if the Frogs have made her look all weird.'

'Your man should know better than to fecking gossip about such things,' said the Irishman, folding his arms. 'Him a petty officer an' all. So what were you lads after, anyways? Apart from the shameless spreading of tittle-tattle.'

'I was thinking on how we ain't had the occasion for no dancing this voyage,' said Hobbs. 'If you've finished your vittles, perhaps you might play for us, like? You being the best fiddler on the barky, an' all.'

'Is it flattery, you're after trying?' said O'Malley, secretly pleased with the description. He was comfortably the frigate's best musician, at least in his own opinion. 'But what will we do for a drummer, now that Fergus O'Leary has passed on?'

'What became of him?' asked Mudge.

'Hacked down by a brace of Danish feckers at Copenhagen, the hounds,' said the Irishman. ''Twas an awful shame, he being the finest stickman outside of Kerry.'

'If you have a drum, I can play it passing well,' offered Mudge.

'Don't be taking offence at all, Larcum,' said O'Malley holding up a hand. 'I am sure you can strike out a beat as grand as the next fecker, but Irish drumming comes from the soul. None as aren't from across the water can do it right.'

In answer Mudge pulled the empty mess tub towards him, flipped it over and picked up a pair of wooden spoons. They vanished into a blur, like the wings of an insect, and a rapid beat rattled out, the tone rising and falling as he moved the point of contact across the base of the tub. With a final flourish the sailor came to a stop.

'Bleeding hell, that were good,' remarked Evans.

'I daresay your grandma might have been Irish,' conceded O'Malley.

'I doubt that, Sean,' smiled Mudge. 'But we do drum a little in Suffolk too, you know, when we be wassailing in the springtime. In truth I'm out of practice. Weren't much call for dancing on my last ship.'

'That be right?' queried Trevan. 'We always enjoyed a bit of a hornpipe back on the old *Emilia,* but maybe Yankee whalers be different?'

'Eh, that be right Adam,' confirmed Mudge. 'New Bedford captains be dreadful old puritans to a man.'

'So, we going to have ourselves a dance then,' asked Hobbs, who had been patiently waiting during the audition.

'Aye, very well,' said the Irishman, unwrapping his fiddle. 'Give your man a fecking drum, and let us hope he'll not play too ill.'

But O'Malley need not have worried. A wide stretch of planking was cleared close to the fore ladderway, where there was better headroom. Some of the deck's lamps were brought over and set down in a ring to illuminate the space. Then those who were going to dance arranged themselves in two loose lines, self-consciously pulling at their waist bands, or tweaking at their shirt sleeves under the gaze of those around the edge of the circle. More and more sailors gathered, either to wait their turn, or just to enjoy the skill of those performing. Off to one side sat Mudge on a stool facing O'Malley and watching the fiddler intently. On his lap was a small drum with a Celtic knot painted across the skin.

'The *Black Almain*,' announced the Irishman. He stamped his foot on the deck a few times to set the rhythm, Mudge took it up, and O'Malley began to play. The sailors were familiar with the tune, and immediately began to dance. Soon there were a dozen men twirling and stamping to the music that flowed from the two players. In the glow of the oil lamps they sent shadows flickering across the faces of those watching.

Sedgwick stood towards the back of the crowd, a strange, sad look in his eyes. It was many years since he had been dragged away from his burning village and into the West African night, but still the combination of bare dancing feet and the sound of a drum could pull him back. The flickering motion of the dancers seemed to conjure up the ghosts of his long-dead family from among the deep shadows of the lower deck. The men of his tribe had been dancing in the firelight that night too, his father and uncles prominent among them, until the village dogs had suddenly started to bark.

He felt an arm around his shoulder, and he turned to find Trevan beside him, a look of concern on his face. 'Why doesn't you and I go an' watch the moonrise, Able lad,' he said. 'It'll be a fine sight, on a clear night such as this.'

The two men slipped away, unnoticed by the others, and made their way up onto the forecastle. The flow of the music followed them, drifted up through the gratings, but it was muffled a little by the two intervening decks. With a final flourish from O'Malley, the dance ended amid a loud burst of approval. Moments later came a fresh tune, and the sound of a new dance starting. The two friends moved away, across to the rail at the very front of the ship. The wind that ruffled their shirts was deliciously cool and fresh after the stuffy lower deck. The bow of the frigate sliced through the water amid a tumble of foam beneath them, and the dark sea stretched out all around, empty as a desert beneath the stars.

'That dancing gets you every time, don't it, Able lad,' commented Trevan.

'Aye, that it does,' agreed Sedgwick. 'But it was a deal worse the first hornpipe I saw, so that be progress of a sort. I daresay it will fade, in time.'

'That be a comfort,' said his friend. 'They do say as thinking upon something else can serve to shift recollections as is too painful.' Sedgwick obediently shut his eyes and tried to clear his head of thoughts of home. Sure enough, a fresh image formed in his mind.

'What do you reckon of our new messmate?' he asked.

'Larcum?' said the Cornishman. 'I likes him well enough, although I hear he were cheeking you earlier about your race, while I was away fetching our scoff.'

'That be true enough, but he ain't exactly the first to

do that, nor will he be the last,' said the coxswain. 'An' he begged my pardon, handsomely enough.'

'That be good,' agreed Trevan. 'For my part, I hold him to be a decent shipmate, an' he be a proper sailor. Shame about him killing that jack, but if the bugger was about to stick him, that be fair enough. He certainly knows his whaling.'

'He knows his way about a king's ship, an' all,' said his friend. 'I reckon he's served on a few before he reached the *Griffin*.'

'That must be true of many a tar,' said Trevan, 'after all these years of war.'

'Aye, and most are content to yarn about it, with a good few as can barely be stopped,' said the coxswain. 'But not him. Have you marked how he's yet to mention a single man-of-war he's served on? Strange, that, don't you think?'

*****

A week later, the *Griffin* left the blustery Atlantic, and was advancing over the dazzling blue of the Caribbean towards the southern coast of Antigua. The island was close, lying across the horizon and filling Clay's view with forest-covered slopes that rose to the bare tops of Sage Hill and Boggy Peak, off to his left. The blue sea flashed into dazzling white where the surf pounded against the rocky shore. Coming out from the island towards the frigate was a line of three graceful schooners. With their long hulls and delicate spars, they seemed as elegant as greyhounds when compared with the heavy masts and solid build of the *Griffin*, but as they passed close to leeward Clay noticed how shabby they looked. Their bright paintwork was battered, and their sails heavily patched. The nearest one had a long vertical stripe of new white canvas running through the middle of its yellowing mainsail. He acknowledged the friendly wave from the barefoot man at the tiller as the ships passed.

'They may be nothing much to look at, but schooners command the inter-island trade in these waters, sir,' said Taylor. 'Both legitimate and otherwise. The Excise would need a swift cutter to catch one of those three on a dark night.'

'What do they chiefly carry?'

'Food, rum, stores, sir,' explained the first lieutenant. 'Slaves on occasion, from islands with a surplus to where they are required. And sugar, of course. That is the white gold of the West Indies.'

Clay watched the line of schooners for a moment, as they ran away to the south, and wondered if any of their crews might be from the *Peregrine*. He had noticed that a couple of the hands had busied themselves at coiling ropes while the shadow of the big frigate loomed over them. Then he returned his attention to the approaching island. Remember what Earl St Vincent said, he reminded himself. Catching the mutineers would be taken care of by others. He had a ship to find.

They reduced sail to just a single topsail as the tricky approach to the entrance to English Harbour opened in the coast ahead of him. As Antigua grew closer, he began to see where swathes of destruction had been torn across the hillsides. The bright green of new saplings could be seen, busily rising from among fallen tree trunks.

'I collect they were badly struck by a hurricane last year, sir,' commented Taylor.

'I believe so,' said Clay, thinking of what good fortune that had been for the mutineers, able to make their way across a stormy but empty sea.

'I can see the entrance now, sir,' said Armstrong, who

had his telescope to his eye. 'Just appearing off the bow. You can see the flag above the fort on Pigeon Point.'

Clay followed where the sailing master had indicated. There were low brown cliffs with trailing creepers dangling down them, topped by a little stone fort that guarded the narrow entrance. Beyond an inlet twisted its way inland, with more stone fortifications, and the roofs of a settlement. Behind the breakwater guarding the inner harbour were plenty of masts, including one with a blue ensign at its mizzen.

'Take us in, Mr Armstrong, if you please,' ordered Clay, closing his telescope. 'Mr Taylor, the admiral is in harbour. Kindly prepare to salute his flag, and have my barge ready to launch. I suppose I had best shift into my best coat and scrapper.' He eyed the fierce sun overhead, and enjoyed the cool sea air for a last moment, before he went down to his cabin to change.

When Clay returned to the deck, dressed in his heavy broadcloth coat, the *Griffin* was deep into English Harbour. The cliffs and slopes that surrounded them seemed to magnify the hot sun, and reflect it up on him from the surface of the water. He felt the first trickle of sweat forming beneath his linen shirt. The hills seemed to have sheltered the inlet from the hurricane. Tall palm trees with feathery fronds lined the shore, and the grey stone buildings of the dockyard bustled with life. In the port were several more schooners and two other warships. Clay's heart soared as he recognised the sloop of his friend John Sutton lying above her reflection.

'We shall be mooring directly sir,' said Taylor, pointing to the forecastle where Hutchinson was barking orders to his men.

'The other ships are the *Echo*, eighteen-gun sloop of war, Captain Sutton, and the *Stirling*, sixty-four, flagship of

Rear Admiral Sir George Montague. Captain Thompson commanding,' announced the signal midshipman.

'Thank you, Mr Russell,' said Clay. Below him Sedgwick was inspecting the crew of the captain's barge. Each man was dressed in clean white duck trousers, matching green shirts of the same shade as their boat's hull and oar blades, and straw hats decorated with the ship's name. He returned his attention to the frigate as it drifted on. There was a cry from Hutchinson in the bow, and she rounded to, neatly picking up her mooring buoy. A torrent of sailors poured aloft, and the frigate's topsail vanished. The moment the sail had gone, the first gun of the salute crashed out, returned from high on the two-decked flagship.

'That was handsomely done, Mr Taylor,' said his captain. 'You have achieved a great deal with the new hands in the last few weeks.'

Thank you, sir,' smiled the older man. 'They are not quite the seamen I would like yet, and their gunnery leaves much to be desired, but I believe in time they may bring a little credit on the ship.'

'The flagship is signalling, sir,' said Russell, as the last bang of the salute echoed back off a nearby cliff. 'Flag to *Griffin*. Captain to repair on board.'

'Get the barge in the water, there!' roared Taylor. 'Handsomely, I say!' Clay slid a hand into his coat to check that his report was there, together with the dispatches he had brought with him from London.

'Kindly have the squadron's mail sacks placed in the boat, if you please, Mr Taylor.'

'Aye aye, sir.'

*****

'Boat ahoy!' came a hail from the quarterdeck of the admiral's flagship. Clay glanced that way, and saw a line of faces peering inquisitively down at the approaching barge. Among them was the smartly dressed midshipman who had called to them, the brass speaking trumpet in his hand shining like burnished gold in the sunlight.

'*Griffin*!' yelled Sedgwick, holding up three fingers to show that a senior post captain was coming aboard, and then, in a softer growl towards the barge crew. 'Easy there. Oars in, larboard side.' He pushed the tiller across, and they turned in a long, sweeping curve towards the side of the *Stirling*.

'Mind the paintwork, Darky,' called a voice from above, but there was no need for concern. The boat came to a halt, barely kissing the side, adjacent to the flight of steps that led upwards. Although she was one of the navy's smaller ships of the line, the *Stirling* still towered over the boat. From above came the stamp of marines being dressed into line, and the urgent hiss of orders. Clay waited in the stern sheets for the sound of preparations to fade. Beside him in the clear water the curved bulk of the flagship's hull continued below the surface, the copper sheaving gleaming in the sunlight close to, becoming mysterious and dark lower down. Shoals of small fish darted about in the shadow cast by the warship.

When all seemed ready on deck, Clay got up and made his way to the side. He settled his hat on his head and pulled his sword clear of his feet. Two hand ropes dangled down, woven from red and white strands in a pleasing crisscross pattern. He seized them both and pulled himself up the side. His progress was slightly crabbed, as he favoured his right arm; his left shoulder had never fully recovered its strength from the Spanish musket ball that had nearly killed him in these waters, five years earlier. The tumblehome of the side helped him as he neared the top, and he managed to arrive at the entry port with some of the dignity to be expected of a post captain. His hand rose to acknowledge the line of white-gloved ship's boys, boatswain's mates and saluting marines.

Even for a flagship, the *Stirling* was immaculate. The scrubbed planking was almost white and the lines of upper-deck cannon were painted with gloss black paint so thick they appeared to have been lacquered. The ropework all around him showed a profusion of elaborate Turk's Heads and Monkey's Fists, and the officers on the quarterdeck all seemed to be in full dress uniform. Some of the more fashion-minded even wore the hessian boots that were starting to take the place of buckled shoes in the service. A man with a bald pate whose uniform matched Clay's stepped forward with a warm smile and an outstretched hand.

'Welcome on board, Captain,' he said. 'My name is William Thompson.'

'Pleased to meet you, Captain Thompson,' he said, taking the hand. 'Alexander Clay. What an astonishingly well-turned out ship you have! Not occasioned by my visit, I trust? Perhaps the governor is due to inspect her later?'

Thompson made to reply, but noticed the twinkle in his visitor's eye, and smiled in response. 'Ah, you seek to make game of me, Clay,' he said. 'I collect you must have served with Sir George before?'

'Indeed, in the Indian Ocean. Does the admiral continue to keep a private supply of paint, mixed to his own specification?'

'He may even have ventured to improve the formulation since then,' laughed Thompson, leading the way below. 'If you care to accompany me, you can ask him for it yourself.'

Rear Admiral Sir George Montague had changed little since Clay had last seen him. His uniform was as beautifully tailored as he remembered. The short dark hair was a little greyer over the temples, but there was the same haughty look in the eyes that regarded him as he approached. They left his face to flicker over the details of his uniform. Then he rose from behind a desk of carefully arranged items and held out his hand.

'Good to see you again, Captain Clay, and welcome to the Leeward Islands,' he said. 'I trust you will not find us overly dull after all your recent exploits in the Baltic. Here catching privateers and impounding smuggled French sugar are our chief concerns, what?'

'Not at all, Sir George,' said Clay, shaking the proffered hand. He ran a finger around the top of his neckcloth, and shrugged at his heavy coat. 'But goodness, it is certainly considerably warmer than I was acquainted with in those waters.' Montague frowned at his new arrival.

'If you were hoping for permission to remove your coat, Captain, I fear you will be disappointed,' he said. 'We maintain high standards in this squadron, which includes the matter of my officers' appearance. You will find my observations on the matter within your standing orders. But I can offer you the comfort of a chair, at least, before you expire where you stand. Would you care for refreshment?'

'Thank you, Sir George,' said Clay, sitting down, and accepting a glass of sherry from the white-gloved steward who had appeared beside him.

'We are not strangers to inclement weather ourselves, you know,' continued Montague. 'A most powerful hurricane passed through Antigua last year. I witnessed rain and wind the like of which I had scarce thought possible. Noah and his flood weren't in it! It is hard to imagine on a day such as this, but the island was very roughly handled. If I had a shilling for every plantation owner who lost his sugar crop, I could retire the service and renounce my pension, what?'

'I did note some destruction on the hillsides to the west of here, Sir George,' commented Clay. 'How did the squadron fair?'

'Tolerably well, for we do not keep the sea in that season,' said the admiral. 'We were snug enough in English Harbour, double moored with our masts struck below and the hatches all battened down. Of course, we were desperately worried on account of Captain Daniels and the *Peregrine*. Rightly so, as it turned out, although it seems he succumbed to fury of a different stamp.'

'Ain't that the truth,' said Clay. 'Have many of the mutineers been apprehended, Sir George?'

'A dozen or so, but we shall presently find the rest, have no fear, once the bounty on offer for them is generally known,' said Montague. 'Such ill-bred types are hopeless at dissembling. Why, we caught one brazen fool right here in Antigua, this very week. He was found in an alehouse in St John. He partook of more rum than was wise and made some boastful remarks to the company about the mutiny. While he slumbered, his drinking companions decided among themselves how they would share the reward, and then called in the constables. I take it your arrival is not unconnected with that affair?'

'Indeed, I have dispatches here from the Admiralty which explain all, together with my report of my voyage, Sir George,' said Clay, passing the documents across. 'We also brought mail from home with us. I took the liberty of having those letters from Lady Montague separated so that I could give them to you immediately.'

'Thank you, Captain, said his host, placing his wife's letters to one side without a glance. 'I shall attend to those later. Will you excuse me while I read the orders?'

'Of course, Sir George,' said Clay. While the admiral read, he took the opportunity to look around the wide, spacious cabin. The *Stirling* was one of the older sixty-fours in the service, built with the comfort of its officers in mind. Behind the admiral was a run of large stern windows, all open, through which he had a fine view over a bustling stone quayside. Shouted orders and the cries of hawkers drifted on the warm air. There were handcarts laden with tropical fruit or caged birds, while further back a line of black slaves were walking up a gangplank, each man bent under the weight of a heavy sack. Then his attention turned to the arrangement of the windows themselves. Most of them had a locker with a padded seat fitted to the lid beneath them, but there were two that had none. He realised that these must be a pair of concealed doors that led out onto a stern gallery. He had noticed it as he rowed over, projecting out like a balcony over the water. Clay stood to look through the nearest window and noticed the gallery's ornate carved rail.

'It is a pity that such detail is vanishing from our ships of the line, is it not, Captain,' said Montague, following where his guest looked. 'The modern trend for enclosed sterns is doubtless more economic in the matter of space, but I do so enjoy taking my ease out there, of an evening, when we are at sea.'

'It must be very agreeable,' said Clay.

'Mind, that does not bear on the current matter in hand,' said the admiral, tapping the open dispatch in front of him and returning to his customary briskness. 'I collect that you have been sent to find the wretched *Peregrine* and bring her out.'

'That is so, Sir George. His lordship has received information that the mutineers took her into Guadeloupe and sold her to the French.'

'I daresay the blighters did!' snorted Montague. 'Most trouble hereabouts comes from that nest of vipers! Of course, his lordship knows Guadeloupe passing well. He commanded the fleet when we captured the island back in ninety-four. Mind, that was a short-lived triumph.'

'The enemy promptly retook the place, did they not, Sir George?'

'Quite so. Soon as they learned of its fall, the damned Frogs sent out a revolutionary hothead named Victor Hughes as governor, with an army of Jacobin zealots. He retook the place, freed all the slaves, and sent many of their former masters to the guillotine. Now Guadeloupe is full of every mischief this side of Hades, and all within a day's sailing of where we are presently seated.'

'Can nothing be attempted against the place, Sir George?' asked Clay.

'That is easier said than accomplished,' explained the admiral. 'Hughes has armed all the negros and taught them soldiering. There are tens of thousands of the blighters, and with their freedom at stake, you can expect them to resist any occupation like demons. The Admiralty has not seen fit to replace the *Peregrine*, and with the trade to protect, the best I have been able to do is keep one of my sloops bottling up the place. Captain Camelford is on station there at present, in the *Daring*.'

'If she is indeed there, where do you suppose the

Peregrine will be found?' asked Clay.

'Guadeloupe has a few harbours, but only one of note, which is Pointe-à-Pitre,' said Montague, sipping at his drink. He paused to look at the glass, holding it up to the light for a moment, and then rounded on his steward. 'For God's sake, Thomas, this glass is filthy! There is half a finger mark on the base, damn your eyes!'

'Apologies, Sir George, let me replace it,' said the servant, hastening around the desk with a fresh drink.

'Is your glass clean, Captain?' asked Montague.

'Eh, perfectly so,' said Clay. 'You were saying that you thought that the *Peregrine* might be found at this Pointe-à-Pitre?'

The admiral consulted the dispatch once more. 'His lordship says that he believes the appearance of the *Peregrine* may have been changed, and that is the only port with the facilities to accomplish such a transformation in the possession of the enemy.'

'Splendid,' said Clay. 'At least I have some notion of where to start. What orders do you have for me, Sir George?'

'Certainly, you must commence your search at Pointe-à-Pitre. But I can give you very little assistance, for I have to be mindful of all my other responsibilities. I have the Jamaica convoy to consider, which will pass in the next two weeks. But you can naturally call on Camelford and the *Daring* to assist you.'

'A heavy frigate and a sloop,' said Clay. 'That should suffice, Sir George.'

'You might want to examine the place first, before offering such a decided opinion, Captain,' said Montague. 'The Pointe-à-Pitre lies at the bottom of a difficult bay that is full of reefs and islands. There is only one practical entrance for shipping, and that is protected by some notable fortifications. I wish you the best of good fortune getting in there, for I am certain you shall have need of it.’

Chapter 4
Guadeloupe

Clay was busy at his desk, putting the finishing touches to his latest letter to Lydia. His wife had a keen interest in the outside world, and there was much in Antigua that would have delighted her. He had just been describing the line of white pelicans, all beaks and angles, that he could see through the stern window of the frigate. They occupied a line of mooring posts, with one huge bird stood on each, busy preening themselves. He had just completed this task when the expected knock came at the cabin door.

'Come in,' said Clay, laying down his pen.

Midshipman Todd marched across and stood in front of his captain. 'Mr Blake's compliments, and a boat has just put out from the *Echo*, sir,' said the youngster.

'Please give him my thanks, and tell him that I will be on deck directly,' said Clay. Todd touched his hat and returned the way he had come, while his captain looked around the cabin to check that all was ready for the arrival of his friend. The dining table had been reduced to its smallest, and was laden with glasses and silverware, together with a basket of fresh bread delivered that morning from ashore. A pair of decanters stood on a table nearby, beneath the portrait of his wife who smiled down on proceedings. Both the cabin's gun ports and all of the window lights that ran across the stern had been opened to let in a little breeze, although it was still uncomfortably warm. His steward, Harte, came bustling in with a beautiful spread of cut flowers that burst from out of a large copper cylinder. He placed them on the table, and then fussed over their arrangement.

'Compliments of the purser, who was ashore this morning, sir,' he said, by way of explanation.

'They look very fine,' said Clay. 'Please give my thanks to Mr Faulkner. But what, pray is that unusual vessel you have put them in?'

'Welcome as his gift may be, there weren't a vase in the whole barky to stow them in, sir,' explained the steward. 'Which ain't so very strange, seeing as we're not overburdened with flowers out at sea. So, I had the gunner saw the top off an eighteen-pounder canister round, and take out all the musket balls. It don't look so shabby, do it?'

'No indeed,' said Clay, rising to his feet. 'Very inventive. Was Mr Faulkner also able to procure the flying fish?'

'Half a dozen, caught this very morning, cleaned and ready for the pan, sir,' said the steward. 'An' fresh pineapple to follow the cheese. Shall I get you your coat and hat?'

'If you please, Harte,' said Clay, doing up his waistcoat. He would dearly have liked to stay in his open linen shirt, but appearances had to be maintained, especially moored in English Harbour, within easy view of his fastidious admiral. He stood up and held his arms behind him to receive his coat, pulled it straight and accepted his hat as he left the cabin. It was a short stroll to the entry port, where his friend was coming on board without the usual ceremony that even a naval commander was entitled to. Instead a group of the frigate's younger officers replaced the usual boatswain's mates and ship's boys. John Sutton had served with most of them, and was well liked by all.

'My thanks for those lovely flowers, Mr Faulkner,' he said to the ship's purser. The officer gave a stiff bow, his elegantly uniform coat swishing open as he did so.

'It was nothing, sir,' he said, in his aristocratic tone. 'They are to be obtained on the quayside for such a reasonable price, I purchased some for the wardroom too.'

'Aye, for which we give thanks,' said his friend Macpherson. 'They at least serve to mask some of the ranker odours emanating from the hold.'

'Or Mr Corbett's ill-washed linen,' added Blake, whose cabin was next to that of the ship's surgeon.

'Boat ahoy!' yelled the midshipman of the watch from the quarterdeck above them. Clay leant forward and saw his friend sitting in the stern sheets of the approaching launch.

'*Echo*!' came the reply, followed by the clatter of the boat coming alongside. From the sound of the muttered oaths from below, one at least of the sailors had failed to get his oar clear in time. A moment later the beaming, darkly handsome face of the sloop's commander appeared in the entry port as he bounded up the side. There was much hand shaking and laughter among the officers, and then his friend was stood before him.

'Good to see you, John,' said Clay, pulling his visitor into an embrace.

'It has been much too long, brother,' said Sutton, holding him close. The two ship's captains parted, and Clay led the way towards his cabin. As soon as both men were inside, they quickly shrugged off their coats, and surrendered them to Harte.

'How is your delightful wife?' asked his friend, gesturing at the portrait.

'In good health, I thank you, John,' said Clay. 'In fact, she was quite blooming when I left England. We have hopes that our little family may be extended shortly.' Clay took his place at the table and hastily touched the surface, while his friend sat down opposite.

'Why that is wonderful!' exclaimed Sutton. 'Some wine here, Harte, if you please.' When both men had been served, he held his glass aloft. 'To the health of Lydia Clay.'

His dark eyes sparkled with pleasure, touched with something sadder. Clay leant across and placed a hand on his friend's sleeve. 'Betsey's time will come, soon enough, I am sure.'

'Not if the Admiralty persists in stationing me on the far side of the Atlantic,' said his friend. 'She yearns for a family, Alex, and while being an aunt again will bring her joy, it will come with a little envy too. How was she when you last saw her?'

'My sister was in the best of health,' said Clay. 'She has started work on a fresh novel, which she tells me is going very ill, and she is naturally missing her husband greatly, of course. But perhaps this peace that everyone speaks of will remedy that.'

'Precious little sign of it breaking out in these waters,' snorted his guest. 'We have to contend with French privateers, Yankee blockade runners, Spanish warships and any amount of smuggling. Which reminds me, I noticed a bumboat selling coconuts to your crew through an open gun port as I approached.'

'Very like,' said Clay. 'What of it?'

'Only that the latest ruse for bringing illicit spirits on board is to drain away the milk and replace it with rum. I believe the hands refer to such refreshment as sucking the monkey.'

'Harte, my compliments to Mr Taylor, and tell him that no coconuts are to be sold to the men other than via Mr Faulkner,' ordered Clay. 'And say he has my permission to drop an eighteen-pounder ball through the bottom of any bumboat that comes alongside intent on selling directly.'

'Aye aye, sir,' said the steward. 'Shall I also fetch the flying fish?'

'If you please.'

'Fish, how splendid!' enthused Sutton. 'That will make a pleasant change from Salt Beef Pepperpot, which is the only local delicacy my steward seems able to produce.'

'I was delighted to find you in port when I arrived, John.'

'Pure good fortune, brother,' said his friend. 'A sprung topgallant yard and an empty hold is what has occasioned it. The moment I have revictualed, I shall be off back to the Mona Passage, hunting down smugglers.'

'Is smuggling endemic in these parts?' asked Clay.

'Rampant,' confirmed Sutton. 'Consider, there are no end of islands of various nationalities, all hard up against each other, with a long history of trading among themselves. They ain't inclined to let the inconvenience of a war in Europe stop all that. Poor Montague would have torn his hair out long ago, if he weren't more concerned with spoiling his coiffure.'

'Yes, I did notice that promotion has not blunted his enthusiasm for a well-turned-out ship,' laughed his host.

'It has made him decidedly worse, Alex!' exclaimed Sutton. 'If the *Echo* spends much more time in English Harbour, we shall presently have polished away every remaining piece of brass on board.'

'Have a care, sirs, for it be brimstone hot!' declared

Harte, placing a sizzling platter in the centre of the table, loaded with charred fish. 'Tatties in the chafing dish, and some manner of local cabbage on the side. May I help you to a flyer, sir?' There was a pause as the two captains were served.

'So what brings you to these waters, Alex?' asked Sutton. 'I take it the First Sea Lord had some greater object in mind than the kindness of renewing your acquaintance with me.'

'I am to hunt down the *Peregrine*, and recapture her if I can,' said his host. 'Did you know much about her?'

'Aye, a little. That was a melancholy affair. She was a nice little sloop, not unlike our old *Rush*. We all believed that she had foundered last year, and some in the squadron thought that a fitting end to an unhappy ship. Then word came from home that some of her crew had been captured, we caught a few more, and the whole sorry tale came out.'

'Did you know Captain Daniels, then?'

'A little, although he thought himself far superior to the likes of me,' said Sutton. 'From the short time I spent in his company, I should say that he was a man wholly unsuited to command.'

'Was he a tartar?' said Clay.

'Very much the brute,' confirmed his friend. 'The admiral warned him enough times not to drive his people so harshly, but it was the usual story. Daniels had such impeccable connections that he was able to defy him. I presume, with no possible remedy in sight, that the crew took matters into their own hands.'

'Yet it was not just a simple rising,' observed Clay. 'The mutineers must have been led with some intelligence, to have vanished so completely.'

'I daresay they were,' said his friend, through a

mouthful of fish. 'When will you commence your search?'

'As soon as I have completed our provisions. But I do not envisage that it will be a very lengthy hunt. His lordship believes the *Peregrine* to lie at Guadeloupe.'

'If it does, it is odd that Camelford has not reported it,' said Sutton. 'He commands the *Daring* and is tasked with patrolling those waters.'

'Sir George mentioned the *Daring,* and said I could call on her for assistance. I would have sooner had you by my side, John, but he says he cannot spare you.'

'He is right on that point,' said Sutton. 'Without the *Peregrine*, the squadron is short-handed. I am sure he is not seeking to frustrate you, but it is a shame not to spend more time together. It will be touch and go, it seems, for us both.'

'Perhaps we shall have the opportunity to see one another when Camelford and I return with the *Peregrine*.'

Sutton put down his knife and fork and sipped at this wine for a moment before replying. 'A word of caution, Alex, where Camelford is concerned,' he said. 'He is a decent enough captain, but he is a deuced odd cove.'

'In what way?'

'For one thing, he is decidedly bookish,' explained his friend. 'The stern cabin of a sloop of war ain't what you would call spacious, as you will recall, but he has had his shelved from deck to deckhead to accommodate his collection. I tell you; his quarters are more like a bookseller's shop than anything you would associate with a man-of-war.'

'Are they, by Jove,' chuckled Clay. 'That does sound strange, I grant you, but hardly sinister. As the husband to a novelist, I might have expected you to be more approving.'

'He is also prey to the most violent of passions,' continued Sutton.

'On all occasions, or just when he finds one of his volumes to have been placed on the wrong shelf?'

'I am serious, Alex. As a midshipman he was disrated for assault when he threw a fellow officer down a ladderway, and a year back he killed an American gentleman in a duel. They fought on the beach around the point. It was some dispute over a lady here in Antigua.'

'He sounds more rakish than bookish,' laughed Clay. 'My thanks for the warning. I doubt if I shall have time for any affairs of the heart while I am in these waters, but I shall certainly insist he precedes me down any steps.'

'Very droll,' said his friend. 'Do you know where in Guadeloupe the *Peregrine* may be found?'

'Sir George thought at Pointe-à-Pitre.'

'Pointe-à-Pitre!' exclaimed Sutton. 'Best of luck cutting her out from there, brother.'

'Yes, the admiral was of much the same opinion. What is so formidable about this place?'

'Where shall I start?' said his friend. 'The entrance is deuced narrow and turns about an island that serves the port like a breakwater. On that island is a large battery that will pound you all the way in. Once you are through that, you pass beneath a fortress with no end of guns to cover you. Oh, and the garrison can call on legions of freed slaves to oppose you. Get through all of that, and taking the *Peregrine* will be as easy as kiss my hand! Save that to get her out, you will have to go by the same route as you came in.'

'But I suppose if this port is so widely considered to be impregnable, at least the French will not expect an attack,' offered Clay.

Sutton smiled at this, and leant across the table to pat the top of his friend's arm. 'That is what I have always admired most in your character, Alex,' he said. 'Your unfailing optimism!'

*****

'We touch, and before we have had time to draw breath, we go again,' sighed Macpherson. He was standing at the stern rail of the *Griffin*, and was staring down on her churning wake, a bold white line drawn across the blue sea, leading back towards Antigua. 'To think that I joined the marines to better acquaint myself with the world. I was looking forward to the diversions of that wee island. I even have a relation who owns a plantation at some place named Saddle Hill, you know?'

'I do, for you can't have mentioned him above a dozen times last night, over that third bottle of Madeira, Tom,' said Blake, looking up from the sketch he was working on. 'It was ever thus in the navy, where we are always in an unseemly rush to be somewhere other than where we chance to be. But this voyage will at least be of limited duration, my friend. No sooner will we have sunk English Harbour, than Guadeloupe will appear in all her splendour.'

'That's as may be,' said the marine. 'But what occasion shall I have to visit that island? Apart from wading ashore at the head of my men, with my claymore in my hand?'

'And what of the painting of English Harbour I was going to produce?' protested his friend. 'I have completed little more than a few preliminary drawings. I shall be obliged to finish the work almost entirely from memory.'

The marine came around and looked over his fellow officer's shoulder, but it was not a harbour scene that lay on the page. Bold lines curved across the paper, conjuring up the lean, weathered face of a sailor with fierce eyes and a hawk nose.

'I know that man,' said Macpherson, stroking one of his bushy sideburns. 'Is it not the volunteer I recruited in Devon? The one with a singular name?'

'Larcum Mudge,' confirmed Blake, pointing with his pencil to where his model stood among the other members of the afterguard. 'He does have the most engaging features, does he not? I did ask him to sit for me, but he was very reluctant, so I am forced to capture his likeness unawares.'

'Aye, I do recall his countenance,' confirmed the Scotsman. 'The moment I clapped eyes on him, I resolved to get him on board. I must obtain his services as a model for my particular friend John Blake, I told myself.'

'Very obliging of you, I'm sure,' laughed the artist, bowing in mock gratitude.

'You have set him down right enough,' said Macpherson. 'I see you have caught some of the swagger I remember from when he signed on. As if he did me a favour by condescending to grace our ship with his presence.' From across the quarterdeck, Mudge seemed to be aware of being discussed. He glanced across at them, his fierce eyes lost in the deep shadow of his wide-brimmed hat.

'Deck ho!' yelled the lookout, sitting high on the fore royal yard. He had one arm looped nonchalantly around the mast and the other raised to shade his eyes. 'Sail off the larboard bow! One of them schooners ag'in!'

Preston, who was officer of the watch, crossed to the mizzen shrouds, his telescope in his hand. He trapped the brass eye piece under his chin, extended the tube, rested it on a rattling and then focused on the horizon.

'Edward grows very adept at performing his duties one-handed,' commented Macpherson.

'Indeed so,' said Blake, closing his sketchbook and rising from the quarterdeck carronade he had been sitting on. 'What have you found for us, Edward?'

'Another of these little local trading craft,' said Preston. 'We shall pass within hailing distance on our current course. Mr Todd!'

'Yes sir,' replied the midshipman.

'Kindly give my compliments to the captain, and tell him that we are closing with another schooner. Showing British colours.'

'Aye aye, sir,' said the youngster, wheeling off towards the ladderway.

'Are we especially interested in such wee craft?' queried the Scotsman. 'I understood that we have come here on the hunt for more substantial prey?'

'Standing orders in the squadron,' explained Blake. 'Any ship encountered is to be investigated, although it would be a bold privateer or smuggler who sailed up to a Royal Navy frigate in broad daylight, as this one is currently doing.'

Both the *Griffin* and the unknown schooner were travelling swiftly, so that when Clay arrived on deck the other ship was easily visible, up over the horizon already. He examined it in a perfunctory way, and then closed his telescope. 'Kindly signal to them to heave too, if you please, Mr Preston, and bring me within hailing distance.'

The flag signal had to be made twice before it was understood on board the approaching ship, and she eventually came up into the wind and wallowed in the swell. On her delicate twin masts, a mass of fore and aft sails shivered and flapped in the breeze. Her narrow hull was almost a hundred feet long, and lay low and heavy in the water. Her bulwarks were pierced with a half dozen gun ports per side, at each of which stood a six-pounder cannon. Her crew seemed a motley collection of various nationalities, mainly black or Hispanic. A red-faced man in a straw hat and a bright green waistcoat stood by the wheel, barking instructions to the crew.

'Ahoy there!' shouted Clay through his speaking trumpet. 'What vessel is that?'

'The *Saint Christopher*, out of Bridgetown, Barbados, sir,' came the reply. 'My name is Adams, and I am her owner.'

'What cargo do you have, Mr Adams?'

'Sugar and logwood for the most part,' came the reply. 'We are bound for Antigua.'

'You are very heavily armed for a simple trader, Captain,' continued Clay, indicating the line of guns.

In response the man barked an order, and four crewmen gathered around one of the cannons. A moment later they lifted it bodily off the deck.

'What the deuced …' exclaimed Macpherson, turning to Blake beside him, who was chuckling to himself. The man in the waistcoat gestured to the sailors to put the cannon down, and pointed his speaking trumpet back towards the *Griffin*.

'The pair in the bow are real, but the rest of my pieces are Quakers, sir,' he explained. 'They serve to frighten off privateers, but will answer for little more.'

'Am I to understand that all those other cannons are false?' queried the marine.

'Quite so, Tom,' smiled Blake. 'Wood and canvas, for the most part, I would think. They are convincingly done, I grant you.'

'Have you passed by Guadeloupe, Captain?' continued Clay.

'Aye, that we did,' said Adams. 'And were stopped by another king's ship for our troubles. I would hold it very kind, if you have completed your enquiries, to let us pass. I should like to make port before it grows dark. That is when these waters belong to the French privateers. And guns that they cannot see will not serve to distract them.'

'I understand, Captain. You may proceed. Have a safe passage,' concluded Clay, turning away from the rail. 'Have the encounter noted in the log, Mr Preston, and then put us back on our original course, if you please.'

'Aye, aye, sir,' replied the lieutenant.

The big frigate ponderously turned back across the wind, rather more slowly than the sleek schooner. Macpherson continued to look after her as she sped away towards Antigua, the island marked by a few puffy white clouds on the horizon.

'Tell me, John, how distant is Barbados?' he asked. His friend considered for a moment.

'Mr Armstrong is the man to answer that question, but I should say it lies perhaps three hundred miles away, off beyond Guadeloupe,' he said, pointing towards the south. 'Why do you ask?'

'Did you not mark the strip of fresh canvas on that ship's main sail?' said the marine. 'I would wager my commission that she is the same craft as we passed on our way into English Harbour when we arrived. I am no authority on navigation, but I should say that yon schooner has made a very swift passage indeed, if she has truly gone so far for her cargo.'

*****

Later that afternoon, the *Griffin* was sailing south, with the island of Guadeloupe filling the eastern horizon. Big white clouds dotted the sky above a chain of dark green forested mountains that soared thousands of feet up from out of the blue water. At the southern end of the range was the highest point, the lofty cone of a volcano. One of its slopes was green with scrubby vegetation, while just beside it was a scree of blackened lava. Against the sky, a line of smoke could be seen, drifting up from the summit. Through his telescope Clay examined the little settlements dotted at the mountains' feet and the occasional fishing boat working close in to the shore.

'This half of the island is named Basse-Terre,' explained Armstrong, who was standing by his side. 'It is forest for the most part. The other half is much flatter, and it is there that all the sugar plantations lie. The two portions are a little like the wings of a butterfly in shape. The place that they touch is where Pointe-à-Pitre is to be found, on the far side of those hills.'

'The French once produced a deal of sugar in these parts, I collect,' said Clay.

'Heavens, yes!' exclaimed the sailing master. 'Volcanic dirt, together with all the sun and rain hereabouts makes cane grow like weeds. Guadeloupe planters were rich as kings, back before the war. Why, at the end of the War of Seven Years, the French traded all of Canada for the return of this island, certain that they had struck a bargain.'

'But all of that is to be found beyond these mountains?'

'Yes sir. When we round the southern point, we shall open up the bay that contains Pointe-à-Pitre.'

'I very much wish to find the *Daring* first,' said Clay. 'I would sooner not announce our presence just yet. The admiral said she was generally to be found close to the Saintes.'

'Those little islands will appear presently, sir,' said

Armstrong. 'They lie off the southern end of Guadeloupe.' He waved towards the bow, just as the lookout hailed from the masthead.

'Deck ho! Sail ahoy! Man-of-war from the look of her!'

As they approached, the other ship appeared from beyond the southern cape of the island, and stood out to investigate the new arrival. She was a neat little sloop, ship rigged with three masts, just like a half-sized version of the *Griffin*. Her black hull had a broad yellow stripe along it, and a carved figurehead of a goddess in a flowing blue dress stared out from beneath her bowsprit.

'She is very like my first command,' said Clay, closing his telescope. 'Mr Russell, kindly make the squadron recognition signal, followed by our number.'

A line of coloured bundles rose up to the masthead, and the flags broke out in response to a deft snap of the halliard from the sailor assisting the midshipman. After a pause, the sloop replied.

'That is the correct response, sir,' said Russell. 'She is the *Daring*, sixteen-gun sloop of war, Master and Commander Stephen Camelford is her captain.'

'Kindly signal for him to come on board, Mr Russell,' ordered Clay. 'Mr Armstrong, please have Captain Camelford shown down to my cabin when he arrives.'

'Aye aye, sir.'

*****

Clay heard his visitor long before he saw him. The frigate had hove to in order to receive him, and the clatter of his boat's arrival alongside was accompanied by a flurry of shouted oaths, one of which was entirely new to him in spite of his two decades in the navy. When Captain Camelford arrived in the cabin, he proved to be a large young man with a prominent head and thin red hair. His solid face was bracketed by bushy ginger sideburns and spotted with freckles. He came through the door with a face like thunder, banging his hat into the hands of Harte and striding over. Clay regarded his visitor with surprise. To a lowly commander, a senior post captain like himself was considerably superior in rank, yet he could detect little of the deference he might have expected. Like the volcano the *Griffin* had passed earlier, Camelford seemed ready to erupt at any moment.

'Pleased to make your acquaintance, Captain,' Clay said, rising to shake his hand. His guest's grip was firm, yet slippery at the same time.

'Your pardon, sir, 'tis only seawater. I splashed my arm coming up the side,' he growled.

'No matter, do please take a seat,' said his host. 'Harte, a towel for the captain, followed by some madeira, if you please.' Slightly mollified, Camelford settled into the chair.

'I was unaware of the presence of your ship in the Leeward Islands, sir,' he said, dabbing at himself. 'Damnation! My whole bloody sleeve is sopping.'

'Surrender your coat to my steward, I pray,' said Clay. 'Before you catch a chill. Harte, kindly take it to the galley, and have it dried, if you please. That is much better, I am sure. As for my presence, I have only newly arrived in these waters.'

'I see,' said his guest, retaking his seat. 'May I ask why I have the pleasure of this visit, sir? I am generally left to guard the French hereabouts without assistance.'

'So I understand,' said Clay. He opened the top drawer of his desk, took out a sealed packet and passed it across. 'Here are fresh orders for you from Sir George covering how we are to work together. To answer you directly, I have been dispatched from home to perform a specific enterprise, which you may be able to assist me with.'

'I see, sir,' said his guest, making as if to slide his new orders into the inner pocket of the coat he no longer wore. A fresh frown of annoyance settled between his eyes. 'And what, pray is the nature of this enterprise?'

'Do you recall the sloop *Peregrine*?'

'Captain Daniels's ship, sir? The one that was supposedly lost in a storm last year?'

'The very same,' said Clay. 'What did you think of that incident?'

'Daniels was such a bloody fool, it came as little surprise to me that he had lost his command. I was quite prepared to believe that the lubber had foundered, but as it transpired, he succeeded in provoking his people to revolt before that could happen. How such coves are elevated to positions of authority is beyond me.' His eyes flickered briefly over Clay's coat, with its double epaulettes, and then he drank thirstily from his glass. 'Capital drop of wine, that, sir,' he said.

'Then let me pour you a little more, Captain, in my steward's absence,' said Clay, collecting the decanter and refilling both glasses. 'The character of the late Captain Daniels need not long detain us. I am more concerned with the location of his former ship. Since it is known that the *Peregrine* did not sink, as was supposed, I have been ordered to find and recapture her.'

'Good luck with that, sir!' snorted his guest. 'Why, she has over half a year's start on you! She might have fetched Botany Bay by now.'

'She might, but the Admiralty think not. They have seized a number the mutineers, and in one respect, their stories are all in accord. After they seized the *Peregrine* and murdered her captain, the rebels took her into Guadeloupe over there and sold her to the French.' Clay pointed towards the green slopes of the island visible through the stern window lights.

'Impossible, sir!' exclaimed Camelford. 'I should know if such a ship were here.'

'But would you?' mussed Clay. 'Consider, she would not have arrived until the hurricane season was at hand, when the *Daring* was withdrawn. Then the enemy will have had considerable leisure to alter her appearance.'

'It would take more than a lick of paint and a few new spars to fool me,' bristled Camelford. 'The *Peregrine* and *Daring* sailed in company on several occasions. I can assure you I am quite familiar with her general appearance, sir.'

Clay turned the stem of his glass between his fingers. 'So doubtless you would have noted her departure?' he said.

'Of course, sir. I know how to perform my duty!'

'Then I am at something of a loss, Captain,' said Clay. 'It is certain that the *Peregrine* was brought here by the mutineers, and yet you assure me both that she cannot still be in that port, and that she cannot have escaped your vigilance to slip away? How are such opposing views to be reconciled? Surely the only conclusion is that she must continue to lie in Pointe-à-Pitre. Is that not so?'

Camelford's face had flushed to a dangerous shade of red. Forewarned by Sutton of his volcanic temper, Clay held up a hand.

'I do not wish to vex you, Captain, but I have my duty to perform and you have fresh orders to assist me,' he said. 'Come, let you and I put all this to the test. We shall close with

Pointe-à-Pitre tomorrow, and conduct a thorough search of the place. I have a man on board who once served on the *Peregrine*, and should be able to see through any French trickery. If she is not in Guadeloupe, then I shall own I was wrong and take my search elsewhere. Will that answer?'

'But it is a fool's errand, sir!' insisted Camelford. 'I know what I am damned well about!'

'What did you just say?' said Clay icily, glaring at the younger man. 'Did you just describe my proposal as that of a fool?'

'No sir, of course not, sir. I was only offering my opinion,' said Camelford, his face blotched and angry.

'I have no objection to constructive suggestions, if they are framed in an appropriate way,' said Clay. 'Have the goodness to use language that reflects the difference in our rank, Captain.'

'I only seek to avoid the unnecessary, sir,' said his guest.

'But I say that it is necessary. If you have nothing to offer above simple contradiction, that is an end to the matter.'

There was a long pause as the furious Camelford stared into the cold grey eyes of Clay. 'If those are your orders ...' he said, at last.

'They are,' snapped Clay. 'I shall come across to the *Daring* shortly after dawn tomorrow, while the *Griffin* will remain out in the offing. The French will be familiar enough with your ship for us not to arouse suspicion. Should it come to an attack on Pointe-à-Pitre, I would sooner not alert them that a more powerful warship is in the area.'

'I remain troubled by your refusal to accept my assurances on this matter, sir,' growled Camelford.

'For God's sake, man, can you not see that I am trying

to be reasonable with you?' demanded Clay, his patience at an end. 'Would you prefer me to have you stand at attention during our meetings, while I bark orders at you?' His guest looked up sharply, his eyes hard with rage. 'Come, my good sir, let us not quarrel over this. You know the way the service operates. I can hardly report back to Sir George, and tell him I gave up without having set eyes on this place, now, can I?'

'I suppose not, sir,' muttered his guest.

Clay rose to his feet. 'Good, that is settled,' he said. 'Until tomorrow, Captain. Pray let me escort you back to the side.'

Camelford collected his hat and damp coat from Harte, putting them on without a word of thanks. The two men left the cabin in silence and made their way back to the entry port. When they arrived, Camelford pushed his hat down firmly on his head, and gave a perfunctory salute, rather than offering to shake hands.

'Oh, there was one further matter, Captain,' said Clay, stopping him with one foot already on the first step. 'Did you chance to encounter any trading schooners yesterday?'

'No, I can't say that I did, sir,' replied Camelford. 'I chased a privateer two nights back, but that has been all. Am I to be answerable to you for all my activities now, sir?'

'Of course not,' snapped Clay, wondering how it was that this difficult young commander had managed to limit the number of duels he had fought to only one. 'Till tomorrow, Captain.'

Chapter 5
Pointe-à-Pitre

Dawn the following day, and the sea was pearl beneath a sky flushed with a delicate shade of rose. Clay paused for a moment at the entry port to take it in, before he clambered down the side of the frigate and stepped into his barge. The movement of the sea was gentle and he had little difficulty making his way to the rear of the boat. He settled himself down next to Sedgwick in the stern sheets. It was deliciously cool this close to the sea's surface, and it was only his dignity as a captain that made him resist the urge to reach over the side and trail his fingers through the water. Instead he looked at the crew, all immaculate in their matching white and green. One sailor dressed in a check shirt and waistcoat broke the symmetry. He was a heavily built man with a dark pigtail threaded with a little grey. Andrews, Clay reminded himself, the boatswain's mate who had served six years previously on the *Peregrine*. He looks solid and competent, Clay decided. The French will have had to make considerable changes to his former ship to fool him.

He turned towards his coxswain. 'Get us underway, if you please, Sedgwick,' he ordered.

'Aye aye, sir,' he replied. 'Shove off in the bow there! Back water, larboards! Easy all! Whole crew, give way!'

The two ships were only a few cables apart, both hove to. Clay looked over the little sloop as they approached. In spite of his impossible temper, or perhaps because of it, Camelford seemed to keep a smart enough ship. Even close too nothing seemed out of place. Her rigging was worn but well maintained, and the paintwork on her battered hull was clean. As the gap to the *Daring* narrowed, Clay's thoughts moved from the ship to her strange, angry captain. His face set into a scowl of determination. I'll take no more nonsense from that young man, he told himself.

He climbed up the side of the sloop and in through the entry port, his eyes darting around ready to find fault with what he saw. But just like the exterior of the ship, all on the main deck was as it should be. The line of ship's boys all had white gloves, the correct number of boatswain's mates twittered away on their calls, and the sloop's small contingent of marines displayed all the white pipeclay and gleaming brass buttons to be expected of them. Even the ship's commander seemed to have decided to be civil today.

'Welcome aboard, sir,' Camelford said, once the ceremony was over. He indicated the dark mass of Guadeloupe behind him, with only the highest peaks illuminated by the rising sun. 'It will take us a good hour to close with Pointe-à-Pitre, so I thought you might care for some breakfast?'

'I should like that very much, Captain,' said Clay. 'There is a sailor in my barge who once served on board the *Peregrine*. Would you kindly have him brought on board and made welcome?'

'See to it, Mr Laidlaw, and have the ship put before the wind, if you please,' ordered Camelford to the officer of the watch, before leading the way below to his cabin. As they went, the deck began to heel a little as the sloop got underway.

'Have a care with the headroom, sir,' warned

Camelford, at the door to his cabin. 'The *Daring* offers a good inch less headroom than you will be accustomed to on your frigate.'

'My first command was a sloop of war,' said Clay. 'I well remember the limitations of the accommodation, although at the time I was newly promoted from lieutenant and thought the cabin one of limitless space, after the little gloomy box I had inhabited before.'

Space, limitless or otherwise, was not freely available in the aft cabin of the *Daring*, however. Sutton had not exaggerated when he had described it; lines of book spines seemed to run away from Clay in all directions. Every one of the bulkheads had been shelved, and every inch of shelving was occupied. More books overflowed from cases on the floor, or were stacked against the carriages of the two twelve-pounder carronades that stood one on each side of the ship. Even the stern lockers that ran beneath the windows were covered in volumes. In the small area of deck that remained unoccupied stood a tiny desk, a little table laid out for breakfast and two chairs. That was all.

'My, what a deal of books!' exclaimed Clay, looking around him. 'Where, pray, shall I sit?'

'Why, just here, sir,' said Camelford, collecting up the three slim volumes that lay on top of one seat, and patting it invitingly. 'Bring through the coffee directly, Smith!' he bellowed towards the cabin door.

'My thanks,' said Clay. He sat down and tried to spread out his legs, but soon met an obstruction. 'Ah, capital. More books,' he said, peering under the table.

'Yes, I am afraid I am inordinately fond of literature, sir,' said Camelford, for once a trifle abashed.

'You don't say,' muttered Clay, as he sipped at his

coffee. 'How long does it take you to clear for action?'

'Not as long as you might suppose, sir,' said his host, looking around for somewhere to put the books in his hands. He eventually settled on the deck beside him. 'You'll note that my carpenter has fashioned bars that fit across the front of each shelf, to retain the books in place. They are required in any event, in case we meet with heavy weather. Then the shelves themselves detach from those above and beneath. My men are really quite well versed in breaking it all down. Are you fond of literature, sir?'

'Tolerably so,' said Clay. 'I certainly enjoy reading, but my sister is the truly bookish one. She is acquainted with a number of authors and poets, and has published several works. Mainly romantic literature.'

'Has she, by God? Any that I might have come across, sir?' The angry young man of yesterday had vanished, and his eyes shone with interest.

'Perhaps her first work,' offered his guest. 'I believe it was tolerably reviewed and has something of a following. It was named *The Choices of Miss …*'

'*… of Miss Amelia Grey*!' completed Camelford. 'But, my dear sir, that is a work of genius! It is one of my favourite novels! Why, the scene in which Miss Amelia and Mr Lavery first dance together is exquisitely crafted. You must be so very proud of her.'

'Eh … yes, I suppose I am,' said Clay.

'Salt bacon and eggs, hot from the galley, sir,' announced the steward, placing a chafing dish between them. 'Might I help you to some, sir?'

'Yes, indeed,' said Clay, holding out his plate. 'Have you tried any of her other books?'

'I have read them all,' enthused his host, who then

embarked on a fulsome dissection of Betsey Sutton's various works, his breakfast congealing in front of him. Clay contented himself with nodded agreement between mouthfuls.

When both the meal and the literary evaluation had run its course, he drained the last of his coffee and dropped his napkin onto the table. 'Thank you for a most excellent repast, Captain,' he said. 'Perhaps we might now discuss this morning's reconnaissance, while we yet have time?'

'Of course, sir,' said the bookworm. 'Kindly clear all this away, Smith, and bring us the chart.'

The map that Camelford spread out on the table was worn with use and covered in little corrections and additions, all made in a neat hand. 'I have patrolled these waters for some years, you'll collect, sir,' he explained. 'I flatter myself that I have become quite the pilot, where the approaches to Guadeloupe are concerned.'

'So I see,' agreed Clay. 'Might I trouble you for a copy of the relevant part before I leave?'

'By all means, sir,' said his host. He turned to his steward. 'Kindly ask the sailing master to prepare one, Smith.'

'Aye aye, sir.'

'This large bay here is known locally as the Petit Cul de Sac, sir,' resumed Camelford. 'The chart originally showed it as devoid of hazards, but as you can see, over time, we have surveyed it with tolerable thoroughness. In truth, it is quite full of reefs and sandbanks.' He pointed them out with a sweep of his hand, before settling his finger on a substantial inlet at the bottom of the bay. 'And there is your Pointe-à-Pitre.'

Clay examined the map with care. The French port was built around a wedge of sea driven into the narrowest part of the island. The eastern side of the entrance was dominated by a large fortress, while blocking the entrance itself was a small island, perhaps a half mile wide, a little way out to sea. At one end of the island someone had added a rectangle of shading. Peering close, he read the small letters printed beside it. '*Gun battery, 8 x 36 pdrs*.'

'The Isle of Pigs is how the French name it, sir,' explained Camelford. 'It is no more than a low sandbank, in truth. Covered in vegetation, of course, as any stretch of ground left alone for five minutes in this part of the world swiftly becomes. It can only be passed at its eastern end, between that battery I have marked on, and the guns of the fortress. Between them they offer a prodigiously murderous crossfire. The deep-water channel bends around that end of the island, requiring any ship to make her turn just at the point where the fusillade is hottest.'

'What prevents a ship passing to the west of the island instead?' asked Clay.

'Coral reefs and a modest sandbank, sir. You can wade from that end of the island to the shore, and the water will seldom reach above your chest.'

'It does seem formidable defended,' mused Clay. 'Has a successful attack ever been made on Pointe-à-Pitre from the sea?'

'It has, but that was almost eighty years ago, sir. Blackbeard led a fleet of buccaneers against the port, and burned the place to the ground. It was his attack that prompted the French to build such formidable defences facing the sea, and the memory of that day is why they maintain them in such good order. Are you sure that your mission is not futile, even if the *Peregrine* is to be found in the port?'

'Have you had a change of heart, Captain?' joked Clay. 'Only yesterday you thought her presence here an impossibility!'

Camelford reddened at this, slammed down his coffee cup and rose to his feet. 'If I have attempted to save you from a wasted journey, sir, I am sorry for it, I am sure. But since you will not take my word on the matter, let us proceed on deck, where perhaps the evidence of your own eyes will persuade you.'

*****

Camelford stormed across the main deck towards the forecastle of the sloop, with Clay trailing in his wake. As he marched, he glared around him.

'Mr Laidlaw!' he roared, pointing at one of the carronades that lined the sides of the ship. 'The breeching on this gun is in a shocking state! Where did you learn your damned seamanship?' Clay looked at the offending rope, which was at best slightly frayed.

'My apologies, sir,' said the lieutenant. 'I shall have it replaced directly.'

Slightly mollified, the captain of the *Daring* climbed up the ladderway and onto the forecastle, and then waited at the top for Clay. From the front of the sloop, there was a splendid view of the approaching land. Clay opened his telescope and looked about him.

The *Daring* was sailing under topsails alone across a bay of deep blue sea, dotted with paler patches where sandbanks and reefs lay near to the surface. The western shore was of rock cliffs, with steep, forested slopes behind. The occasional silver thread among the blanket of green marked where waterfalls tumbled down the mountainside. Higher still were the peaks, wreathed in mist, with the smoking cone of the volcano just visible in the distance. On the eastern side the character of the island changed; white sand lined the shore, backed by feathery palm trees.

The land was of rolling hills, dotted with buildings. Some were modest whitewashed cottages, roofed in thatch or terracotta tiles. A few were more substantial, such as a grand white block faced with columns and porticos and surrounded by a cluster of outbuilding that faced towards the sea. Between them the hillside was a chessboard of cane fields, linked together by a network of red-earth tracks. Through his telescope Clay could even see a field being worked. A line of tiny figures showed against the vivid green curtain of sugar cane, their steel machetes twinkling in the early morning sun. An overseer in a broad straw hat sat behind them on his horse.

'They continue to harvest sugar, I see,' said Clay, pointing towards the field.

'Yes, sir,' said Camelford. Clay waited for more, but his companion stared resolutely forward, his face still tinged with red, his jaw set. Touchy bastard, concluded Clay to himself. He turned his attention to Pointe-à-Pitre.

It lay between the two halves of the island. The Isle of Pigs, in front of the port, was much as Clay had imagined it: a low dome emerging from the sea like the back of a whale, and covered with bushy mangroves and palms. At the eastern end of the island the trees had been cleared from in front of the battery. He could see a line of grass-covered embrasures beneath a tricolour that flapped languidly in the gentle breeze. Clay fancied he could even see the black muzzles of some of the cannons, pointing towards him. To the left of the island was an area of disturbed sea, with small waves breaking over obstructions in the water. To the right was the deep-water channel, with the fortress beyond.

It sat on top of a low cliff of brown rock, with lines of

imposing grey walls and some terracotta roofs peeking up just proud of them. Another, even larger tricolour here, and many more guns. Beyond the fort and the Isle of Pigs, he could see a cluster of masts in the port, mostly the slender ones of schooners, but a few more solid-looking spars. Of the town itself, only the higher parts were visible above the island: a cluster of houses, most painted white, but others in ochre or yellow, rising up the hillside. In their midst rose the stone tower of a church.

As the sloop came closer there was a puff of smoke from the battery on the island, followed by a chain of splashes on the water heading towards them as a ball skipped across the sea. The last splash was a good quarter mile from them, and was followed by the low boom of a cannon.

'Where is it your practice to observe the port from, Captain?' asked Clay, continuing to examining the approaching land.

'I can't say that we have a regular place, sir,' said Camelford.

'Really?' queried Clay. 'You favour a more distant blockade then?'

'I do, sir.' Again, the bare minimum that duty required.

'No matter,' said Clay, after a pause. 'Here will serve as well as any other spot. Can you kindly have the ship heave to. I shall then need a couple of reliable young gentlemen to conduct the observations for me from the masthead. Can you also pass the word for the sailor who came aboard with me?'

'Aye, aye, sir,' said Camelford. 'I shall attend to it now.' He strode off, calling for Lieutenant Laidlaw.

The two midshipmen who appeared a little later were gangly youngsters, all elbows and knees. One had a face dotted with acne, in spite of his deep tan. The other had large, awkward hands that a recent growth-spurt had left a good two inches proud of his coat sleeves. But both seemed excited by the task being asked of them, and had come equipped with their telescopes, notebooks and pencils.

'Now, gentlemen, I want you each to take a masthead, and have a good look into the port for me,' Clay said gravely. 'Take your time, and note down everything that you see. I am particularly interested in vessels with hulls of a similar size to this ship. Is that clear?'

'Yes, sir,' they chorused.

'Do either of you have some aptitude at drawing?' he asked.

'Thorny here does, sir,' said awkward hands, indicating his colleague with the point of his elbow. 'I mean Mr Thorne, sir,' he added.

'Excellent. Then perhaps you could produce a plan of the port for me, Mr Thorne, with all the various ships marked on. This man here is Andrews, and he will be accompanying you aloft,' he concluded, indicating where the former *Peregrine* stood with his arms folded. 'A spy glass for Andrews, if you please, Mr Laidlaw. Any questions? No? Then away with you.'

The two young officers flew to the shrouds, and began to run up them, clearly engaged in some sort of race. Thorne took the foremast, accompanied by a more sedate Andrews.

When they were safely installed on the topmast crosstrees, Clay turned back towards the *Daring*'s captain. 'Now we shall see whatever is to be seen,' he said, trying to engage him in conversation again.

'Indeed, sir,' said Camelford. 'And may I ask what you will do if the *Peregrine* is not in the port?'

'Then I will leave you to your blockade, and search the

other harbours in the island,' said Clay. 'If that too should prove fruitless, then I will proceed to the other enemy-held islands in the Caribbean. My orders are quite clear. Indeed, I find myself almost hoping that you are correct, and that she does not lie in Pointe-à-Pitre.'

'Why so, sir?' asked Camelford.

'Because if the *Peregrine* is here, I am duty-bound to attempt something against her, Captain,' replied Clay. 'There is very little moon for the next few nights, which will serve as a good opportunity for us to attempt something, but the defences of Pointe-à-Pitre appear every bit as formidable on close inspection as you promised. I don't see any prospect of taking the *Griffin* and *Daring* in without enduring some fearful punishment from that battery and fort. Even if we could somehow fight our way past them and into the port, the commotion would rouse the whole place, which would make taking the *Peregrine* most uncertain.'

'If you can take her at all, sir,' added Camelford. 'Remember that the governor has an army of negros at his disposal, any number of which he may have stationed on board.'

'Quite so,' said Clay. 'And then, to cap it all, the ships have to come out by the same channel that they went in, running the gauntlet once more. If I had command of a first rate, I would still think twice before hazarding it!'

'I did urge caution, sir,' said Camelford, looking a little more pleased with life again.

'You did, but I do not have the luxury of ignoring my orders,' said Clay. 'So, if sailing in like Blackbeard in his pomp won't answer, another way will need to be found. Perhaps an assault in boats? They will have more chance of slipping into the port, undetected.'

'They will, sir,' agreed the *Daring*'s captain. 'Although they will be very vulnerable if spotted by the enemy. The Frogs have several guard boats that patrol the harbour entrance, and I have yet to see how the *Peregrine* is to be got out, once the alarm is raised.'

'No, that is the nub of the problem,' agreed Clay. 'Perhaps a landing of marines to take the battery?'

'That might help, but would leave the fortress in place, and warned by the sound of fighting from the island, sir,' said Camelford. 'But perhaps such speculation will prove unnecessary. Maybe she is not here at all.'

'Maybe,' murmured Clay, walking across to the forecastle rail to stare at the land. He focused his telescope back on the island. The line of cane cutters had completed their field, and were now busy loading the long rods onto a wain. For some reason the scene troubled him, but search as he did, he couldn't think why. After a while he heard a cough from behind him.

'I believe the young gentlemen may have completed their observations, sir,' announced Camelford.

The two midshipmen slid down the backstays and formed a huddle, agreeing what they had seen. A little farther back stood Andrews, listening to what the two youngsters said. The pages of the officers' notebooks flapped in the breeze as they ordered their thoughts, and then they came over at last.

'Gentlemen, what have you to report?' asked Clay.

In answer, Midshipman Thorne held out his notebook. Across two pages was the plan he had made of the harbour. It was carefully drawn, with hatching to indicate the shore, leaving the water blank white. Various crosses were marked on, each with a little note beside it.

'Most of the shipping is on the eastern side of the inlet, sir,' he began, indicating one side of his picture. 'Just behind the fort is a breakwater, with perhaps two dozen small fishing boats.'

'Maybe more, sir,' supplemented his colleague.

'We didn't do a complete count, because none of them are large enough to be the ship you are looking for, sir,' explained Thorne.

'I understand,' said Clay. 'What else could you see?'

'Beyond the fishing harbour are most of the wharfs, sir. Plenty of activity there, with five sail of large schooner, and a brig warped in close. At first I thought the brig might be your ship, but she only has two masts, and is a fair bit shorter than the *Daring*, so we don't hold her to be the one. Andrews here agrees.' The boatswain's mate nodded from his place a little behind his superiors.

'It is as I feared,' said Camelford. 'No sign of your quarry, sir.'

'There is another ship, moored away from the others, sir,' continued the midshipman. 'Her hull has been painted black, and she is certainly the right size.'

'What did you make of her, Andrews?' asked Clay.

'*Peregrine* for sure, sir,' said the sailor, coming forward to join the group.

'How can you be so certain, man?' demanded Camelford.

'Because I know every inch of her, sir,' insisted Andrews. 'Them sly bastards has done their best to make her look wrong, what with hacking off her gingerbread, an' rigged her up all foreign. But I would still know her on a night as black as a Newgate lock hole, if only by the rake of her bowsprit.'

'The rake of her bowsprit!' protested Camelford, glaring at the petty officer. 'Surely, we need more than such trifles, before contemplating a most uncertain attack, sir.'

Andrews turned towards Clay in appeal. 'It ain't just that, but all manner of stuff. Like she had her starboard cathead shot away back in ninety-four, when we fought ag'in the *Ville de Chartres*. The dockyard fashioned a replacement, but it ain't never looked quite the same. It be her, right enough.'

'You are quite sure, Andrews?' asked Clay.

'May I be struck dumb if I'm wrong, sir.'

'And where was the *Peregrine* moored?'

'Over here, sir,' said Thorne, pointing to a cross on his drawing, with a question mark beside it. 'In this bay on the western side of the inlet, between us and the moored ship of the line.'

'The what!' exclaimed Clay and Camelford together.

'The ship of the line, sir,' repeated the officer, pointing to a second, larger cross. 'She is a big two-decker. Probably a seventy-four.'

'Or even an eighty gunner,' added his colleague.

'Is she moored close to the *Peregrine*?' demanded Clay.

'If the *Peregrine* it is,' muttered the sloop's commander, under his breath.

'Not hard against her, but perhaps a half mile away, sir,' said Thorne.

'Maybe as much as a mile,' supplemented awkward hands.

'Why the hell can't she be seen from here, if she is so damned large?' demanded Camelford.

'The French have struck their upper masts on deck, doubtless to conceal her. And of course, there is the island in the way, sir,' explained Thorne. 'She is plain to see from the masthead.'

'A ship of the line, out here in Guadeloupe,' said Clay. 'That is certainly unexpected. I wonder what she can be about?'

'I have never heard of the like in my time,' said the *Daring*'s captain. 'There were plenty of French warships hereabouts in the past. Perhaps she has escaped from one of the Atlantic ports, although for what object, I am sure I don't know.'

'Sir George did mention the Jamaica convoy would pass close by, in a couple of weeks,' said Clay. 'Might there be a connection?'

Camelford blanched at the thought. 'That must be it!' he exclaimed. 'Such a powerful ship loose among all those fat merchantmen. It doesn't bear thinking upon!'

'Then we must see that she does no such thing,' said Clay. 'Could you put the ship about, please, Captain, and let us re-join the *Griffin*.'

'Mr Laidlaw! Have the ship stand out to sea, if you please,' bellowed Camelford towards the quarterdeck.

'Aye aye, sir.'

'Thank you, gentlemen, for your observations,' said Clay. 'And for your assistance too, Andrews. Mr Thorne, perhaps you can copy up your plan in a fair hand for me, before I leave the ship, together with a note of all of your observations?'

'Aye, aye, sir,' said the midshipman, touching his hat and withdrawing with his fellow officer. Andrews knuckled his forehead and disappeared too.

'And might I have the use of your cabin, together with pen and paper? I need to report this all to Sir George.'

'Of course, sir,' said Camelford, ushering him across to the head of the ladder that led down to the main deck. 'After you, sir.'

'No, after you, Captain,' Clay insisted, as something Sutton had said returned to him.

Once he was alone at Camelford's little desk he worked quickly, dashing off his report to the admiral. The two midshipmen arrived at one point, to present him with their findings on Pointe-à-Pitre, written out in Thorne's crabbed hand. When he had finished writing, Clay called out to Smith to bring some wax seals. A little while later Camelford came in to report that the sloop was closing with the *Griffin*.

'Excellent, Captain,' said Clay, passing over the two sealed packages. 'Here is my dispatch for Sir George, and these are your orders. You are to make all haste and find the admiral. When you do so, you are to bring him back here. He has the only ship of force in the area.'

'If she truly is a French eighty-gunner, she will heavily outclass the little *Stirling*,' observed Camelford. 'They carry thirty-six-pounders on their lower deck, against the flagship's twenty-fours.'

'Perhaps all those layers of paint Sir George has added to the exterior will serve to armour her,' smiled Clay. 'But you forget the *Griffin*. We cannot challenge this Frenchman alone, but I daresay between myself and the admiral, we shall give a decent account of ourselves.'

'And who will take my place before the island, sir?'

'I will do that,' said Clay.

'With respect, the blockade of Guadeloupe is the *Daring*'s responsibility, sir,' said Camelford, a frown creasing his forehead. 'Are you quite sure that is the right course?'

Clay finally reached the end of his patience with this

annoying young man. 'That is my decision,' he snapped, rising from behind his host's desk. 'I do not propose to discuss it any further. Kindly go and find Sir George, as I have instructed, and give him my dispatch. It covers the bald facts of the situation here. I shall leave you to explain to him how it was that you managed to let a French ship of the line slip past you into a port that you were tasked with observing. Good day to you, Captain.'

Chapter 6
Alone

Long after the *Daring* had disappeared over the horizon, the *Griffin* remained stationary with her topsails backed, wallowing to each fresh wave that ran beneath her. The sun rose higher, the sea grew a little bluer, and the dark mass of Guadeloupe remained on the horizon. All those on deck watched the lonely figure of the captain as he paced along the weather side of the quarterdeck, back and forth, back and forth. His hands were clenched behind him, his head was bowed and his calm grey eyes were blind to all that went on around him. A passing rain squall briefly wetted the planking, bringing Yates, his servant, out onto the deck armed with his master's oilskins, but he was waved away as the remorseless striding continued. Even the bustle of the watch changing over failed to interrupt him.

Released from duty, the sailors returned to the lower deck. Here it was close and muggy, in spite of the wind chutes that had been installed to bring a little air down into the hull. The faces of the sailors glistened in the lamplight as they sat around their mess tables. In spite of the uncomfortable motion of the ship as it remained hove to, Trevan had got out a large sperm-whale tooth he was working on. The ivory was polished to a smooth buttery-yellow by long handling, and on one face the shape of a ship was appearing from a mass of tiny cuts.

'That be a nice piece of scrimshaw you got there,

Adam,' commented Mudge. 'Must have come from a good-sized beast an' all – eighty barrels at least, maybe more.'

'Aye, it were a bull we caught off the Cape back when I were on the old *Emilia,* afore I was pressed,' confirmed the Cornishman. 'That bugger fought like a demon. Near smashed our boat to splinters before we managed to lance him.'

'What be the ship?' asked Mudge. 'She looks too big for a whaler.'

'That be our old barky, the *Titan*, thirty-six,' said Trevan. 'She be no more, alas, but I can still bring her lines and rig to mind.'

The other former *Titan*s nodded at this, and O'Malley looked over his friend's shoulder. 'That's her, to be sure,' he said. 'Uncommon quick, so she was. You've got her just so, Adam.'

'Wish this bleeding barky were uncommon quick,' moaned Evans, as the frigate continued to wallow in the swell. 'Ain't Pipe decided what to do yet? I'll be puking me guts up if we don't get underway soon.'

'What be making him linger so, Able?' asked Trevan. 'One peep at the Frogs and now he seems minded to wear a hole in the deck.'

'He be caught as to what to do, I reckon,' said Sedgwick. 'Andrews says that *Peregrine* be there, right enough, but what he can't fathom be how we shall come at her.'

'Pointy Point be a proper tough place to enter, I hear,' said Trevan. 'No end of cannon, and a right tricky entrance. I hope all that walking about in the sun ain't giving Pipe the notion to try.'

'How come you know so much about it, Adam?' asked Mudge.

Larcum Mudge

The Cornishman pointed across the lower deck with his clasp knife, and picked out a wiry-looking sailor on another table. 'Abbott were here back in ninety-four, on the old *Vanguard,* when we took the place from the Frogs. Course, it didn't last any. Some bugger from Paris showed up with an army and freed the slaves, who fought like tigers for him. He reckons the place is tight as a clam.'

'If it were that tough to crack, how did it come to change hands at all?' asked Evans.

'They landed an army down the coast and walked in,' explained the Cornishman. 'It's as easy as kiss my hand to seize from the landward side, if you has the soldiers, that is. Not sure our forty Lobster will answer.'

'It's worse than that, lads,' said Sedgwick. 'Andrews told me there be a Frog two-decker moored in the place, and a proper big bastard at that.'

'A two-decker!' exclaimed O'Malley. 'We should be leaving that fecker well alone! Ain't no call for pulling that bugger's tail, I'm after thinking.'

'So, why be it taking Pipe so bleeding long to make up his mind?' queried Mudge. 'He can't be thinking of sailing in against them odds, can he?'

'Proper deep one is Pipe,' observed Trevan. 'If there be a way to come at that *Peregrine*, he'll find it, though he has to pace the deck till Doomsday.'

'Maybe he's thinking of cutting the bugger out, with boats, like we did that Frog slaver a couple of years back,' suggested Evans.

'And maybe his orders don't give him no choice but to try,' added Sedgwick.

The sailors pondered this for a moment, and then looked up towards the main deck overhead. With a slow creaking from the frames around them, the frigate started to swing through the water. The wallowing eased, and the gurgle of passing sea began to tremble through the oak wall beside them.

'Oh, that do feel better,' said Evans.

'Not sure as I likes the sound of that,' said Trevan. 'I reckon we be heading back towards Pointy Point.'

Sedgwick held out his hand and touched the ship's side. 'For good or ill, he's gone an' made up his mind, lads.'

*****

The following night, after the molten sun had dropped below the horizon in a fiery blaze, it quickly grew dark. The sky was covered with occasional puffs of cloud, the clear patches between them alive with stars. Down on the surface of the sea, the big frigate went about and started to close with the shore, pulling a line of ship's boats behind her like a mallard with her ducklings.

For once the *Griffin* was almost completely dark. No navigation lamps winked out from high on her mastheads. No amber lanterns shone on her main deck, where her crew were quietly gathering. Only by her wheel was there the light from the binnacle, illuminating the large figure of Jacob Armstrong as he stood quietly conning the ship. The chart produced by the *Daring*'s sailing master fluttered in his hand as he angled it towards the faint glow.

There is more light outside the ship than within, thought Clay to himself, as he stood by the rail, allowing his eyes to adjust to the dark. Where her hull swept through the water beneath him, it left faint tendrils of phosphorescence curling in the sea. What starlight there was caressed the tops of the lapping wave crests. The dark bulk of the island lay all about them as they entered the bay, dotted with a net of yellow points from homes and farms on shore. And over all was the volcano, spitting out a dust of tiny vermillion sparks high up above them.

Clay extended out his night glass and focused on the cluster of lights that was Pointe-à-Pitre. There was the fortress on the cliff, a dark block with only a few orange points showing. The dark bar of the Isle of Pigs stretched across the entrance, its battery invisible and a gentle line of silver beach showing below it. He turned his attention to the island's western end, with its reefs and sand bars, linking it to the land. Somewhere behind were the *Peregrine* and the ship of the line. What the hell are you thinking of? he asked himself again, just as he had been doing for hours. Attacking this place against such odds? Surely the discovery of that huge warship had changed everything? No one would blame you for turning back.

He closed his telescope with a snap; breathing in the warm tropical air, he forced himself to be calm again. Have a little faith, he told himself. The judgement you reached on the quarterdeck earlier was sound. Once you had discounted everything that was impossible to achieve, what was left was the bones of something promising. The men all know what they need to do. It will work. He turned away from the rail and walked back across to the group of officers by the wheel.

'Have we much farther to go, Mr Armstrong?' he asked.

'Another few cables, sir,' said the American. 'That volcano off the larboard quarter makes for a useful mark.' Clay went to nod, and then realised how useless the gesture was in the dark.

'Very good,' he said, and went forward to look down onto the main deck. He could sense more than see the groups of heavily armed men who were forming up, under the hissed instructions of their officers.

'To me, launch crew,' said the voice of Preston, from close under the forecastle.

'Blue cutter over here,' said Midshipman Russell. 'Have those packages the gunner gave you ready for inspection.'

Just below where Clay stood was an oasis of calm among all the movement. There could be no mistaking the carefully arranged block of men, perfectly aligned with each other, even if he couldn't see their red coats and cross belts. From almost directly beneath his feet came Macpherson's voice.

'Corporal Edwards, have you checked that every man's piece is uncocked?' he asked.

'Yes, sir,' came the reply. 'Private Conway had his on half-cock, so I've stopped his grog for a week to learn him.'

'And you have the shuttered lantern?'

'I got it here, for when you should have need of it, sir.'

'Good man,' said the marine. 'Should we encounter any sentries posted on the beach, cold steel only, lads. The man who fires before I give the word will taste a dozen at the grating in the morn.'

'Bring her up into the wind, helmsman,' ordered Armstrong at the wheel, and the frigate started to turn. 'Mr Sweeny, my compliments to Mr Hutchinson, and tell him he can get in sail and let go the anchor.'

The youngster scampered off along the gangway, almost colliding with his captain in the dark.

'Steady there, Mr Sweeny,' Clay said. 'No need for

such unseemly haste. Remember you are a king's officer and the eyes of the men are on you.'

'Aye aye, sir,' said the chastened midshipman, before disappearing into the night.

'Are you ready to depart, Mr Macpherson?' Clay called down.

'Aye, sir,' replied the Scot.

'Very well, we shall await your signal. The best of luck to you.'

The first of the frigate's two cutters had drawn up alongside and the marines made their clumping way down into it. With a few hissed instructions, and a clatter of oars, it pulled away, a nucleus of black against the starlit water for a moment before it vanished altogether. Clay watched it go, and then turned as someone appeared beside him.

'Ship is at anchor, and showing no sail, sir,' said the first lieutenant.

'Thank you, Mr Taylor,' said his captain, returning his attention to the island. He was willing for a sign, and dreading that it might be the sudden prickle of musket fire.

'Tom knows what he is about, sir,' said Taylor, 'and he has a few men skilled in moving in the dark without rousing suspicion.'

'Yes, former poachers, for the most part. But I am sure it is proceeding satisfactorily,' said Clay, with a forced calm he didn't entirely feel. 'Is all in hand down on the main deck?'

'All is as it should be, sir,' said the first lieutenant. 'Mr Preston and Mr Blake have their men in hand, and I made young Mr Russell repeat his orders to me, one last time.'

They resumed their vigil of the island, waiting for the signal. Time stretched out for the watchers as the night filled with sound. The groan of the anchor cable against the hawse hole. The chink of equipment and the occasional cough from the men stood waiting down on the main deck. The lap of water against the hull beneath them.

Now Clay's head began to run with all the details that he would have liked to have checked over with Taylor, knowing that he shouldn't ask. The older man was much too good an officer not to have attended to them all, and might be offended by the implied lack of confidence in him. Clay sighed to himself, remembering when he had been a first lieutenant. Back then he had dreamed of being a patrician captain, freed from worrying about all the mundane detail behind an attack like tonight's. Yet now that he had reached that position, he was busy fretting over being excluded. His natural good humour came back to save him, and he chuckled to himself. Then an orange light appeared at the western end of the Isle of Pigs, and started to wink. Three flashes, a pause, and then two more.

'That is the correct signal, sir,' said Taylor. 'Shall I give the word?'

'Yes. It's time.'

*****

The last boat to leave the frigate's side was the cutter commanded by Midshipman Russell. It was the smallest of the frigate's four boats, a fact that became apparent as the larger members of the storming party made their way to their places.

'Shift yer great fecking arse there, Sam Evans,' hissed O'Malley, as he tried to give himself enough room to pull on his oar.

'Not so bleeding easy, with Larcum hard by on t'other side,' complained the big Londoner. 'How about if I take your cutlass and pistol, and shift up into the bow?' The night filled with clanking and muffled oaths, and the cutter was set rocking.

'What *is* going on there?' demanded the voice of the midshipman from the stern of the boat.

'Just finding me place, Mr Russell,' said Evans.

'There be no room here, Sam,' protested Trevan, who was occupying the bow seat. 'And I've got these crowbars to mind an' all.' More shifting followed as the big man returned to his original place and sat down heavily.

'Settle down, Evans,' growled Sedgwick. 'None of us fancy a swim this night.'

'Easy for Able to bleeding say, taking his ease with the Grunters,' muttered Evans. 'And how comes that Andrews bloke gets to sit with them?'

'He's to be our fecking guide,' replied O'Malley. 'Knows that barky we're after like the back of his hand.'

'Silence in the boat!' ordered Russell. 'Get us underway, if you please, Sedgwick.'

They pushed off and rowed gently away from the frigate, each dip of the oars accompanied by brief rings of phosphorescence. The cliff-like side of the *Griffin* rose up behind them, her lofty masts and rigging a net for the stars. Two dark shapes grew from out of the water on either side.

'Easy all,' ordered Sedgwick, and the cutter ran on a little before slowing to a halt.

'Mr Preston, are you ready?' came the voice of Blake from the stern sheets of the longboat.

'Yes sir,' replied the launch.

'Mr Russell?'

'Cutter's ready, sir,' replied the midshipman.

'Absolute silence, gentlemen, if you please,' urged

Blake. 'Follow my lead.'

In line ahead, the three boats turned towards the shore. The dark water of the bay was dappled by starlight, swirling in silver pools where the sea broke over the coral reefs and sandbanks that lay all around them. Ahead was the port, and the island spread across the entrance, a bar of dark shade against the faint lights of the town beyond, growing ever larger as they came near. A fluke in the wind brought the mouldering smell of dank vegetation, just as the first sound of waves lapping against the shore reached them.

'Western end of the island, Sedgwick,' muttered Russell. 'As far from that damned battery as can be achieved.'

'Aye aye, sir,' whispered the coxswain. 'I reckon I can see where Mr Blake has beached.' He pointed at a dark shape against the white sand with a cluster of figures around it. The launch ahead was turning off to one side of it, so Sedgwick pulled the tiller across and headed the other way.

'Backs into it lads!' he hissed. The boat surged into a gentle wave, the bow lifting at first and then tilting forward to surf down the far side.

'Easy all!' said Sedgwick as the boat rushed forward amid a welter of foaming water. The bottom caught for a moment, ran free, and then grated to a halt.

'Over the side, lads,' urged Russell. 'But keep those packages dry!' He stepped out of the boat, braced for cold water soaking into his shoes and stockings. The sea was warm as milk, a surprise that was remarked on with chattering pleasure by the barefooted crew of the cutter.

'Silence!' he ordered. 'Sedgwick, take charge while I go and find Mr Blake. Keep the men together, and above all quiet.'

'Aye aye, sir.'

Larcum Mudge

Russell stumbled across the sand towards the sound of gentle voices ahead. They had landed at the extreme western end of the Isle of Pigs. The beach was narrow here, backed by the curved trunks of palm trees, the dark forest beyond. Off to the east, towards the gun battery, the sandy shore vanished into a mass of mangroves, their serpentine roots black against the white surf as they curled like claws and dipped into the sea. On the other side of him the beach turned around the end of the island. Stretching between here and the coast was a mass of disturbed water, with banks of white sand proud of the sea in places. The sound of the wash and ebb competed with the hum of insects and the shifting of night creatures among the trees.

'Cutter arrived, sir,' he reported to the figure of Blake.

'Splendid to hear that, Mr Russell,' said the lieutenant. 'What was less good was the sound of your men skylarking as they landed. Kindly keep them in hand. Once we get into the harbour proper, such levity will cost us dear.'

'Aye aye, sir.'

'Very well. Tom, what have you to report?'

'That my men have secured this end of the island,' said Macpherson. 'There is a path that leads through the woods in the direction of the battery. I have placed pickets to guard it. Also, we have had the leisure to look at possible ways to bring the boats through these shallows and into the port. Corporal Edwards here has found a promising-looking wee channel that runs close alongside the beach.'

'It's shallow, mind, sir,' reported the marine. 'No deeper than me knees in places, but only fifty yards long at best. With a deal of hauling, I daresay the boats will squeeze through.'

'What sort of bottom?' asked Preston.

'Sand for the most part, some rock towards the far end, sir,' said Edwards.

'Any sign of the enemy?' asked Blake.

'Aye, but taken care of,' said Macpherson, indicating a pair of dark shapes beneath the palm trees. Russell realised that he had seen them when he landed, but had dismissed them as rocks. 'Mind, they will be missed presently, when their watch is over, so I suggest you gentlemen make a start with getting the boats through. My lads will hold this part of the island until your return.'

They started with the empty cutter. The channel that Corporal Edwards had found proved easy to follow, even in the dark. It swirled with water, moving between the beach on one side and a smooth dome of sand that rose proud of the sea on the other. The crew of the cutter were able to run their boat through, with it only grounding lightly in two places. Next came the bigger launch, which proved more troublesome. That needed the combined manpower of two boat crews to drag her across the shallowest parts. At times the men were straining and slipping among the churning water, hauling the heavy boat forward a foot at a time. Which left the much larger longboat to come.

'We can lighten her by taking out the gratings and oars, and carrying them along via the beach,' suggested Preston, rubbing at the stump of his left arm.

'I can get some my lads to porter them,' offered Macpherson.

'I daresay we can get her through, with a deal of effort,' said Blake. 'My worry is the return trip, with the enemy alerted, and perhaps pressing us hard. That ship of the line could put twice our numbers into her boats, not to mention any relief coming from the shore.' The officers stood on the beach, imagining the chaos that would follow them trying to pull the stubborn longboat through, under attack from swarms of Frenchmen.

'Not an attractive prospect,' said Preston.

'I think I have it!' exclaimed Macpherson. 'Leave the longboat where she lies, on the outer side of this wee piggy island, for me and my marines to use when the time comes to return to the *Griffin*. In her stead, use the cutter that brought my men across.'

'It will leave us short for the attack on the *Peregrine*,' mused Blake.

'Aye, but what you do is to be but a diversion,' urged the marine. 'It is Mr Russell here who is will land the telling blow.'

Blake looked up to the starlit sky for a moment, and then made his decision. 'Very well, let us make it so,' he said. 'Get the other cutter pulled through, and let us start this night's work in earnest.'

*****

Protected by the Isle of Pigs and all the shallows, the harbour beyond was a calm pool. On its broad surface was faithfully mirrored every light in Pointe-à-Pitre on the far side of the inlet. Only where the deep-water channel ran beneath the black walls of the fortress was the sea disturbed, setting the reflected lights to flash and wink. Midshipman Russell looked across at the wharfs and buildings of the sleeping town. Faint noises drifted on the night air. The call and reply of the watch as they patrolled the quayside. A burst of sound from an unseen party of revellers. The single bell-stroke from the clock in the church tower.

'One in the morning,' he muttered to himself, as he settled in the stern sheets of the cutter. 'Kindly follow Mr Preston's launch, Sedgwick.'

'Aye aye, sir,' said the coxswain. 'Shove us off there, lads.'

The boat slid down into the water as the last of the crew clambered over the sides and took their places, and the attack party set off into the harbour.

They hugged the western side of the inlet, as far from any watchers in Pointe-à-Pitre as possible. Here the shore was sparsely populated, with only the occasional light up on the hillside. Where land met water there was a low cliff, fringed with trailing creepers. In the deep shadow at its foot, the line of boats was almost invisible as it crept along. Sedgwick found himself straining forwards, as he tried to follow the faint wake of the launch ahead.

'Bow, ship yer oar and keep an eye out for rocks,' he ordered, in a faint whisper.

The boats stole on, deeper and deeper into the inlet. A tiny cove opened off to one side, where starlight flashed on a cascade of water tumbling noisily down to a little beach.

'Around the next headland, ain't it, sir,' breathed Sedgwick to the officer beside him.

'That's right,' murmured Russell, tightening his grip on his sword at the thought. The line of boats pressed on, turning about the narrow point and opening up the rest of the inlet. A mile farther up Sedgwick could see the huge bulk of the ship of the line. She was bow on to them, her sides spreading wide, before angling back again. Her lower masts were like the thick columns of a temple, each capped with a fighting top, but strangely truncated without any upper masts above them.

Larcum Mudge

'That fecker must be broad as a first rate,' muttered O'Malley, peering over his shoulder as he rowed.

'Quiet in the boat!' urged Russell. 'She is no concern of ours this night.'

The cutter continued to turn, entering a sheltered bay. Anchored in its heart was a much smaller ship. Lamps hung in her rigging, and more light spilt out from her hull and the windows that ran across her stern.

'She don't seem prepared to resist us, sir,' marvelled Sedgwick. 'Every gun port must be agape to catch the sea breeze!'

'Why would she be fearful, anchored in the heart of a fortified port with an eighty-gunner for company?' commented Andrews, from beside him.

'And she is truly the *Peregrine*?' asked Russell.

'Oh aye, that be her, right enough, sir,' confirmed the sailor.

'Easy all,' whispered Sedgwick, and the cutter drew up beside the other two pools of dark on the water.

'Mr Preston, are you ready?' came the voice of Blake from one.

'Yes, sir,' replied the other.

'Mr Russell?'

'Yes, sir,' confirmed the midshipman.

'Starboard forechains for us,' continues Blake, 'larboard for you, Mr Preston. See that both our assaults are truly set before you make your move, Mr Russell.'

'Aye aye, sir.'

With a glimmer of starlight on water, the two shadows vanished, their courses diverging, leaving the cutter crew resting on their oars. Time dragged for the waiting sailors.

'Surely they must have reached her by now?' muttered

Russell. Then something, a flash of white on the calm surface, as an oar stroke was missed. Moments later a challenge rang out, followed by the thump of a boat against an oak side.

'One guinea, two guineas, three guineas,' intoned Russell.

A pistol flashed, startling bright after so much dark, followed by the bang of a shot, and then a ragged cheer from beneath the forechains of the ship.

'Twenty guineas, twenty-one guineas,' continued the midshipman.

The sound of fighting rolled across the water towards them. Shouts of fear and rage, the clash of steel on steel, the banging of more pistols, up on the forecastle of the *Peregrine*.

'Fifty guineas, fifty-one guineas.'

The second boat arrived on the far side of the sloop, unleashing more attackers. Orders were shouted in French and fresh sounds rang out. The crash of a grating being dropped in haste on the deck, the rumble of feet thundering up a ladderway.

'Ninety-nine guineas, one hundred and time!' said Russell. 'Lay us under her counter, Sedgwick.'

'Aye aye, sir.'

The boat shot off, impelled forward by the tense crew.

'Row steady there!' urged Sedgwick. 'It ain't no blooming race.'

The boat settled into a longer stroke, sweeping forward towards the ship. In the glow of the lamps hung from her rigging her whole forecastle was a swirling melee of struggling figures. At the other end of the *Peregrine*, all seemed quiet.

'Ease off, there,' whispered Sedgwick. The cutter slid through the dark water towards her stern. They had almost reached the ship when a head appeared over the rail, muttered a curse and in the faint light a musket was levelled at them. For a moment Russell thought the weapon was pointing straight at him. It crashed out with a flash of blinding light, and then the cutter was under the shelter of the sloop's counter, with her weed-covered rudder just beside them. Sedgwick leaned heavily against him as the boat came to a halt.

'What are you doing!' whispered the midshipman.

'It ain't me, sir,' protested the coxswain. 'It's Andrews! He's been shot!'

'He can't have been!' exclaimed Russell. 'We need him! Is he alive?' In answer Sedgwick hauled the boatswain's mate into the light shining down from the stern windows above their heads. His open eyes stared towards the heavens, white and lifeless.

'Damnation!' exclaimed Russell. 'What the bloody hell are we to do now! He is the only one who knows his way around the *Peregrine*!'

Chapter 7
HMS *Peregrine*

While Midshipman Russell was transfixed by the stiffening corpse of Andrews, the crew of the cutter rested on their oars, waiting for the next order. The stern of the ship rose like a damp wall beside them, curving over their heads to form the counter, protecting them from above. As they waited there in the dark, other sounds came to them. Clashes and cries from the fight on the forecastle, echoing through the ship. The distant sound of a drum from the fort across the water, as the guard was called out. The clang of a church bell sounding the alarm in Pointe-à-Pitre. Beside Russell, Sedgwick stirred in his place.

'We can't be a waiting here all night, sir,' he whispered. 'It be a shame about Andrews, an' all, but we got to get on. Maybe this sloop will prove much the same as the old *Rush*. You and me served on her, as did some of the others.'

'You're right, Sedgwick,' said Russell, coming back to the present. 'Search the lower counter for a port, men. Andrews said we should find one close to the water.'

'Larboard side search, the rest hold us steady,' supplemented the coxswain. 'Oars flat on the surface.'

'There be something here, sir,' announced the voice of Trevan. 'Hard by the rudder.' A hollow sound rang out as he banged his fist against the cover.

'Good work!' enthused the midshipman. 'Prise it open with one of the crowbars.' Grunts and oaths sounded from near the bow for a moment, and the cutter surged and knocked against the sloop.

'She be bolted pretty tight, sir,' announced the Cornishman, through gritted teeth.

'Here, you get that side, and I'll get this,' said the voice of Evans, a massive presence as he rose up, kneeling on the thwart, and clattered another crowbar into place. 'When I says three, give it some bleeding brawn. One, two and three.' The straining oak cover groaned as the two men heaved.

'Shift, you bleeder!' urged Evans. At last there was a loud crack, the port lid swung open and orange light poured down onto the wildly rocking boat. The bright square vanished as Evans wormed his head and shoulders through it.

'Wardroom, sir,' came his muffled report. 'Looks to be empty. Shall I nip through, like?'

'No, I shall lead,' said Russell, making his way up to the broken lid. 'Trevan and O'Brien, wait here with the cutter. The rest of you follow me.'

Standing on the thwarts, the midshipman could push his whole upper body into the cabin beyond. It was a modest-sized space, lit by two oil lamps that swung from the beams overhead. At the far end was the thick trunk of the mizzen mast as it passed through on its way to the keel. To either side were canvas partitions, the nearest of which had its flap open. Through it he could see a cot suspended over a sea chest, with an officer's coat hanging on a peg beside it. Everywhere he looked there were signs of hasty departure. A nightshirt lay crumpled on the deck. A scatter of cards spread across the table, together with several half-filled glasses. A chair knocked over and left where it lay. He pulled himself up through the port, and the other sailors followed him.

'Evans and Mudge, come with me,' he ordered. 'The rest of you check the mattresses in the officer's cabins. If they're straw-filled, bring them along.'

The three men approached the single door in the bulkhead that led out from the wardroom into the rest of the ship. Russell was just leaning forward to place his ear against it, when the brass handle began to turn. He stopped in alarm, and the door swung away from him to reveal a portly man with a thin black moustache. His eyes opened wide with horror.

'*Mon Dieu …!*' he started to shout.

'No you bleeding don't!' said Evans, pushing past the midshipman and smashing his fist into the man's face. He was not set properly, so the blow only stunned the Frenchman, but this left him in no position to dodge the thrust from Mudge's cutlass as it ran him through. By the time that Russell had ripped out his own sword out, the fight was over.

'Well done, men,' said the midshipman, stepping over the body and advancing onto the lower deck. There were more doors here, to right and left, and then the ship opened out. Rows of hammocks lined both sides, while beneath them were more signs of a hasty departure. A shoe lay on its side under the nearest one, next to the discarded scabbard of a cutlass. The sound of fighting from the front of the ship echoed down through the grating overhead.

'What we be looking for, sir?' asked Mudge.

'A way down to the orlop deck,' said Russell.

'I reckon there's sure to be one hard by the main mast, sir,' said Evans, advancing towards the thick column. 'Here we bleeding go!'

Russell looked behind him as O'Malley came struggling through the door of the wardroom, dragging a mattress behind him.

'Ah, splendid,' said the midshipman. 'Bring that along with you.'

'Is it a fecking kip we're after having?' the Irishman muttered to Sedgwick, as the coxswain joined him with a second one. The pair set off after the others, manhandling their mattresses around the mast and down the steeply pitched steps to the deck below.

The orlop was a close, forbidding space, full of dark passageways that led off in different directions. The deck height was a bare five feet, and large openings gaped in the floor, through which could be glimpsed the curved tops of huge barrels packed into the hold beneath them. Russell unhooked a lamp that hung at the bottom of the ladderway, and peered about him.

'Close to the aft magazine but not too close,' he muttered to himself. He advanced uncertainly down one opening and then turned to beckon the others to follow. 'Come on lads, this way.'

The short section of corridor between bulkheads ended in an open area, lined with more doors and the dark entrances of two more passageways. The atmosphere down here was close and musty, full of rank odours rising from the bilges beneath them. Through two levels of deck, the sound of their fellow Griffins fighting on the forecastle was faint. Then came a loud boom, accompanied by the rumble of gun trucks on oak from overhead. The sailors looked at each other in the glow of their lamp.

'That was a fecking cannon, or I ain't never heard one,' exclaimed O'Malley.

'Summoning help, I daresay, sir,' added Sedgwick. 'Best get a shift on.'

'This place will serve well,' said the midshipman. 'Cut open those mattresses, and pile the straw up here. Evans, Mudge, open up some of these doors and see what you can find that will burn.'

With frantic urgency, the two men set to with their crowbars, levering open doors and peering in. 'Sail room, sir,' reported Mudge, from the shattered frame of the first opening. 'Ain't sure as musty canvas be what we're after.'

'Here we bleeding go!' exclaimed Evans from the next room. 'Carpenter's store, sir!'

'Excellent!' enthused Russell. 'You men, get some lumber piled up on all this straw.'

While Evans and Mudge investigated further, the others pulled out odd pieces of wood, building their pile of straw into what was becoming a considerable pyre, heaped up against the bulkhead.

'That will do nicely,' said the officer. 'Set your combustibles deep in among the kindling, and let us get this lit.'

Every member of the cutter crew had a lanyard around his neck from which a bulky package of oilskin hung. They all slipped them off, tore them open and pulled out the contents. Each one contained a tar-soaked rag, wrapped tight around a bundle of slow match. The kneeling men thrust them deep into the straw, while Russell crouched down and lit his length of slow match from the lantern. He passed the lamp to Sedgwick, and whirled the end of the match into spluttering life. A trail of grey smoke curled up from the glowing end, and the smell of burning sulphur filled the air. Then the young officer went around the perimeter of the pile, lighting each package in turn. Hungry yellow flames blossomed up, and spread quickly among the straw.

'More lumber, lads,' urged Russell, stepping back from the blaze. Further planks and beams were dragged from the wood store and thrown on. In response the flames rose higher, licking along the lengths of wood, and sending clouds of acrid smoke catching at the men's throats. More wood was piled on, and the sailors began to pull their neckcloths up over their mouths and noses. They were forced to step back as the fire spread, lines of little flames running out along the walls as the bulkhead began to catch. The heat was growing intense, forcing them to duck low to escape the hot smoke that was filling the upper part of the space. Then the figure of Evans appeared, doubled over a small but heavy-looking keg he was clutching to his chest.

'Mind yer backs!' he warned, before hurling the barrel into the heart of the blaze. At first it sat there, a dark shape among all the red flame, like the egg of a phoenix in the midst its fiery nest.

'What was that, Big Sam?' asked Sedgwick.

'Something I found back there, in the boatswain's store,' said the Londoner. 'I think it might be lamp oil.'

'Lamp oil!' exclaimed the coxswain, the eyes above his mask swelling with horror. 'Everyone! Get back!'

As the barrel staves burned and twisted, the oil poured out, instantly trebling the intensity of the blaze. The blast of heat was unbearable, forcing the sailors to flee. Sedgwick held his arms up to protect his face, and felt the agony of them scorching, and his nostrils filled with the smell of burning hair. The fire had become a volcano of yellow light, with bright tongues rushing out over the deckhead above the men like the branches of a flaming tree.

'We've got to get out, sir!' he yelled to Russell, dropping to his knees to escape the flames and smoke.

'How?' protested the officer, pointing to the way they had come, now engulfed in flame.

'This way!' shouted Evans. 'I saw another passage beyond the boatswain's store.' The men started to crawl after the big Londoner, when another voice cut through the bang and roar of the fire.

'No! Stop! You'll all perish. 'Tis a dead end! Follow astern of me!'

After a moment of hesitation, the men turned to follow Mudge, as he led them to the other side of the sloop. Hard against the inner skin was a narrow passage, no more than two feet wide, that ran behind the store rooms. Without hesitation, he crawled into it and vanished from sight.

'How the bleeding hell am I going to fit down there?' coughed Evans.

'With your fat arse aflame, I daresay you'll find a way,' yelled O'Malley, diving in after Mudge and wriggling through like a snake. Pursued by the heat and flames of the fire, the rest scrambled through. Even the big Londoner managed it, with Sedgwick and Mudge pulling him by the arms. Then they all stumbled after Russell, until the ladderway they had come down appeared through the smoke. They dashed up it to arrive, coughing and retching, back on the relative calm of the lower deck.

'How the fecking …' began O'Malley.

'Silence!' snapped Russell. 'Back to the cutter, men! Before those flames reach the aft magazine. Go swiftly, now!'

While the sailors ran back into the wardroom and tumbled out through the broken port, Russell stood by the column of hot smoke that was pouring up the steps from the deck below. It was thick and dark now, with the odd glowing ember whirling upwards in its heart. Beside him stood

Sedgwick, waiting for the young officer. The midshipman pulled out his whistle from around his neck, and put it to his trembling lips. The first trill was faint and uncertain, but as he regained his breath, he was able to blow it properly. Three blasts, a pause, then three more. On the third repetition, the faint sound of an answer came from the forecastle.

'Good, we can depart now,' he said. In response Sedgwick whipped out his pistol and fired it at the grating in the deck above them. There was a loud thump, and a face appeared, pressed against one of the square openings.

'He'll be smoked like a kipper, presently,' said Russell, giggling with relief after so much strain. Sedgwick took his arm and guided him towards the wardroom. 'We've got to go, sir,' he urged. 'Afore that powder blows us back to the barky without call for rowing. You may not be able to feel it through your boots, but this deck be growing mighty hot underfoot.'

*****

As soon as Russell and Sedgwick turned their backs on the hatchway, the first flames appeared around its rim from the deck below. The coxswain glanced back over his shoulder to see the column of rising smoke swell with glowing light. He slammed the wardroom door shut against the pursuing fire, and raced across to follow the midshipman out of the open port and down into the waiting boat.

It was wonderful to be out of the ship, to draw clear air into smoke-filled lungs, and to feel the cool evening breeze waft across blistered skin. From farther forward the sound of battle was changing. They heard Blake and Preston yelling at their men, and the French shouts turning to jeers as the British withdrew. Then came the first cry of alarm.

'Push off larboard side!' gasped Sedgwick, coughing and spitting to clear away the last of the smoke. 'Together, both, and put your backs into it!'

The cutter ran smoothly away from the *Peregrine*, floating on water that was turning to molten gold in the light of the burning ship. Russell looked back and saw long tongues of flame licking out of the sloop's stern most gun ports, and lines of yellow racing up her mizzen mast. Soon the whole back of the ship was engulfed, while from on board came the urgent bark of orders as her crew tried to save her. Backlit by a growing wall of fire came the two other boats, rowing in haste towards them.

'Wait for the others here, Sedgwick,' ordered Russell. 'We should be out of range now.'

'Easy all,' ordered the coxswain, turning around to watch the spectacle. The flames had reached the main mast, and balls of fire were following each other up her tarred rigging as this too caught fire.

'Holy Mary fecking save us,' muttered the voice of O'Malley. 'Hell must be very like to that.'

'Them Frogs ain't never going to put it out, sir,' commented Sedgwick.

'I think some of them are of your way of thinking,' said the midshipman, pointing to a boat that had been launched from the stricken sloop, with men tumbling down her side into it. Closer too was the first of the *Griffin*'s two launches. Between the lines of oarsmen lay a group of injured sailors.

'Good work, Mr Russell,' said Preston, as his boat drew level. 'Although it looks to have been a close-run thing, to judge from how scorched you all seem.' The blazing ship was now lighting the whole bay. In the glow Russell looked at the blackened faces and clothes all around him. Sedgwick had lost both his eyebrows, and a good piece of hair from his scalp, while one of Mudge's bristling sideburns had vanished altogether. Wherever he looked, he could see painful burns and missing hair. He glanced down at his own clothes, and realised that the white lining of his coat was visible through a large burn in the sleeve. His left hand felt as hot as if it was still on fire.

'Come, gentlemen, there will be time for discourse later,' said Blake, as his launch came up on the cutter's other side. 'We must depart before the enemy recover themselves. Look, they are already busy launching craft!'

Now the whole of the harbour was illuminated by the blazing sloop. Across an expanse of glittering water, he could see the wharfs and buildings of Pointe-à-Pitre lit in a wash of amber. Faces where appearing in windows, and people were massing on the quayside to watch the spectacle. Beneath the walls of the fortress, the main harbour entrance was blocked by a line of rowing boats, with more hastening from the shore to join them. Several had small boat carronades mounted in their bows, others had lamps hung from spars, and all were packed with men.

'Fortunately, they seem to be expecting us to leave by the front door,' shouted Preston. 'Let us hasten to the tradesmen's entrance, before they realise their error.'

'Follow astern,' ordered Blake. 'Make haste!'

The boats had hardly set off before a massive blast deafened them. Russell felt himself knocked forward, as if the cutter had been shunted heavily from astern, and night rushed back.

'Keep rowing!' yelled Sedgwick beside him, his voice woolly and distant through the ringing in Russell's ears. The dazed crew of the boat picked up a faltering stroke, just as fragments from the destroyed ship plunged down around them, throwing up columns of water. Moments later a wave rushed under them, lifting the boat with it and sending them surging forwards. Russell looked behind him at the bay, but all that remained of the *Peregrine* were a few smouldering timbers floating on the water, and a ball of black cloud rising up and expanding out into the starry sky.

One ear popped, and he could hear again. He turned his attention to the boat. Sedgwick had the men back in order, and the cutter was heading steadily towards the western end of the island, where they had crossed the shallows. The French boats clustered at its eastern end looked like fireflies in the night, with their bobbing lanterns, but search as Russell might, he could not see any between him and their escape route.

'Ha! I do declare we have the French properly foxed,' he exalted to Sedgwick beside him. 'See how they are all set to prevent us leaving in the *Peregrine*. The captain's plan has worked splendidly.'

'Aye, that it has, sir,' said the coxswain. 'Shame for the lost prize money, mind, and I ain't sure as my whiskers will ever grow back.'

'Oh, but what a triumph,' continued the youngster. 'We might get a whole page in the *Chronicle*! Think of that!'

'We done alright, sir,' agreed Sedgwick. 'An' I shall give you joy of your page, just as soon as we are safely back in the barky, an' not bobbing about in an enemy harbour no more.'

The young midshipman sat back against the thwart and considered this, but it was hard for him to keep still. He had been both excited and scared in equal measures ever since Clay had given him the critical role in the attack. Keeping it all suppressed and maintaining the calm expected of an officer had been a sore trial for the teenager. But now they had succeeded, not even the pain from his scorched hand could prevent him from bubbling over with relief.

'Mr Russell, sir,' said the sailor pulling on the stroke oar. 'I reckon I can see a brace of launches astern. Going like the clappers, they is, which is how I marked them. Reckon they've come from that big Frog bugger, maybes.'

Russell looked around, and saw the boats instantly, even in the dark. They were bow on to him, and both were pulling hard, their oars splashing and foaming to either side. The nearest was perhaps a half mile behind, but was gaining on them fast.

'Put your backs into it, lads,' he urged, and the cutter gathered pace.

'Keep the stroke clean, mind,' added Sedgwick beside him, before turning to whisper an explanation to the young officer. 'The lads will be tired with all we've done this night, sir, while I daresay them Frogs was kipping in their hammocks until not half an hour ago.'

Soon the cutter began to overhaul the launch.

'What are you about, Mr Russell?' demanded the voice of Preston. 'It is not the damned St Ledger, you know?'

'Two big enemy launches closing from astern, sir,' reported Russell. 'From the size, I would judge them to have come from that ship of the line.' There was a pause while Preston looked behind him.

'They may prove troublesome, but if they are as large as you say, they will struggle to follow us across the shallows,' he said. 'See, we are very nearly at the island.'

Russell looked to where the Isle of Pigs filled his view. On this side the trees seemed taller, rising in a thick dark mass against the night sky, with a faint line of white beach at their feet. Just ahead of him, Blake's launch had turned aside, and was heading straight for the channel at the island's end. Russell indicated for Sedgwick to follow. They had almost reached the sand when a challenge rang out.

'Who goes there?' demanded the bass voice of Corporal Edwards, from somewhere in the shadows.

'Griffins,' replied the voice of Blake.

'I should get hauling those boat across as swiftly as you can, Mr Blake,' said Macpherson, calm as always. 'You have brought a brace of friends with you, I collect.'

'Wounded to stay on board, crew disembark,' ordered the lieutenant, the moment the launch grounded in the shallows. 'Handsomely there.'

The other two boats arrived alongside Blake's, and the crews tumbled out.

'Mr Russell, I shall need your men to assist to get the launch through, before returning to help Mr Preston,' ordered Blake.

'Aye aye, sir,' said Russell. 'Sedgwick and Trevan, stay with the cutter, the rest of you clap onto the boat.'

Soon the combined crew were busy hauling the first boat through the shallow channel, the water glowing with phosphorescence as the men splashed along beside her in their haste to drive her onwards. The night was full of curses and oaths as the salt water found the more painful of the cutter crew's many burns.

'Barrel of fecking lamp oil!' muttered O'Malley to Evans. 'Why stop there, and not chuck on a powder keg, an' all?'

'Aye, perhaps I did get a bit carried away,' acknowledged the Londoner. 'But what a bleeding fire, eh!'

While Russell waited for the two larger boats to be hauled through, he went and stood beside the elegant marine officer as he watched the approaching enemy.

'We managed to destroy the *Peregrine*, sir,' he reported, trying to keep the excitement from his voice.

'Oh, did you, laddie?' queried Macpherson. 'And there was I thinking a fresh volcano had erupted in the bay.' Russell turned to walk away, but the Scotsman pulled him back. 'Stay a moment. You did a hard thing very well. I only make light of it in jest. I have much to attend to at present, as do you, so don't let a fine tale spoil with a hasty telling. When we are safe back on board, I shall want to learn all you have done this night. Now away with you, and let me think how to stop the enemy spoiling your triumph.'

Russell returned to the cutter, and left the marine stroking one of his sideburns with his gloved hand. He looked across at the slowly moving British boats, and then at the rapidly approaching French pair. Then he came to a decision.

'Still no sign of anyone advancing from the battery, Corporal?' he asked the figure beside him. 'No sir, not a peep.'

'Excellent. Have the pickets withdrawn to join the others, and then I want the men to fall in here, in a close order line.'

'Yes sir,' replied the corporal. 'Shall we be giving them Frogs a quick volley, and then scarper back to our own boat?' Macpherson looked at the nearing French. They were so close he could hear the rattle of their oars and see the glint of starlight on the muskets of the soldiers. His right hand closed around the hilt of the old claymore he always wore.

'No, they are too numerous and press too close for that to answer,' he said. 'We shall have to make them fear this island first. Bring the men swiftly, now.'

*****

Earlier, Lieutenant Etienne Albert of the French eighty-gun ship of the line *Centaure* decided that he was not having a good night. It had started promisingly enough, with an excellent dinner ashore hosted by the officers of the garrison. Most had left France over six years ago, and had been starved of news from home for much of that time. The arrival of the *Centaure* the previous month had been a godsend for the homesick soldiers, who had long since tired of each other's company. In honour of the occasion, some of the best wine the fortress's cellar could offer had been produced. This had been followed by a particularly fine cask-aged rum from a local producer who had learned his craft among the vineyards of Armagnac. It was after midnight that Albert and his fellow naval officers, all now thoroughly drunk, had returned to their ship, singing loudly as they made their unsteady way to their cabins to be undressed by their servants. It was only after considerable persistence from a burly young midshipman that he had been roused from sleep, a half hour later.

'Wake up, monsieur!' the youngster had urged, shaking the lieutenant's cot until its snoring occupant was forced into consciousness. 'The captain wants you! The enemy are in the port!'

Five minutes later, Lieutenant Albert burst out onto ship's huge quarterdeck, still buttoning his shirt, with his neckcloth stuffed in a pocket. From somewhere he could hear the distant pop and bang of small arms fire. Closer at hand, the ship was alive with activity. Down on the main deck the boatswain and his mates were bellowing orders to a party of men who were at work on the booms. They were struggling to extract two of the ship's bigger launches from all the upper masts and yards that had been struck down on deck. From farther forward the ship's company of marines were being bawled at by their sergeant. On both sides, the cannon were manned by their crews. Lines of smoke rose like incense in a church from all the smouldering linstocks, making him gag a little. He looked up at the stars and breathed deeply, hoping that a few lungfuls of tropical air might halt the constellations from turning across the night sky in such a disturbing way.

'Where is your sword, Etienne?' demanded Jean Senard, the first lieutenant, stepping from his place beside the wheel.

'Er … my sword? Now, let me think, sir,' he said, looking around him as if the missing weapon might chance to be lying on the deck.

'Are all of my officers drunk, Senard?' raged the *Centaure*'s captain, joining the pair. His fury at having been pulled from his bed in the middle of the night was only matched by his annoyance that he had been obliged to dine with the island's teetotal governor that evening.

'I … I assure you I will be quite able to perform my d–duties, sir,' said Albert, stifling a belch.

The captain exchanged glances with his first lieutenant, who shrugged in response. 'Dupont continues to be sick, and Bisset can't get up the ladderway, sir,' he explained.

'Come with me, both of you,' barked the captain, setting off along the ship's starboard gangway with the two lieutenants trailing in his wake. He reached the forecastle rail, high above the waters of the port, and pointed towards the dark bay scooped into the western side of the inlet.

'Do you see that damned mutineers' ship?' he asked.

'The English are trying to cut her out.'

In truth, Albert could see two damned mutineers' ships, but the night air had sobered him up sufficiently to realise that letting his captain know this was unlikely to end well. Instead he narrowed his eyes in concentration, forcing the twin images to merge. Although the *Peregrine* was at least a mile away, he could still detect the fierce struggle taking place on board from the prickle of small arms fire on her forecastle. His captain passed across a night glass, and the scene became much clearer. Now he could also see the shape of the two launches bracketing the sloop's bow. Something in the scene troubled him, but search as he might, he could not think what it was.

He rubbed his temples, trying to massage some life into a mind fogged by drink. 'How did the English pass the fortress, and the guard boat undetected, sir?' he asked.

'How does the Royal Navy achieve half the things they do?' snapped his captain. 'Perhaps the garrison were too busy pouring rum down the gullets of my officers to watch the harbour entrance properly? But never mind that! The enemy must not seize that ship! Monsieur Senard, I want you to take the longboat. Monsieur Albert, you shall command the blue launch. Arm the crew, and take a file of marines each. Go and end this nonsense, swiftly.'

'Aye, aye, sir,' replied the two officers, touching their hats in salute.

By the time the boats were launched, Albert had managed to gulp down some water, complete getting dressed and recover his sword from its place in his cabin. Feeling a little more alert, he climbed down the ship's side and into the stern of the launch. The boat was packed full, with the normal crew supplemented by a double row of soldiers seated along the centreline. Each man held a musket upright in front of him.

'Push off,' he ordered to the coxswain, 'and follow Lieutenant Senard in the longboat.'

It was dark on the water, after the lamp-lit main deck of the *Centaure*. The boat passed along the bulging side, and then underneath her bowsprit, which sprang out from the hull for almost a hundred feet, pointing the way like an enormous compass needle. Directly above Albert was the ship's figurehead, silhouetted against the night sky. The prancing centaur looked enormous from beneath, almost the size of a small elephant. Then he turned his attention to the sloop ahead, in its little bay. The fighting was as intense as ever, still concentrated on the forecastle. From behind him three bell strokes sounded from the ship of the line, and he began to realise what might be wrong.

'When were the first shots heard?' he asked the coxswain beside him.

'A little after two bells, sir,' replied the sailor.

'Almost half an hour ago!' exclaimed Albert, 'and yet the Roast Beefs have got no farther than the forecastle?'

'Yes, our men must be fighting very well, sir.'

'Fighting like the devil himself, you mean,' scoffed the officer. 'A sleepy anchor watch, surprised by two boatloads of attackers? Are the Republican Guard manning the ship? The English should have swept the deck clear in an instant, and be halfway to the open sea by now.' He bowed forward and massaged his temples once more. His forehead touched the metal of his sword scabbard, cooling his brow. 'Think, Etienne, think,' he muttered.

'Sorry, sir. Did you say something?' asked the sailor at the helm.

'I am trying to work out what the enemy is truly about.'

'They don't just want their ship back, sir?'

'They are setting about it in a very odd way if they do,' said Albert. 'I was at Toulon back in ninety-four, when they cut out *L'Utile* from under the noses of two shore batteries. The first the gunners knew about it was when she was heading out of the harbour.'

'Perhaps this time they have made a dreadful error, sir,' gloated the coxswain.

'Maybe, in which case, why not retreat? What attacker keeps fighting for half an hour, once he has no surprise ...'

His voice trailed off, and he looked towards the harbour entrance. The dark walls of the fortress were invisible on their cliff, but he thought back to earlier in the evening, when he had been on the ramparts, admiring the sunset with one of the garrison's officers. The man had been boasting how impregnable the port was, with an airy sweep of his glowing cigar. He had slapped the solid breech of one of the heavy cannons that dominated the deep-water channel. Then he had pointed out the difficult turn that forced ships across the face of the battery on the Isle of Pigs. He remembered how a guard boat had been setting out from the little jetty beneath them, and how there had been a flotilla of others, tied up and ready.

'*Sacré Bleu*! That must be it!' said Albert at last.

'What is, sir?' queried the coxswain.

'The English! They haven't taken the ship, because that is not what they are here for,' said Albert. 'Even if they captured her, they could never bring her out. The entrance is too closely guarded.'

'Then what are they doing, sir?'

'That,' said Albert, grimly, 'is what we need to find out.'

Over the water came the faint sound of a whistle,

trilling out what sounded like a signal. It was soon taken up by another, louder one, repeating the call. The *Centaure*'s boats had barely covered a quarter of the way, but even at this distance it seemed to Albert as if the intensity of the fighting had changed. A few more shots rang out, accompanied by some shouts of derision. Then the ship fell silent.

'What now?' muttered Albert, straining to see ahead.

A new light appeared in the night, brighter than the others, shining through an open gun port near the stern, like the eye of a demon. Soon it was joined by a second light in the port beside it, and the mast and rigging of the sloop appeared, lit from beneath. Moments later the first flames began to lick up the mizzen mast, and as the blaze grew, the bay filled with yellow light.

'Fire! Of course!' exclaimed Albert. 'An attack to draw our crew away, while a determined man with a tinder box does the rest. They cannot cut their ship out, so they destroy her.'

'Boats on the water, sir,' said the coxswain, pointing. 'Three of them, over there.'

The *Peregrine* was soon fully ablaze, sending a whirling column of sparks high into the night. Against the fire, the silhouettes of the *Griffin*'s boats stood out, like black insects as their oars worked backwards and forwards. Albert looked at the sloop and felt rage in his heart. The crew had abandoned any attempt to quell the blaze. Some of the luckier ones had managed to launch a boat. The less fortunate were starting to throw themselves over the side to escape the inferno. He watched as one desperate sailor did so with his clothes ablaze.

He tightened his grip on the sword scabbard he held in front of him. 'Pick up the pace! Faster!' he yelled at the rowers. 'None of those bastards escape us, understand?' There was a growl from the crew and the launch surged forwards.

Albert's boat had almost caught up with the *Centaure*'s longboat when the *Peregrine* exploded. They were fortunate to be farther away than the *Griffin*'s boats had been, although the surge that swept out of the dark was powerful enough to set the big launch pitching and tossing and water slopped in over the side.

'Marines! Get bailing,' ordered Albert. 'Use your hats, if you need to. The rest of you, keep rowing.'

'Lieutenant,' called the voice of Senard, from the dark longboat alongside. 'Have you sight of the enemy? I was looking at that ship when the damn magazine went up, and I am blind to all else. Are they making for the harbour entrance?'

Albert peered into the dark, and saw a little tell-tale swirl of wake on the starlit water ahead. 'No, sir,' he reported. 'They are making for the island.'

'The Isle of Pigs?' queried Senard. 'What on earth can be there for them? Are you quite certain?'

'Perfectly so, sir,' said his colleague.

'Strange, but no matter. They may be seeking to hug the shore, and pass our gun boats in that way. You had best lead the way.'

With their crews still fresh, the French set off in pursuit of the three boats ahead. Albert soon realised that his launch was swifter than the longboat, and he began to open a lead. No matter, I have enough men on board to deal with the enemy, he told himself, as he urged his crew on. Lieutenant Senard was mistaken about the enemy's intention. If anything, their course was taking them towards the far end of the island, and away from the entrance to Pointe-à-Pitre.

Larcum Mudge

The little glimpse of wake he was following grew steadily into dark shapes on the water as the French boat drew nearer. Then they vanished once more, merging into the greater dark of the forest-covered island that loomed ahead. Albert strained from side to side, trying to see through the thicket of muskets held by the soldiers in the boat. Eventually he rose to his feet, balancing precariously.

'Where have they gone?' he muttered, staring ahead. The beach was white sand. Surely boats would show against that?

'Over there, sir,' said the coxswain, pointing. Then he saw them, clustered around the far end of the island. There was white water, breaking against a reef of some kind, in the midst of which he could see dark figures in the shallows, hauling a boat through the surf.

'Is there a passage to the west of the island?' he demanded.

'None that I have ever heard of, sir,' replied the coxswain.

Albert thought for a moment, and then he pointed the way ahead. 'Land on the beach over there. Quickly! The enemy is escaping!'

A rock appeared to one side of the boat, as the water shelved towards the shore. The sound of hushed orders and the collective grunts of the British sailors dragging their boats through the shallows sounded in the night, seemingly from just ahead. Now the beach appeared, silent and abandoned, backed by dark forest. The white sand was strewn with a tide line of debris.

'Easy there,' ordered the coxswain, and the launch ran up into the shallows with a jolt that threw many of the men backwards.

'Come on!' yelled Albert, leading the way over the side. Then he heard an order in English, shockingly close.

'Marines will stand,' barked the voice. The line of debris got to its feet, and resolved into a solid wall of men, not ten yards from the boat.

'*Mon Dieu*!' exclaimed the coxswain.

'Present arms,' said the voice. Starlight glistened on a row of muskets as they were levelled at the boat, each one tipped with a long bayonet. The calm authority of the marines was in sharp contrast with the surprised crew of the launch. Some who had left the boat tried to scramble back in. Others began to push it back out to sea, while the majority remained seated inside, open mouthed.

'Fire!' ordered the voice, and a volley crashed out, a chain of brilliant light in the darkness. Men tumbled down around Albert in the packed launch. The coxswain beside him spun backwards, falling half out, his head and shoulders trailing in the water. After the first shocked silence, the wounded began screaming in pain.

'All of you! Get out of the boat!' Albert yelled, coming to life at last. 'Sergeant, get your men in hand! Form a firing line!'

'The sergeant is down, sir,' reported a soldier who was supporting a wounded man. Albert could just make out the stripes on his arm.

'Marines will advance!' ordered the voice. The soldiers came striding down the beach towards them, still in a close order line and Albert's command dissolved into blind panic. Some men fled along the shallows, flinging away their weapons as they went. Others waded out to sea. Those who remained were in no position to resist the remorseless wall as they charged home. Albert ripped out his sword, just in time to parry a savage bayonet thrust. As his sword jarred and slid down the barrel, he was defenceless to avoid the bayonet of the next marine in the line. He felt agony, deep in his gut, and he staggered back from the blow, sinking to his knees.

'Marines will fall back,' ordered the voice, in its remorseless, calm, matter-of-fact way and he saw the officer at last. He was no more than a few feet from where Albert knelt, an upright figure, gesturing with the long sword in his hand. The soldiers were vanishing back into the dark as quickly as they had appeared, leaving a pile of French dead and wounded in the shallows around the abandoned boat.

Then the white sand of the beach rushed up to meet him, and Albert lay at peace, feeling strangely calm. He could no longer feel the wound in his stomach. Instead he was on a tropical beach, beneath the stars, with water lapping against his legs. But where the water had been warm at first, it was growing steadily colder, until he could barely feel his legs as the chill spread. But at least his head seemed fine at last, pillowed on the soft sand. He felt tired, after his long night. Why did I drink so much, he muttered, as he closed his eyes and let the tropical breeze waft him to sleep.

Chapter 8
A Flag of Truce

The follow day the *Griffin* was patrolling off Guadeloupe, standing in towards the coast on a long, sliding run across the dazzling blue water, as if about to attack Pointe-à-Pitre once more. She had been sailing across this same stretch of sea since dawn. Just as she neared the point where a long-range shot from the battery on the Isle of Pigs might reach her, she came up into the wind. Amid a welter of flapping canvas, she slowly turned about, flaunting her big naval ensign, before coming onto the other tack and sailing out to sea once more. Each time she turned, the guns of the French battery had opened fire, cloaking the island in smoke, and raising fountains of water from the sea. None were closer than a hundred yards to the frigate's side, and as she gathered way again, the battery fell into brooding silence.

Unconcerned with the sound of gunfire, or the manoeuvring of his ship, Clay sat with his clerk, working at his report on the previous night's events. Normally his dispatches were coldly factual, dashed off with the minimum of fuss, but this time he was making more of an effort. The bloody mutiny on board the *Peregrine* had been greeted with outrage by the news sheets and journals back home, which meant that news of her destruction would be widely reprinted. Time for some care and attention, he told himself. The skylight above his head was open to its fullest extent, as was the line of window lights that ran across the rear of the cabin, allowing the warm sea breeze in to ruffle his shirt sleeves and tug at the various officers' reports strewn across his desk.

'Read me back the first part again, Mr Allen,' he said. 'Where I explain why we destroyed the *Peregrine*.'

The clerk scratched at his wig with the top of his pencil until he found the relevant passage and cleared his throat.

'*… having concluded the defences of Pointe-à-Pitre to be of too formidable a character to permit the cutting-out of His Majesty's former ship* Peregrine, *and mindful of the import placed in my instructions on the aforementioned ship not remaining at the disposal of the enemy, I resolved on the vessel's destruction*.'

'Hmmm, I suppose that will answer,' said the captain. 'What must we attend to next?'

'We have covered Mr Blake's account of the general assault, together with Mr Russell's report on the fire,' said Allen, running a finger down his rough draft.

'Yes, that was most illuminating,' said Clay, smiling across the desk.

'Do you think so, sir?' said the clerk. 'I thought it set down very ill, although I understand the young gentleman has scorched his writing hand.'

'No, I was making a pun. His report on the fire was very illuminating … oh, no matter.'

'Ha ha. Very droll, sir,' said the clerk, his face impassive. 'Although, if I might be so bold, I would urge the avoidance of levity in such a serious report.'

'Good God, man, I was not going to put that in!' exclaimed his captain. 'Now, we must have reached Lieutenant Macpherson's part.'

'Quite so, sir,' said Allen.

Clay lifted up the inkwell that held the marine officer's report in place, just as a gust of wind whistled into the cabin, and the page was off before he could grab it. With a sigh, Allen rose to his feet and recovered it from the base of the bulkhead, where it had come to rest beneath the portrait of Lydia Clay.

'My thanks, Mr Allen,' said his chastened captain. He scanned through the document, to refresh his memory, and then began to dictate.

'*The enemy having been fully roused, our assault party found their retreat challenged by two large ship's boats of the enemy. These attempted to land on the Isle of Pigs, from where they hoped to frustrate the escape of our people. I am pleased to inform you that this landing was foiled in the most handsome manner by Lieutenant Thomas Macpherson, together with the detachment of marines he has the honour to command. They gallantly attacked the French as they disembarked, putting the enemy to flight, which permitted the party to withdraw in good order with no further loss*. How does that sound?'

'Tolerably well drafted, sir,' conceded Allen, scanning through what he had written. Then he looked up towards the skylight. 'Was that a hail from the masthead?'

'It was,' agreed Clay. 'We had best press on. End with '… *I regret to inform you of the loss of* …' – Clay glanced at the sheet supplied to him by Corbett, the ship's surgeon – '… *of six men killed, thirteen wounded and one missing as per the attached list. I beg to remain* … etc, etc.'

'Etc, etc,' echoed Allen. 'I shall draw it up directly, sir.'

'If you please, although I daresay I shall want to change it further.'

Allen leant over the desk to gather up all the various

papers, just as there was a knock at the cabin door.

'Come in!' called Clay, and as his clerk departed, Midshipman Todd entered smartly.

'Mr Preston's compliments, and a schooner is coming out from Pointe-à-Pitre, sir,' the youngster reported.

'Only a schooner?' queried Clay. 'Not that deuced big ship of the line?'

'No, sir,' replied Todd. 'They are all still busy setting up their masts. Mr Harrison says he could have rigged the *Sovereign of the Seas* in the time it has taken them.'

'The longer the better,' said Clay. 'I take it there is still no sign of the admiral with the *Stirling*?'

'No, sir. Nothing yet.'

'Thank you, Mr Todd,' said Clay. 'Kindly tell Mr Preston that I will be on deck directly.'

'Aye aye, sir,' replied the midshipman.

With his neckcloth and coat back in place, Clay ran up the aft ladderway and out onto the quarterdeck. The frigate was approaching the land once more, crossing the bay towards the cane fields and lush slopes of Guadeloupe. The schooner had just slid from between the Isle of Pigs and the fortress on the cliffs. She was a smaller craft than the *Saint Joseph* they had encountered a few days back, but her fore-and-aft rig was almost identical. From her main mast flew a faded French tricolour, with something else fluttering above it.

'Kindly have the ship hove to, Mr Preston,' he ordered.

'Aye aye, sir.'

The frigate came up into the wind, blocking the route towards the open sea, and showing her long row of gun ports towards the harbour entrance. Unperturbed, the schooner turned around the end of the island, and headed directly towards them.

'She comes on very bold, does she not, sir,' said Taylor. 'Surely she cannot mean to fight us?'

'I doubt that, sir,' said Preston, who was examining her through his telescope. 'She lacks even wooden cannon to challenge us with.'

'What do you make of her colours, Mr Preston?' asked Clay.

'It looks to be a flag of truce, sir,' said the officer of the watch. 'But surely she can't be a warship?'

'Perhaps it is a ruse to permit her to close with us, sir,' said Taylor. 'She could have a hold crowded with boarders, or perhaps she is a fireship, come to pay us back in our own coin. With your permission I'll turn up the watch below.'

'She rides very high in the water, for a ship packed with men,' said Clay. 'But it will do no harm to have the guns manned. Tell her to stay under our lee, Mr Preston.'

'Aye aye, sir.'

In spite of Taylor's fears, the approaching ship seemed innocent enough as she drew nearer. Search as they might, they failed to detect the twinkle of weapons from beneath her hatch covers, or any trails of smoke drifting away downwind. Instead they could see that she was in the same battered state as all the local schooners they had encountered. The dark blue paintwork on her hull was patched in places and worn away altogether in others. Her bleached sails were thin and old, and her crew seemed unconcerned by the pair of eighteen-pounders directed towards them, as she came up into the wind close by the *Griffin*. Most of her crew were black with a sprinkle of Europeans among them. Many were dressed in ragged clothes, but beside the binnacle stood a more smartly dressed man, in a long grey coat over pale yellow britches. He raised his hat politely towards Clay, revealing a head of curly auburn hair, and then picked up a speaking trumpet from the becket in front of him.

'May I have your permission to come aboard, Captain?' he asked, in heavily accented but perfectly understandable English.

'You can come across, in a single boat with an unarmed crew,' replied Clay. 'No ceremony, if you please,' he added, in an aside to Preston.

'Aye aye, sir.'

'What do you make of their quartermaster?' asked Taylor, who had continued to examine the schooner. 'I would wager my commission he was once in the navy.'

Clay looked at the seaman. He was a big, thickset man, wearing high-waisted trousers and a checked shirt. He stood with his back to the frigate, as if reluctant for his face to be seen, but that only served to highlight the thick braid of dark hair that reached down between his shoulders. The sleeves of his shirt were hitched clear of bulging forearms that were blue with tattoos.

'He certainly has that look, I grant you,' said Clay. He focused his telescope towards Pointe-à-Pitre, searching for any clues as to why this ship had come. The tricolour continued to flutter above the battery, its colours brilliant against the green trees behind it. Deeper into the inlet the foremast of a substantial warship reared up above the island, looking strangely unbalanced without a main or mizzen in place behind it. A swarm of tiny figures were working aloft, swinging up a big yard, thickened by its closely furled sail. Otherwise all seemed normal. There was no sign of any other vessel passing down the deep-water channel behind the island. Clay closed his telescope, cupped a hand next to his mouth and yelled up to the frigate's lookout.

'Masthead there! Anything happening in the harbour?'

'Deck there!' came the reply. 'There be a proper cluster of boats all round where that *Peregrine* were moored, sir. Pulling stuff from the water, and towing busted timbers to the shore, for the most part. That big bugger be setting up her masts, of course. But that be all.'

'A jolly boat is approaching from the schooner, sir,' reported Preston.

'I shall return to my quarters,' said Clay. 'Have our visitor shown below when he arrives, if you please.'

'Aye aye, sir.'

Back in his cabin, Clay took his place behind his desk once more. He removed all the documents and books from its surface, and locked them in a drawer. Then he sat back, uncomfortably hot in his coat now that the frigate was no longer moving.

'Shall you be wanting to offer this Frenchie a glass, or shall I have a pot of coffee fetched up from the galley, sir?' asked Harte.

'Too damned hot for coffee,' said Clay. 'And I shall certainly not be extending him any hospitality until I am a deal clearer as to why he is here.' Through the open skylight came the hail and reply as the schooner's boat arrived alongside. There was a long pause, and then the sound of approaching footsteps outside his door, followed by the expected knock.

'Come in,' said Clay. Midshipman Russell entered, accompanied by a short, deeply tanned young man. The red hair that Clay had noticed earlier was accompanied by a full ginger moustache set above a smile of flashing white teeth. Close to, his visitor's clothes seemed expensive. The grey coat was beautifully tailored and lined with satin, and his pale yellow britches were accompanied by a waistcoat of yellow calico and a cream silk neckcloth. One of his thumbs was hooked into his pocket; he extended the other hand towards Clay.

'This is Monsieur Boisgard, owner of the schooner *Étoile D'espoir*, sir,' reported the young officer.

'Thank you, Mr Russell,' said Clay. 'Will you wait outside, please.'

'Aye aye, sir.'

The French visitor remained standing with his hand extended, and Clay rose to his feet and grasped it.

'Welcome aboard, monsieur,' he said. 'Will you take a seat.'

'Thank you, Captain,' said Boisgard. He pulled his coat tails apart and settled himself on the chair. Then he pulled out a small silver box from his coat pocket. 'Would it inconvenience you if I took a little snuff?'

'Please do so,' said Clay, 'after which you can provide me with an explanation for your presence here.'

Boisgard smiled his thanks, flipped open the box, revealing a tiny rural scene painted in enamel on the surface, and transferred a generous pinch of brown powder onto the top of his hand. With his other hand, he snapped the box closed, returned it to his pocket, and after a brief rummage, reappeared with a large handkerchief. Then with a deft bob of his head, the Frenchman loudly inhaled the snuff. A pause followed while he looked past Clay for a moment, his dusty nose aloft and his eyes blinking. Then he released a gargantuan sneeze into the handkerchief, and blew his nose loudly.

'My thanks, Captain,' he resumed. 'A dreadful habit, I confess, but one I am quite unable to stop. And may I congratulate you on your attack last night? A bold move, full of the dash we have come to expect from the English navy.'

'It is kind of you to say so,' said Clay. 'But surely you did not come out from Pointe-à-Pitre just to offer me compliments, monsieur?'

'No, I had other reasons for my visit,' said Boisgard. 'The garrison are recovering bodies from the harbour as we speak. Many are beyond recognition, as might be expected after such an explosion, but others are not. If we were to find any from your crew, we would be happy to return them to you, to deal with according to your customs.'

'Thank you, that is kind,' said Clay, watching his visitor carefully.

The young man crossed his legs and brushed some particles of snuff from his britches. 'We had no idea that such a fine vessel as yours was so close at hand,' he commented.

'Surprise is often important in warfare,' said Clay.

'So I understand,' said his visitor. 'Well, you achieved it in a most admirable fashion last night.'

'I am certain that we are both busy men,' said Clay. 'I do not want to be impolite, but may I ask again? Why are you here, monsieur?'

'I am a close friend of the governor of Guadeloupe, who asked me to call on you.'

'I see,' said Clay. 'Do you have any credentials to confirm that?'

'No, Captain,' said Boisgard. 'My visit is made in a more private capacity, if you follow me.' Clay didn't, but there was something in his visitor's manner that intrigued him.

'I think I may understand,' he said. 'Harte, would you serve the Madeira.' Once both men had drinks, Clay continued. 'What may I do for his excellency?'

'He wishes to understand if you are to stay long in these waters, Captain?' said Boisgard.

'And why would he think to ask such an impertinent question, monsieur?'

'Because we have grown accustomed to the presence of Captain Camelford and his *Daring*,' said Boisgard. 'Will he be returning soon, Captain?'

'Surely the governor must know that I am not at liberty to discuss such matters with you,' said Clay. 'Our nations are at war, after all, monsieur.'

'Regrettably they are at present, although I understand from the captain of the *Centaure* that negotiations have begun between our governments, and are progressing at a satisfactory pace.'

'The *Centaure*, sir?' queried Clay. 'Would that be the handsome seventy-four currently setting up her masts?'

'Seventy-four? I believe I heard tell of eighty guns, although I am sure you understand these matters better than I,' said Boisgard.

'Eighty guns, of course,' said Clay. 'She will be one of Monsieur Sané's magnificent creations, I don't doubt. Harte, some more Madeira for my guest, if you please.'

The Frenchman accepted a refill from the steward, and then regarded Clay over the top of his glass. 'In Captain Camelford's absence, am I to understand that your ship will be blockading Guadeloupe, Captain?'

'Things can change quickly during a war, but let us assume that is correct,' replied Clay.

'And did you and Captain Camelford have the opportunity to discuss the situation here, before his departure?'

'We spoke of many things.'

'That is excellent to hear,' said the Frenchman, looking at his host in an expectant way.

'Where exactly is all this leading, monsieur?' asked Clay. 'Can you not speak with a little more candour?'

'Candour can be difficult, with a person one has only just met,' said Boisgard.

'Monsieur, I slept very little last night, and I have much to occupy my time,' said Clay. 'It is you who wanted to see me. I understood you to say that you spoke on behalf of the governor. What is it he wants to say to me?'

Boisgard looked at Clay for a moment, and then put his glass down. 'His excellency would like to know, in light of the events of last night, if his agreement with Captain Camelford remains in place.'

Behind his calm, steel-grey eyes, Clay's mind was a whirl. An agreement? With the French? What treachery was this? But beneath his simple outrage, he was also busily searching his memory. Almost immediately another battered trading schooner came to mind, similar to the one that had brought this strange, dapper little man across.

'He did indeed speak of an arrangement that might prove advantageous to me,' said Clay, pressing his fingers into a steeple. 'If I was to permit the odd vessel to pass, such as the *Saint Christopher*.'

'Ah, monsieur, for a moment I thought I was dealing with a zealot!' The Frenchman let out a sigh of relief, and then wagged a finger towards Clay. 'You seemed very angry for a moment there. I could see it, in your eyes.'

'Sorry to have alarmed you,' laughed Clay. 'But Captain Camelford was not able to give me the particulars of how the agreement worked, exactly.'

'Oh, as for that, it is simplicity itself!' exclaimed Boisgard. 'You and I agree the odd day when you will choose to inspect another portion of Guadeloupe's extensive coastline. In your absence, a trading schooner or two come and go from Pointe-à-Pitre, and a deposit is made with a representative of your choosing in Antigua.'

'Of course,' said Clay, smiling at his guest as everything fell into place. 'These vessels take French sugar out, I collect?'

'Naturally, and return with some of the necessities we lack in Guadeloupe.' The Frenchman tapped the pocket of his coat. 'Snuff, for example.'

'How elegant an enterprise,' enthused Clay. 'Might I be in the presence of its architect?'

Boisgard bowed low in his chair. 'So, I can inform the governor that the arrangement can continue?'

Clay gave his guest a beaming smile. 'No, you most certainly cannot,' he said.

'No!' repeated the Frenchman. 'But I understood you to say …'

'Harte, would you pass the word for Mr Russell, and ask the marine sentry outside my door to step this way.'

'What are you doing!' said his guest, rising from his chair.

'Pray remain seated, monsieur,' barked Clay. 'Mr Russell, my compliments to Mr Taylor, and he is to send an armed party to take possession of the *Étoile D'espoir*.'

'But this is an outrage!' exclaimed Boisgard. 'I came under a flag of truce!'

'Is your vessel a national ship of France, monsieur?' asked Clay.

'No, Captain, it is a private vessel …'

'And are you an officer of the French state?'

'I am a simple planter and ship owner,' said Boisgard. 'But I come on behalf of the governor.'

'Without a letter or any credentials to confirm your position,' said Clay. 'You have no right under the rules of war to the protection of a flag of truce. Why, you are little more than a smuggler and a blockade runner! From your own mouth you are guilty of corrupting one king's officer, and of attempting the same on another here today. A scrap of white cloth will not deflect me from my duty. Furthermore, I suspect your ship to be sheltering at least one Royal Navy deserter.'

*****

Without her captain on board, and menaced by the *Griffin*'s huge eighteen-pounders, the *Étoile D'espoir* put up no resistance to the boarding party that swarmed onto her deck from the frigate's longboat. Taylor's sullen deserter was apprehended and taken across to the frigate, the captured schooner was sent off to Antigua with a prize crew, and the *Griffin* resumed her patient watch on Pointe-à-Pitre. Each of her sweeps across the bay ended with gunfire from the battery, while inside the port, the upper masts and yards of the *Centaure* rose steadily into the Caribbean sky, like so many huge black crucifixes, as the warship prepared for sea.

Meanwhile the routine of the frigate continued. The morning's sail drill had been completed before the schooner had come out, and after she left, the afternoon was devoted to gunnery practice. Watch followed watch, through the day, until the sun disappeared behind Guadeloupe's smouldering volcano, and the waters of the bay turned to silver in the fading light. Enjoying the balmy evening on the frigate's lee gangway was a group of off-duty sailors, sitting taking their ease.

'Plum duff tonight, lads,' commented Evans as he sniffed the air. 'Bleeding lovely!' A waft of heat from the galley chimney had brought the smell of cooking streaming across the forecastle.

The air temperature was still uncomfortably warm, and most of the group had burns that throbbed hot beneath the dressings that covered them. In spite of this, the prospect of eating steaming suet pudding in the tropics didn't seem to distress any of the hungry sailors.

'Them feckers on Hog Island are done burning powder for the night,' said O'Malley, who was standing at the rail watching the battery. 'Maybe's they're after having their own scoff.'

'I ain't sure as we should be vexing them, sailing so close at each pass,' commented Mudge. 'That big ship over yonder be fully rigged now. It'll be hell to pay when she comes out.'

'It be a touch late for that, Larcum,' commented Trevan. 'Pipe taking that schooner will have them in a proper fury, coming after us slipping into Pointy Point, as easy as kiss my hand.'

'Easy as kiss my arse, you mean!' exclaimed O'Malley. 'You and O'Brien was sat in the fecking boat, while we was all getting braised. 'Twas like a foretaste of hell! Christ only knows when my whiskers will come back.' There were mutters of agreement at this.

'Good to be alive, mind,' said Sedgwick, his face shiny with goose fat and strangely altered with both eyebrows gone. 'And all thanks to Larcum here.' He leant towards Mudge, and slapped his shoulder.

'I doesn't want no fuss,' mumbled the sailor.

'Not sure as Midshipman Russell will agree,' commented the coxswain, 'Good Grunter, is Rusty, who ain't the sort to take credit as is due to another. He reckons last night's work might make the news sheets. Fancy that!'

'Fancy,' repeated Mudge quietly, looking out to sea.

'Come along there, mate,' urged Evans. 'No call for turning shy! We was done for, afore you found that bleeding bolt hole for us to scarper through.'

'Every barky has the same, to let the carpenter come at the ship's side,' explained the reluctant hero. 'Wings, they calls 'em. There ain't no call for carrying on about it.'

'Wings, eh? I suppose that must be right,' said the Londoner. He scratched idly at his shirt and then paused to sniff the cloth. 'Bloody hell! I stink like a chimney sweep.'

'Did I hear tell of some turncoat they found on board that there schooner?' asked Trevan.

'Aye, one of our jacks as had taken up with the Frogs,' confirmed Sedgwick.

'What became of him?' asked Mudge.

'Pipe's keeping him close,' said the coxswain. 'He didn't send him into Antigua with the prize. Instead the Lobsters have him, down in the lock-up.'

'Ugly looking fecker,' said O'Malley. 'Big lad, so he was, with an old scar running across his gob.' The Irishman ran his finger over one side of his face. Mudge watched the track it followed, his face expressionless.

'Be it a match for Powell's?' asked Trevan, indicating where the heavily scarred boatswain's mate stood on the far side of the forecastle, chatting to a fellow petty officer.

'No,' conceded the Irishman, 'Powell's is proper nasty, but 'tis a fecking beauty, all the same.'

'My Pa used to say how there weren't no call to fear blokes with scars,' said Evans. 'It's the bleeder what scarred them you needs to be alive to.'

At that moment four bells rang out from the belfry

close by them.

'Scoff at last!' exclaimed O'Malley, and the sailors rose to their feet, stretched like cats, and joined the mass of hungry sailors all heading towards the lower deck.

In the midst of the swirling movement, Sedgwick found himself alongside Mudge, by accident or design. He leant over and whispered in his ear. 'You keep your secrets close, mate. There ain't none here as will grass on you, but be warned. There be plenty of shrewder heads on board than Big Sam. The next time you be asked about last night, I should have a decent yarn to hand, if I were you.'

*****

Their steaming bowls of plum duff seemed to have had little detrimental effect on the crew of the *Griffin* later that night. Nor did the stifling atmosphere on the lower deck, warm as a cattle shed, with only a trickle of air filtering down from the world above. Most of the crew had taken part in the previous night's attack on Pointe-à-Pitre, and all had endured a sleepless night full of alarms and tension. As a result, even those with painful burns had little difficulty in sleeping. They lay in packed rows of hammocks, a carpet of humanity suspended between the planking below and the deck above, swaying as one to the gentle motion of the ship. But in the heart of the snoring, breathing mass lay a figure who remained awake. The dark eyes set either side of his hooked nose stared beyond the oak a foot above him, into another hot, tropical night, many months before.

It was not the first time that he had relived the events of the mutiny. In the aftermath, images had crowded his dreams constantly, but some of the immediate horror had then faded with time. Yet tonight, he had only to close his eyes and he was back there again. Swept along in the midst of that drunken throng as they poured aft. He saw again the marine sentry before the cabin door, desperately fumbling for his bayonet. The soldier had been stabbed a dozen times and then trampled in the relentless crush. The door burst open, and officers leapt up from a table strewn with half-empty plates and splattered with wine. There was the look of anger on Daniels's face, turning first to disbelief and then terror as the first clumsy cutlass blow struck home. Then his struggling, blood-sodden body had been manhandled across to the open stern window and pitched out. He could almost hear the captain's pitiful cries in the dark, slowly retreating as the *Peregrine* sailed on.

Mudge turned over in his hammock with a groan as he thought of what had followed. That night he had felt fear as he had never known it before. John Graves had been remorseless, revelling in the power that he held. He had sat in triumph on the capstan, like a king upon his throne, declaring judgement on the battered and bleeding as they were dragged before him. He had listened to their sobbing pleas for mercy before ordering each one to be tossed over the side once there was no more sport to be had from them. When the red dawn finally came, none but mutineers remained. The sloop was far out into the Caribbean, still followed by the sleek fins of sharks and the squabbling of seabirds.

When the terror Mudge had felt that night faded, shame had quietly filled the void. Why had he not intervened to stop the slaughter? Many of the crew had looked up to him, yet he had done nothing with what power he had. Nothing to check the murderous violence as it had moved from the guilty to the innocent. As soon as he could, he had run from the events of that night, but somehow, they had now followed him. The mutineer who had recognised him on the brig in mid-Atlantic. The shrewd guesses of Sedgwick, and the knowledge he was probably not alone in suspecting. Suddenly the sailors on either side seemed to press a little closer. The deck above his head began to push down, like the lid of a coffin. All seemed to have gone wrong, after that fateful day when he had felt drawn to the companionship of four sailors, taking their ease in the warm sunshine before a tavern.

He stared this way and that at the barely visible shapes that surrounded him in all directions. He felt his hands grip the canvas edge of the hammock tightly. What if the coxswain was wrong about the crew, and one of them did betray him? And what of the prisoner from the *Etoile D'espoir*, just beneath him in the hold?

His face set into a look of grim determination. He had killed before to keep his identity hidden. He would just have to do so again.

Chapter 9
The *Centaure*

Clay awoke next morning to find Yates in his night cabin, clattering around the washstand, making just sufficient noise to wake his captain. In the amber glow of the lantern he watched the young man pour steaming water into the tin bowl, and then set out his razor, soap and towel.

'What time is it, Yates?' asked Clay, stretching languidly in his cot.

'Two bells, sir, as you requested,' answered the servant. 'It's been raining for much of the night, but that has cleared away. Mr Blake says it will be light in half an hour, and the wind is a gentle westerly. Perfect for that Frog ship, should she care to come out.'

Mention of the enemy propelled Clay from his bed. He pulled his nightshirt over his head, bundled it into Yates's hands, and began lathering his face.

'Tell Harte I will break my fast later,' he ordered. 'But have him bring coffee, if you please.'

'Aye aye, sir.'

Once he was washed and dressed, Clay came striding up onto the quarterdeck. The glow from the binnacle lamp was just visible, throwing light onto the face of the quartermaster at the wheel. In the east a pink blush was washing across the sky above the horizon of dark sea. Lines of rope and curves of sail were beginning to appear above Clay's head as the light grew, most of it damp from the rain in the night. The mountains of Guadeloupe remained shadowy, but the summit of the volcano was tipped with gold.

'Look sir, the enemy has been busy this night,' said Blake, pointing towards Pointe-à-Pitre. Spots of light dotted the slopes of the town. There was the fortress, on its cliff, and the Isle of Pigs with its thick pelt of dark forest. Just beyond the island was a very large ship, its hull invisible behind the trees, but its presence obvious from the huge masts that towered up above them. The light had grown sufficiently for the colours of her big tricolour to be made out.

'She is damnably big, sir,' commented Blake. 'Why, her main mast must be close on two hundred feet high!'

'She is the *Centaure*, one of those new French eighty gunners,' said Clay. 'Thirty-six-pounders on the lower deck, with twenty-four-pounders above them.'

Blake whistled. 'Goodness! Why, she will be able to throw much the same weight of ball as one of our second rates, sir.'

'Indeed,' said Clay. 'They must have warped her down to the harbour entrance during the hours of darkness.' He looked around as Taylor came up on deck to join them.

'Good morning, sir,' said the first lieutenant. 'Good morning Mr Blake. I see those lubberly French have got their masts and yards set up at long last.'

'Good morning to you,' said Clay, opening his telescope to examine the French ship more closely. 'If I am not much mistaken, they also plan to use them presently.'

The others joined him at the rail to examine the enemy ship. A swarm of ant-like figures had appeared above the tree line, clambering up her foremast shrouds. Soon they spread out along the topsail yard like pearls on a string. Taylor pulled out his pocket watch and flipped open the cover. Back on the *Centaure* the top sail began to appear, a ghostly grey mass in the gloom. It fell free, was sheeted home, and the three masts began to advance towards the harbour entrance.

'They make sail a deal less swiftly than we would have it done, sir,' reported the first lieutenant, 'but it was not performed as ill as I have seen on some Frenchmen.'

'So I should hope, setting sail in the calm of a harbour!' commented Blake. 'I would like to see how they will manage in a blow.'

'Consider, they have crossed the Atlantic, gentlemen,' said Clay. 'She is a foe we must respect.'

The *Centaure* was gathering speed as she headed towards the open sea. Her long bowsprit appeared from behind the island, and a triangle of jib flapped and spread as it was sheeted home. Next to appear was her gilded figurehead, catching the first of the morning light as the sun cleared the horizon. Like a creature emerging from its lair, the hull followed, sliding into sunlight. Its long, double row of gun ports seemed to go on forever. Then she made her turn around the end of the island, and headed directly towards them. It had become very quiet on the frigate's deck.

'Mr Blake, have the ship put about, if you please,' he ordered. 'Head for open water, and you had best set our topgallants.'

'Aye aye, sir,' said the officer of the watch.

'All hands!' roared the boatswain's mates. 'All hands to wear ship!'

The watch below came pouring up the ladderways, and rushed across the deck to their places. Topmen bolted up the shrouds and out onto the lofty topgallant yards, as the frigate swung away from the island. The moment she had completed her turn, fresh sails blossomed in the morning sun, and the *Griffin* surged forwards.

'I do hope they are noting our time over there,' said Blake, pointing towards the *Centaure*, which had only just sheeted home the last of her topsails. 'That should give them pause for thought.'

'And this from the man who wanted me to neglect sail drill in favour of practising the crew with his beloved guns, sir,' said Taylor, in an aside to his captain. Clay smiled at his officers, pleased at how relaxed they seemed, in spite of the huge ship that was setting more and more canvas in the hope of catching them.

'Once the sails are trimmed and drawing, kindly see that the men have a good breakfast this morning, Mr Taylor.'

'A good breakfast, sir,' repeated the officer, his eyes wide with alarm. 'Does that mean you intend to fight with them?'

'No, but I am quite certain that they mean to fight with us, if they are able,' explained Clay. 'And she has the look of a fast ship.'

'She does, sir,' conceded Taylor, 'but a well-founded ship like the *Griffin* should have the beating of her, barring any accidents aloft.' The first lieutenant reached forward to touch the ship's rail as he said this.

'Nevertheless, we may well be in action later this day,' said Clay. 'We need to hold her interest, giving her some hope that she might overhaul us, so that she will follow close. That way we can lead her, like a bull by the nose, towards Antigua. Captain Camelford should have reported to the admiral by now. I have some hope that we shall encounter the *Stirling* coming towards us. Then things may become interesting.'

The two ships reached the edge of the bay; first the

frigate, and then her pursuer rounded the mountainous western half of Guadeloupe. Their sudden appearance caused the cloud of little fishing boats working the western coast of the island to scatter back towards the shore. Meanwhile the warships headed out for the open sea. The *Centaure* had been steadily setting more and more canvas as she came and the breeze grew as they left the land behind. Each new sail set by the French ship was matched on board the British frigate, until both were heeling far over, throwing curtains of white water down to leeward. Clay stood at the windward rail, with one arm hooked into the mizzen shrouds and the deck sloping down away from him towards the boiling sea. The rope against his arm was as stiff as iron, and gave off a low hum.

Without warning, a line of glossy grey backs curved out of the water alongside.

'We have dolphins for company, sir,' grinned Blake. 'A good omen, I think. We must be moving swiftly to have won their favour.'

'Perhaps they come to warn us that we are over-pressed, sir,' said Taylor, eyeing the bulging canvas and straining yards. Clay looked back towards the French ship, measuring the distance between them in his mind.

'Very well, put another reef in the topgallants, Mr Taylor,' he ordered. 'I do not wish to leave her too far behind.'

'Aye aye, sir.'

With the area of sail reduced, the motion of the frigate became a little easier. The green hump of Guadeloupe, ridged like the back of a dragon, shrank behind them, while the *Centaure* still bounded along astern. She was magnificent, viewed from ahead like this. Her huge masts were mountains of white, towering up above her big hull. Her foretopsail spread far out on both sides, while the gilded centaur beneath her bowsprit seemed to be rearing up from out of her tumbling bow wave.

'I believe we are out of range of her bow chasers, sir,' commented Taylor.

'But still no sign of Sir George and the *Stirling*?' mused Clay. 'Where can they be?'

A puff of dirty white smoke appeared briefly high on the forecastle of the *Centaure* and a tall splash rose up in the frigate's boiling wake a good hundred yards behind them. The bang of the cannon arrived a little later.

'The French don't seem to be of your way of thinking, Mr Taylor,' said Clay. 'Kindly set whatever sail you see fit to maintain us at this distance, and have me called if the situation changes. I shall go below to my cabin.'

'Aye aye, sir,' said Taylor, touching his hat.

There was something breathlessly exciting about being chased by a more powerful ship. On the quarterdeck, Clay had felt that those around him shared his reckless mood. Most of them were seaman enough to know that, barring an accident, they had the swifter ship. Yet the knowledge that such awesome, destructive power was thrashing along behind them, just out of range, made the men bubble over with excitement.

In the calm of his cabin Clay tried to concentrate on the breakfast that Harte brought through for him. The fried salt pork was spluttering hot, and the fresh eggs from the frigate's chickens just the way he liked them. Yet he found himself hurrying the meal, his eye relentlessly drawn towards the run of glass windows at the rear of the cabin, and the ship that filled them.

When he had finished eating he went to his desk, resolutely turning his back to the *Centaure* and concentrating on the blank sheet of paper in front of him. He had written his report on the capture of the *Étoile D'espoir*, with word of the deserter he had recovered, but had yet to record Boisgard's revelations about Camelford. This was not a matter he could intrust to the gossipy Allen. Accusing a fellow officer in an official document was a tricky business, and what he wrote might well be the main piece of evidence at a court martial. Ideally, he would have wanted to speak with Camelford first, to have seen in his eyes his guilt or otherwise, but heaven knew when that opportunity would come.

He chewed at the end of his pen, but somehow the words wouldn't come. This is ridiculous, he chided himself. He stole a glance towards the *Centaure*, and then turned around in his seat. Surely, she was closer than he remembered? A fresh plume of smoke belched from high on the forecastle of the enemy ship, and the bang of a cannon firing sounded through the thick glass. For a moment he held his breath, wondering if the ball would crash through the window and into the cabin. The splash, when it came, was just as far behind the frigate as the previous one. With a sigh, almost of disappointment, he returned to his report.

He tweaked the blank sheet in front of him a little straighter, took a deep breath, and dipped his pen into his inkwell. Still nothing formed in his mind. Clay sat poised, a black drop of ink forming on the nib, waiting for revelation to come. Then a hail from the masthead drifted down through the cabin's skylight.

'Deck ho! Sail on the bow!'

Clay wiped his pen clean with relief, returned the virgin sheet of paper to its place, and awaited the arrival of a messenger. It was only when the knock sounded at the door that he realised he was sitting at a completely empty desk.

'Come in!' he called, pulling the ship's watch list from

out of a drawer, and spreading the pages in front of him. An excited Midshipman Todd strode into the cabin, and stood to attention in front of the desk. After a brief pause, Clay looked up.

'Mr Taylor's compliments, and a sail is in sight, bearing north-north-east, sir,' said the youngster. 'He believes it to be a warship.'

'Thank you, Mr Todd,' said his captain. 'Please tell him that I shall be up directly.'

When Clay returned to the quarterdeck, most of his officers were there already, straining towards the horizon ahead, or glancing behind them at the following ship.

'What do you have for me, Mr Taylor?' he asked.

'Upper sails of a large warship in sight ahead, sir,' reported the first lieutenant. 'The lookout also believes he can see a second, smaller ship behind the first. I have just dispatched Mr Todd to the masthead with our best spyglass.'

Clay glanced up and saw the small midshipman taking his place beside the lookout, who was pointing ahead. He saw him extend his telescope out and settle it on the horizon.

'Deck there!' called the youngster. 'The *Stirling* for sure, with either the *Echo* or the *Daring*, astern I should say, sir.'

'Not both?' muttered Preston, who had replaced Blake as officer of the watch. 'We shall need every vessel in the squadron to best this foe, sir.'

'The *Echo* will be away on patrol,' said Clay. 'Three ships, if briskly handled, should suffice. Kindly make more sail, if you please, Mr Preston. Let us close with the admiral and report.'

Guadeloupe had vanished beneath the horizon, while Antigua had yet to appear, leaving an enormous disc of blue ocean with two pairs of ships rushing from its rim towards the centre. From the south came the *Griffin*, with the *Centaure* several miles astern, while from the north came the *Stirling* with her consort. At the speed the ships were converging, it wasn't long before the upper sails of the flagship and her companion could be seen from the deck of the frigate as tiny squares of white, a little more solid than the pale sky at the horizon

'That sloop is *Daring*, I think, sir,' reported Taylor. 'Her foremast has a bit more rake than Captain Sutton's *Echo*.'

'Maybe,' said Clay, staring at the horizon until his eye began to water. More sails were becoming apparent as the range came down.

'Deck there!' called Todd. 'The other ship looks to be the *Daring*!'

Shame, thought Clay. He would have much preferred his efficient friend to the mercurial, possibly untrustworthy Camelford.

He turned towards the signal midshipman. 'Send this, if you please, Mr Russell,' he said. "*Griffin* to flag. Enemy in sight bearing south by west. Single ship of the line".'

'Aye aye, sir,' said the officer, chalking the message onto his slate. By the flag locker the signal rating was already pulling out the correct flags and attaching them to the halliard.

'Flagship acknowledges, sir,' reported Russell.

'Thank you. Now send "enemy is French national ship *Centaure* of eighty guns".'

'Sir, sir!' exclaimed Preston beside him. 'The enemy is hauling her wind.'

Clay turned and looked at the French ship. She came ponderously sweeping around up into the breeze. Her starboard side slowly appeared, with a white stripe running along each of its gundecks.

'Flagship acknowledges, sir,' said the signal midshipman.

'Thank you, Mr Russell,' said Clay, continuing to watching the *Centaure*. 'Can you report that the enemy is going about, if you please.'

'Aye aye, sir.'

Centaure's jib began to shiver as she approached the eye of the wind, and then flapped free as it was hauled across. Her big yards were turning on her masts, forcing her bow around, until she settled at last on the other tack, heading away from the *Griffin* and towards the empty heart of the Caribbean.

'I daresay that she doesn't like the look of all these new sails on the horizon, sir,' commented Taylor.

'We may have the beating of her in a race, but that tub *Stirling* will not catch her, sir,' said Preston. 'Those old sixty-fours were never the swiftest.'

'Then we shall need to alter matters, gentlemen,' said Clay. 'Time for us to do some chasing, I declare. Mr Preston, kindly follow the enemy about, and I'll have the topgallants drawing again so as to bring her within range.'

'Aye aye, sir,' said the lieutenant.

'Mr Russell, another signal to the flag, if you please. "Submit, *Griffin* engage the enemy to slow her progress".'

Preston and Taylor exchanged glances at this, but neither passed comment.

'Aye aye, sir,' said the midshipman, already leafing through his signal book. Soon the long line of flags was climbing up the mizzen mast. After a pause, a signal broke out on board the *Stirling*.

'Flag to *Griffin*,' translated Russell. 'Proceed.'

Clay closed his telescope. 'Mr Taylor, will you kindly

have the ship cleared for action.'

*****

The rattle of the side drum swelled to a thunderous roar as the young marine drummer warmed to his task. He stood close to the base of the main mast, a spot from which the sound of his instrument could carry throughout the frigate. In response to its urging beat, the crew ran to prepare their ship for battle.

Some disappeared down below the waterline, like the gunner and his mate. Both men emptied their pockets of any metal, tied back each other's pigtails into a compacted knot and pulled on their soft list slippers. Each made a final turn in front of the other, bumped fists, and pushed their way through the heavy felt 'fearnaught' screen into the copper-lined magazine beyond, where enough gunpowder awaited them to destroy the *Griffin* several times over.

Farther aft, in the cramped gloom of the cockpit, preparations of a different kind were underway. Richard Corbett, his coat laid to one side and his shirt sleeves rolled up, was having his leather apron tied around his waist. The front of the garment was black and stiff from previous patients, and brown flakes showered down as the material flexed around him. Another of his assistants was lashing a canvas cover over an operating table fashioned from sea chests, while off to one side, a third man laid out a long line of saws, knives and probes.

Two levels above their heads, the first sound of gun trucks could be heard, rumbling across the planking of the main deck as the crews tested that their weapons were running freely. After the cathedral quiet of the hold, the noise here was deafening. Orders were barked over the sound of busy hammering from the carpenter and his mates. They were dismantling the last of Clay's quarters, the bulkheads and furniture quickly vanishing towards the hold, to leave the entire sweep of the main deck free and unencumbered. Each of the big eighteen-pounders that lined the sides was surrounded by its crew. Some were rigging gun tackles, others were testing their equipment or stripping off their shirts and rolling their neckcloths into bandanas to protect their ears. O'Malley, who was captain of one of the cannons, pressed a leather bucket against the chest of the nearest member of his crew.

'Larcum, go an' fill that fecker, will yous,' he ordered.

'Right you be,' said Mudge, heading off to join the queue that had formed by the pump.

'She be rigged,' announced Trevan, standing up from beside the carriage. The Irishman looked over the gun, checking all was as it should be. The flint in the lock was sparking brightly, Evans had the flexible rammer cradled against his chest and the rest of the crew were lined up along the tackles. He next tested the deck, scuffing the soles of his feet on it to see if enough sand had been scattered to give the men grip, then he looked around him for the ship's boy allocated to the gun. The lad was standing off to one side, his leather charge case draped over one shoulder, giggling nervously with the boy from the gun next in line.

'Mind what you're about, Charlie, and leave your fecking mate be,' he growled.

The other lad went back to his post, while Charlie adopted a more sober attitude.

Mudge returned with a brimming bucket of water, and paused in front of the boy. 'Someone be a knocking at your door, nipper,' he said, his face solemn.

Charlie grinned in response, recognising the start of the formula. 'Who be that a knocking at my door?' he asked.

'It be John,' replied the sailor.

'John who?'

Quick as a flash, Mudge dipped his hand into the bucket and splashed water in the boy's face. 'Why, John the Baptist, of course!'

The powder monkey squealed with delight, while the listening crew all chuckled appreciatively.

'John the bleeding Baptist!' repeated Evans. 'Ha ha, I like that.'

'Ain't you got your piece sorted yet, O'Malley?' demanded the petty officer in charge of the gun section.

'Aye, Shango be ready, Mr Fletcher,' said the Irishman, ignoring the gun's official number in favour of the name painted across the barrel by her proud crew.

'The Brimstone Belcher be ready an' all, Mr Fetcher,' added the crew of the eighteen-pounder next in line.

Slowly calm spread across the frigate, as each preparation was completed and each man reached his station. Clay, now in his glittering full dress uniform, leant on the rail and looked down on the crowded main deck. He was quietly satisfied with what he saw. Months of drill and the action against the *Peregrine* had served to blend the new recruits with the old hands, until he struggled to notice the difference. Just below him a hefty young man with wild, straw-coloured hair swayed easily with the motion of the ship. Only his lack of a pigtail or any tattoos marked him as one of the volunteers brought in by one of the posters. Then Clay looked beyond the *Griffin*'s long bowsprit at the French ship ahead, growing all the time as they steadily overhauled her. He felt his mouth grow dry. I shall need all of the crew's spirit and training to get through today, he decided.

'The ship is cleared for action, sir,' reported Taylor from beside him. Clay turned from the rail, as if noticing the transformation for the first time. Above his head there were splashes of scarlet among the bulging slabs of white, where marine sharpshooters were positioned aloft. The quarterdeck around him had suddenly filled. All the carronades had been manned, extra quartermasters stood by the wheel, and additional midshipmen waited by the binnacle, ready to carry any messages. Preston stood close by, a telescope grasped under his right arm, and had been joined by Armstrong, while a little farther back Macpherson stood beside his reserve of marines.

'Thank you, Mr Taylor,' he said. 'Would you ask Mr Blake and Mr Preston to join us, if you please.'

'Aye aye, sir,' said the older man, touching his hat.

Blake was the last to arrive, running up the companion ladder from his precious guns on the main deck.

Clay looked at his three lieutenants, noticing the sparkle of excitement in the two younger men's eyes and the look of concern on the face of the more cautious Taylor. 'Here is a pretty situation, gentlemen,' he said. 'A deuced powerful Frenchman loose in the Caribbean, and the Jamaica convoy due in a week or so. Once the *Stirling* and *Daring* join us, I daresay we may have the beating of her, but the enemy don't seem inclined to allow that to happen. So how should we proceed?'

'We need to damage her aloft, to allow the admiral to join us, sir,' said Preston. 'That at least is clear.'

'That will not be so easy to achieve,' said the veteran first lieutenant. 'She can serve out some fearsome punishment with those broadsides of hers.'

'Weight of fire is her advantage, I grant you,' agreed Clay. 'What do we have in our favour?'

'Superior speed for certain, sir,' said Blake. 'And better manoeuvrability to boot.'

'And I will wager my commission we have the best drilled crew,' added Preston.

'Exactly so,' agreed Clay. 'We shall need to be like a terrier, annoying a bull. So long as we stay astern of her, snapping at her tail, we will do very well. I daresay she has a pair of twelve-pounders set close to the water, either side of her rudder, but nothing more than that can bear on us.'

'So, what are your orders, sir?' asked Taylor.

'Mr Preston, I want you to place yourself on the forecastle, with a good sight of the *Centaure*, but where you can be seen by both myself here, and Mr Blake down on the main deck. Use our long nines to pepper her as we close the range. If she continues to run, we shall luff up periodically and give her a broadside, and then resume our place astern of her once more.'

'Firing high, I take it, sir,' said Blake. 'To damage her rigging?'

'If you please,' confirmed his captain.

'And what if the bull turns around to gore at us, sir?' asked the first lieutenant.

'That is why Mr Preston needs to place himself with such care,' said Clay. 'Watch her rudder as if your life depends upon it, as it may indeed. The moment you see it move, signal to us with your hat the direction in which she is turning. We will immediately swing the opposite way, to keep astern of her, and you will have the opportunity to rake her once more, Mr Blake.'

'Aye, that I shall, sir,' chuckled the lieutenant.

'Until Mr Preston gives us his signal, you will have no notion as to which broadside will be required to fire,' cautioned his captain. 'Shall you be able to manage with so little notice?'

'With your leave, I will have both sides loaded and run out, and allocate the men as required, sir,' said Blake. 'I daresay we shall manage well enough.'

'I daresay that you will,' smiled Clay, turning next to his first lieutenant. 'Your part will be sail handling, Mr Taylor,' said Clay. 'Have the best topmen stationed aloft, and the sheets and braces manned. I shall require you to make the old girl dance to a reel, if the situation requires it.'

'Will it answer, I wonder, sir,' mused Taylor.

'Did you note how awkwardly the *Centaure* tacked about earlier?' asked Clay. 'So long as Mr Preston can warn us the moment she starts to turn, all will be fine.'

'Aye aye, sir,' said Taylor.

'Are we all clear?' asked Clay. 'Mr Preston? Mr Blake? Good, then the best of luck to you all, and kindly take your places, if you please. We will be in range presently.'

*****

Clay had commanded men in action since his teens, and warships since his late twenties. All those years of experience had taught him the value of showing only supreme confidence in the face of danger, until he could play that part as well as any actor on a stage. When his officers left him, his face settled into a mask without him realising. Behind that outward calm, his true emotions churned and raced. The risks he was taking were appalling, he reflected, as his ship ploughed along in the wake of the *Centaure*. It was only a year since his last command, another frigate, had been beaten into a broken wreck by a much smaller ship of the line than this one. The slightest slip, or error of judgement, and the *Griffin* might suffer the same fate.

They were growing closer all the time. On the forecastle he could see Preston urging the crews of the two bow chasers to ready their guns, his one-armed gesticulations strange and jerky. Beyond him was the stern of the French ship, a slab of glittering glass windows framed by gilded figures. Carved mermen with coiling tails brandished tridents towards him from either quarter galley, while across the broad taffrail was a curved relief showing an array of muscular centaurs locked in battle. Above the stern her masts soared upwards, lofty as the spires of a cathedral.

Clay opened his telescope to examine her in more detail. Her name was easy to read, painted in block letters across her counter. Beneath that her rudder dipped into the foaming wake, with a square gun port to each side. They hadn't been opened yet, but he could see the hull around them was wet with spray. Best of luck firing from so close to the surface, thought Clay. The gun crews would be doubled over beneath a low deck, with water splashing freely into their faces. The *Griffin*'s two long nines would have a distinct advantage over them, placed as they were out in the open, high up on the frigate's bow.

Something moved in his peripheral vision, causing him to search upwards towards the stern rail. A cluster of French officers had gathered to look back at their pursuer. One was gesticulating busily, the braid on his uniform flashing in the sunlight as he pointed towards the frigate. Behind the group, more figures appeared, making their way aloft up the mizzen shrouds. They had muskets slung on their shoulders, and moved with a slowness that no sailor would display, while from both flanks of the *Centaure* a double line of cannon gradually appeared, pointing out to the sides.

'They too are preparing for battle, I collect, sir,' said a voice beside him.

'They are indeed, Mr Armstrong,' said Clay. 'They also seem to have a deal more soldiers than we have to hand.'

'Sure, but how many are marines, used to the sea, and how many are puking landsmen they have swept up in Guadeloupe, sir?'

Clay lowered his telescope to reply, but then became aware that a small figure was rushing along the portside gangway towards him. 'Yes, Mr Todd?'

'Mr Preston's compliments, and he believes the enemy will presently be in range, sir,' said the breathless youngster.

'My thanks to him, if you please. Kindly tell him that he has my permission to open fire.'

'Aye aye, sir.'

While the midshipman scampered back to the forecastle, the ship's master handed over the brass speaking trumpet he had brought across from its place by the wheel. 'You will have need of this, once matters become warm, sir,' he said.

'My thanks, Mr Armstrong,' said his captain. 'What do you think of our situation?'

'Hazardous, in truth, sir,' said the American, 'but then I reckon such is the fate of a king's officer in time of war. An' I do approve of the fix in which we shall place the enemy. Does he continue to run, while we slowly batter him to pieces? Or will he twist and turn to come at us, which will serve to slow his progress and bring the admiral ever closer?'

'You understand matters well,' said Clay. He looked behind Armstrong, towards the horizon where the other two ships followed. They had grown more distant now, with only their uppermost sails visible. Then a double bang came from the bow, and two fountains of water rose up behind the French ship.

'A little short,' commented Armstrong, 'but well enough directed. We shall find the range presently. Shall I have the time the engagement started noted in the log, sir?'

'If you please, Mr Armstrong.' Clay watched the crews on the bow as they raced through the process of reloading. Beneath him on the main deck, some of the men were pushing their heads through the open ports, eager to see what was going on.

'Back to your places there!' roared an indignant Blake. 'Gawking like damned nuns in a bawdy house! You shall have sight of the enemy soon enough.'

Another double bang from the forecastle sent a dirty ball of brown smoke rolling away to windward. Clay forced himself to ignore the fall of shot, and instead watch Preston. He stood bare-headed in a pool of sunlight, his black bicorn held down by his side.

'A miss off to larboard sir, but I didn't mark the second ball,' said Armstrong, who had his telescope to his eye. 'Ah, I have it. A hit! We have stove in a window. That will teach the blackguards.'

Clay looked at the beautiful stern, and saw the shattered window, third from left in the lower run of glass. Then he noticed that the two stern ports had swung open.

'We shall presently be under fire ourselves, Mr Armstrong,' he said, pointing forwards.

The range had closed further the next time the bow

chasers fired. One missed again, while the other sent splinters flying from low on the stern, leaving a white gash on the counter, like a big full stop between the 'A' and 'U' of the ship's name. A dull roar followed; smoke gushed up from around the *Centaure*'s rudder, and a line of splashes appeared off to one side of the frigate's bow. Then Preston spun around on the forecastle and waved his hat urgently, to his right.

Chapter 10
The Bull and the Terrier

'Man the braces, Mr Taylor!' roared Clay. 'Headsails!' Then he turned to the men at the wheel. 'Two points to larboard, helmsman. Make haste, now!'

'Two points, aye, sir,' repeated the quartermaster, rolling the polished spokes through his hands.

'Mr Blake, have the starboard guns made ready!' Clay ordered, striding forward to the quarterdeck rail.

'Aye aye, sir!' came the reply.

Ahead of the frigate, the *Centaure* was beginning to turn up into the wind. He could see water boiling around her rudder as it came across, gripping the sea. High in her masts, her heavy black yards were creaking around against the blue sky. One long side of her hull, studded with big guns, began to appear from behind her elaborate stern.

'Come on, turn,' urged Clay, banging the rail beneath his fists. He could hear Taylor barking instructions from the windward gangway. Then beneath his feet he felt the angle of the deck change, and his ship began to swing the opposite way, moving back across the French ship's stern.

'Ready Starboards!' yelled Blake beneath him. A line of clenched fists rose into the air as each gun captain showed his piece was ready.

The frigate was gathering pace on her new course, cutting across behind their enemy. Too fast, Clay suddenly realised. Their huge opponent was almost stationary, still ponderously turning, with canvas beating in the wind, while the *Griffin* sailed on. The frigate would soon shoot through the blind spot behind their opponent, and out into the killing zone of the guns on the *Centaure*'s far side.

'Come up a point, helmsman!' yelled Clay. 'Mr Taylor, back the foretopsail! Now! Mr Blake, fire as she bears!'

'Aye aye, sir.'

This was the moment when all the crew's long hours of sail training began to tell. Under the urgings of their petty officers, the lines of men heaved the big foretop yard around, the canvas sail cracking thunderously in protest as the wind spilt from it, until it was pressed back against the mast, and the frigate's progress stuttered to a halt. Clay glanced across at the French ship. The *Griffin* was rocking in the gentle swell, lying across her opponent's stern where all her guns could bear.

'On the up roll, Starboards!' ordered Blake. 'Open fire!'

The broadside roared out, tipping the frigate away from her enemy with the force of the recoil, and engulfing them in a wall of smoke. Beneath Clay the line of big eighteen-pounders shot back inboard, almost perfectly together, and their crews flew through the process of reloading the guns. From the forehatch a pack of ship's boys came running up the ladderway and fanned out across the deck, each one bearing a fresh charge for his gun.

'The enemy is on the move again, sir,' reported the ship's master as the smoke began to thin. 'Coming back on her original course, I reckon.'

'Follow her around, if you please, Mr Armstrong,' said Clay, before raising his speaking trumpet to his lips. 'I'll have that foretopsail drawing again, Mr Taylor.'

'Aye aye, sir.'

As the *Centaure* gathered way, the *Griffin* slid back into her wake. Almost immediately the two nine-pounders in the bow fired again, and a French shot cracked into the frigate's foretopsail, leaving a ragged hole.

'Will you darn well look at that, sir!' enthused the sailing master, his American accent suddenly stronger. 'That broadside has wounded her plenty aloft. And I reckon her progress may have slowed a touch.'

Clay opened his telescope and looked over the enemy. One of her three big stern lanterns hung at a drunken angle, where an eighteen-pounder ball, aimed too low, had broken a stanchion. The rest of the broadside had struck her much higher up. Clay could see plenty of fresh holes in her sails, and teams of men at work high in her rigging, repairing some of the severed lines that hung down. The group of officers at her stern rail had shrunk to just two, both of whom had telescopes focused on him. Clay thought one of them touched the brim of his hat towards him, but his view was masked for a moment by smoke as the bow chasers fired again. Then the two Frenchmen turned as something fell onto the deck behind them.

'What do you suppose they will try next, sir?' asked Armstrong.

'Why should we wait for them to act, Jacob?' said Clay. 'Mr Preston is doing fine service, but it will take a day and a night to disable such a huge ship with only a brace of nine-pounders to call upon. We must close and press our advantage.' Clay returned his speaking trumpet to his lips. 'Mr Blake, have your larboard side guns made ready, if you please. Trained as far forward as possible.'

'Aye aye, sir,' came the reply from the well of the main deck, accompanied by a rumble of approval from the gun crews who had yet to fire.

'Mr Taylor!' continued Clay. 'When we are a cable closer, we shall luff up, and give her another broadside.'

'Aye aye, sir. I shall be ready.'

The ships raced on across the dazzling blue sea, the gap between them closing all the time. From the forecastle the two nine-pounders continued their steady bombardment, hitting the enemy's sails regularly as the range came down. The reply from the pair of French guns was much slower, in contrast, and they frequently missed altogether. Clay looked aloft to see what damage his ship had received. Apart from the hole in the foretopsail, and a line that Hutchinson had a party of hands re-roving, all seemed well. He returned his attention to the dwindling distance between him and the enemy. Almost, he muttered. Just a little closer. He waited for what he judged was the right moment, and then waited a little more. Now, he decided.

'Bring her up into the wind, Mr Armstrong,' he ordered. 'Mr Blake, open fire the moment the guns bear! Mr Taylor, be ready to reverse course once the guns have fired!'

'Aye aye, sir.'

The frigate turned up into the stiff breeze, slowing rapidly as she slewed around, bringing her broadside to bear on to the enemy's stern. Now the distance was increasing rapidly, as the French ship continued to speed on her way, but she was still comfortably within range when the *Griffin* opened fire. Clay could see Blake beneath him, sighting along the barrel of the middle gun in the portside battery. When the *Centaure*'s stern had appeared completely he shouted a warning, jerked back on the firing lanyard, and gestured for the rest of the guns to fire. This time it was a rolling broadside, spreading out from the middle cannon, racing forward towards the bow, and rumbling back down the deck towards him. The moment he heard the last eighteen-pounder bang out beneath him, Clay was issuing instructions.

'Wheel back over, Mr Armstrong!' he yelled. 'Headsails, Mr Taylor!'

The frigate checked its turn, hung for a moment, and then slowly turned back onto its original course. As the last of the cloak of gun smoke parted, the *Centaure* reappeared. Her gilded stern continued to glitter in the sunshine, but she was now much farther away. There was plenty of fresh damage aloft for Clay to see. The mizzen topsail had a big tear in it, and a long streamer of canvas was flapping free. The frigate gathered speed, and the pair of bow chasers barked out again.

'Definitely slower now, sir,' said Armstrong, with his pocket watch in his hand. Clay looked back towards the two following British warships. They still seemed as distant as before, but then the frigate lifted to a wave, and for the first time he glimpsed the *Stirling*'s hull for a fleeting instant.

'A little slower,' he agreed. 'But nothing vital has carried away yet.'

The chase settled back into the same pattern as before. The frigate gained steadily on the French ship, creeping up behind her like a footpad on his victim. On the forecastle the two nine-pounders fired again and again, punching more holes in her sails, and cutting fresh lines in her rigging. Behind the two guns stood the bare-headed Preston, watching their opponent's rudder, his hat by his side, ready to signal.

The frigate was almost close enough to luff up and let fly with another broadside when a ball from the *Centaure*'s stern chasers struck a screeching blow as it hit flush on the iron fluke of one of the frigate's anchors. A shower of sparks flew up, and shards of broken metal scythed across the forecastle. Clay watched as three wounded seamen were carried down to the main deck and away to the surgeon. One man hung limp between the sailors carrying him, his shirt dark with gore. Another howled in pain, one bloody arm cradled across his chest by the other. Clay waited until they had been taken below, forcing himself to harden his heart and returned his attention to the battle.

He swung his speaking trumpet up to his mouth. 'Mr Blake, kindly have the larboard side guns ready once more, if you please.'

'Aye aye, sir,' replied the lieutenant.

'Mr Taylor!' shouted Clay. 'We shall luff up again directly.'

As Clay gave his orders, he felt a strange sense of *déjà vu*. The same sun shone down on the brilliant sea. The *Griffin* was back in the same position, just to windward of the white line of wake thrown out by her opponent, ready to perform the same manoeuvre. He could even see the pair of French officers watching his ship's approach once more, from the stern rail beside the broken lantern. The frigate swept up into the wind as the wheel went across, her way came off, and the portside guns roared out in sequence, masking their opponent in dense smoke. The men clustered around the guns were busy reloading them once more, and then something different happened. A movement, rapid and urgent like the flapping of a bird, caught his attention from the forecastle. It was Preston, waving his hat frantically at him, his arm held out to the right once more.

For a moment Clay hesitated, and then he started barking orders.

'Wheel hard over!' he roared. 'Mr Taylor, haul around the topsail yards!'

The *Griffin* was barely moving through the water at all, and she stalled for a long moment, the sea slapping against her stationary side. All the time the gun smoke was thinning, revealing the *Centaure*, not racing away from them as before. This time she was turning up into the wind too, bringing her starboard battery to bear on the troublesome frigate. She was stern on to them at the moment, but her long side was appearing as she came around, every cannon trained to fire as far aft as possible.

'Bless my soul,' exclaimed Armstrong. 'They must have been waiting for us to luff up and turned the moment we fired, the dogs! Thank goodness Mr Preston was positioned clear of all this darn reek.'

'Get those topsails drawing, Mr Taylor!' yelled Clay, while inside he seethed with frustration. How could he have been such a fool! Of course the French would try something different, rather than let him steadily pound their sails to ribbons.

The two ships were both almost stationary, locked in a race for survival being carried out at the pace of a snail. The French leviathan was inching up into the wind, twisting her side towards her tormentor. Aloft, her tattered rigging and torn sails flapped in the wind like so much bunting. Meanwhile the frigate was turning in the opposite direction, slowly beginning to pay off, desperate to return to the invisible triangle of shelter astern of the *Centaure*.

Macpherson appeared beside him, drawn forward by the unfolding drama. 'Come on, wee lassie,' he urged, stroking his hand along the oak rail before him. 'You can make it.'

'Look at all the damage she has aloft, sir!' exclaimed

Armstrong, from his other side. 'By rights she should be finding it near impossible to manoeuvre.'

The side of the French ship was slowly lengthening. A puff of smoke erupted from her stern most cannon as a gun captain fancied his weapon bore, and a fountain of water rose up from the sea beside them. The boom of the shot was deep and menacing, the water spout far taller than any the *Griffin* had raised. Time seemed to stand still, with the ships perfectly synchronised, as the frigate drifted forward at the same rate as the *Centaure* was turning. Another two puffs of smoke, more huge splashes and Clay held his breath. Then he heard it, a sound as welcome as the tinkle of a stream to a man lost in a desert. It was the gurgle of water as it whispered past the hull. The frigate's big foretopsail flapped loudly as it was hauled around, and then it stiffened into an arc of white as it caught the breeze, and the *Griffin* gathered pace.

'Another broadside, if you please, Mr Blake,' ordered Clay, breathing at last.

'Aye aye, sir. Ready gun captains?'

The curved line of arms rose into the air, and the gun crews crouched down around their pieces, holding their hands over their ears.

'Point to windward, Mr Armstrong,' said Clay. 'Let us come a little closer.'

'Aye aye, sir.'

The enemy's stern rose high out of the water as the frigate bore down on it. Clay could see more of the damage they had inflicted on their opponent. Three of the stern windows had been smashed, and one of the mermen had lost his arm. From her mizzen mast lines of cut rigging hung down like jungle creepers amid the torn sails.

Clay began to hear shouted orders from on board, as

the big ship tried to pay off and get back underway. 'Close enough, Mr Armstrong,' he said. 'Hold her thus, Mr Taylor.'

'Aye aye, sir.'

The *Centaure*'s two stern chasers fired together, and there was a double crash from forward as the shots struck home, followed by a cry of pain, pitched at a level that only one of the ship's boys could reach.

'It seems not even the Frogs can miss at this range,' muttered Macpherson.

'Let us hope we can repay them with interest, Tom,' said Clay. 'Give them another, Mr Blake, if you please.'

'Aye aye, sir.'

*****

The gun crews were getting ready as the enemy ship grew near.

'Pipe be taking us in proper tight this time,' marvelled Trevan, peering through the open port at the approaching ship. 'I hope he knows what he be about.'

'Move yer fecking arse, Adam,' ordered O'Malley, who was trying to sight along the barrel. 'Hand spike men! Shift her a touch towards the stern.' Two of the crew levered the heavy red carriage around. 'Easy there,' called the Irishman, couching low with one eye closed. 'That's the mark, right on the fecker's mizzen top. Places, lads.'

He waited until the others had all dropped into position, and then took up the slack in the lanyard with one hand, while raising the other. From next to the *Centaure*'s rudder came an eruption of smoke, the tongue of flame at its heart seeming to come straight towards him, and a moment later there was a crashing blow on the hull. Splinters rattled against the gun barrel, and one of the crew yelped, pulling his hand from the tackle and sucking at it. There was a scream of pain, as high-pitched as a girl's, and Charlie fell to the deck with a dagger of wood protruding from his thigh.

'Nipper's copped it!' exclaimed Mudge, turning from his place on the gun tackle.

'Leave him be!' roared Fletcher. 'He ain't in the way. Just you attend to your duty!'

'Open fire!' ordered Blake, from his place by the main mast.

'Stand clear!' warned O'Malley. He gave a final glance across at the target and jerked the lanyard. The lock snapped forwards, there was a gush of sparks from the touch hole, and the gun leapt back across the deck. A wall of smoke billowed up beside the frigate, while the men raced to reload the cannon. Mudge knelt down beside the boy, supporting him while he eased the leather charge case over his head and passed the heavy bag of powder to Trevan. Charlie grew quieter, whimpering gently into the sailor's shoulder.

'We're after needing a fresh powder monkey here, Mr Fletcher,' reported the Irishman. 'Charlie's hurt fecking bad.'

'Alright, O'Malley,' said Fletcher, summoning over a replacement. The smoke was rolling clear, revealing the damage the latest broadside had caused. The *Centaure* was further off once more, still sailing away from the *Griffin*, but her profile had changed dramatically. Her mizzen mast had taken the brunt of the frigate's fire, and the upper half hung down in ruin. The mizzen topmast had snapped clean through, leaving a cone of torn canvas and broken spars beneath it. Debris dotted the water behind the stern, and sailors could be seen working with axes clearing away the wreckage. A roar of approval rose up from the watching gun crews.

In the confusion, Mudge picked Charlie up, making light of his thin body, and headed towards the aft ladderway. ‘Come along, nipper,’ he murmured into the boy’s ear. ‘Let’s be a getting you down to the sawbones.’ The youngster nuzzled his face closer, wetting his shoulder with tears.

Blocking the ladderway stood a marine sentry. His musket had its bayonet fitted and he held it across the entrance, barring the way. ‘Halt there!’ he ordered. ‘Only wounded or them as is fetching powder are allowed below!’

‘You got both here,’ snapped Mudge ‘So get your arse out of my bleeding way!’

‘What’s wrong with him then?’ demanded the soldier.

Mudge gently rolled Charlie’s wounded thigh towards him. Red splashes dripped onto the deck, and the boy moaned in pain. ‘Satisfied?’

‘Alright, you can pass,’ conceded the sentry, standing to one side. ‘But there ain’t no call to get bleeding hot with me. You’d be surprised how many folk find cause to go a visiting the hold, once them cannon balls is flying.’

‘Aye, and I dare say there be no shortage of Lobsters as want to guard that prisoner, nice an’ safe down in the lock-up, like,’ added Mudge, from halfway down the ladder.

‘Now, that’s just where you be wrong,’ said the soldier, leaning forward to call after him. ‘All us marines are required to fight up here.’

Mudge passed through the deserted lower deck, with its rows of abandoned mess tables stretching away from him, and continued down into the gloom of the orlop deck. A lamp hung at the bottom of the steps, illuminating an open space with dark passages running away from him. The similarity with the interior of the *Peregrine* was striking. Although the frigate was more spread out, the headroom was just as challenging for a tall man, and he had to bend double over his burden, placing one hand gently on the back of the boy's head to shield it from bumping against the low beams. He paused to get his bearings, and then headed towards the sound of Corbett's voice.

In the cockpit it was relatively calm. Two seamen lay in hammocks strung at the far end, their wounds dressed, emitting loud snores from the combination of rum and laudanum that had eased their treatment. Beneath them lay the shape of a third, motionless and covered.

'Ah, we have a new client,' said Corbett to his assistants as Mudge appeared at the door. 'Pray bring him to the table.'

'Go easy on him please, sir,' said the sailor, as he passed the wounded boy across. 'He ain't no more than a lad.' The assistants carried the patient to the table and laid him on his back. Charlie groaned weakly, his head turning from side to side.

'So I see,' agreed the surgeon, stooping over him. 'Apply a tourniquet above the wound, if you please, Henderson, before this child expires for want of blood.'

'Aye aye, sir.'

'What is the patient's name?' asked Corbett.

'He be Charlie, sir,' said Mudge. 'Charlie Dyer.'

'Well now Charlie, Henderson here is going to give you a little grog for your present relief, after which I shall take a look at your leg,' said the surgeon, smiling down at the boy from behind the steely glint of his little round spectacles.

'D– don't leave me, Larcum,' pleaded Charlie.

'None of that, young man,' said Corbett. 'I shall require you to be gallant for me. Henderson, a gag for the preservation of his tongue, if you please, and then bring over the straps. I shall use my number two saw, I believe. You may return to your duties, Mudge.'

'Aye aye, sir.'

Mudge stumbled out of the cockpit and into the passageway outside. The sound of battle was muted here on the orlop deck. Shouted orders came faintly down to him through the hatchways and gratings from above. Much louder was the double thump of the bow chasers, firing up on the forecastle, and the thunderous rumble of the main guns being run out again. All around him was the renewed creak and groan of the frames as the frigate resumed the pursuit of her wounded opponent. Loudest of all were Charlie's screams of pain, pursuing him all the way to the bottom of the ladderway. He stopped and looked around in the light cast by the lantern that hung close by, but he was quite alone. Ahead of him was the glow of another light, farther forward in the ship.

He stealthily advanced up the passageway until he arrived beside a solid-looking door. It was closed, but had an opening about a foot square cut into the top. This was fitted with bars, and allowed what air and light was available to reach the occupants of the lock-up. From inside he heard a cough and the shifting of a body, accompanied by the chink of metal against the deck. Mudge unhooked the oil lamp that swung in the passageway, and peered into the cell. There was enough room for three or four prisoners, but only one man was inside. He was a heavily built seaman who sat with his back against the far wall with his legs stretched out ahead of him. Both ankles were fettered, and an earthenware jug with a wooden cover rested on the deck beside him. As the light shone in, he looked towards it, shading his eyes with his hand. The lower half of his face was dark with stubble, save where a long scar lay across it.

Larcum Mudge

'Have you come to tell me what the bleeding hell be going on?' demanded the prisoner. 'I can hear broadsides and all manner of tumult, but there be not so much as a guard to pass the time of day with.'

'The Lobsters be all busy,' said Mudge. 'Fighting the Frogs, they claim, although stopping honest folk bringing the wounded to the sawbones seems to be the greater part of it.'

'That be Lobsters all over, mate,' chuckled the sailor. 'Why don't you come in and tell me what be a going on?'

'How does I do that? I ain't no cutpurse as can pick a lock.'

'No need,' said the prisoner. 'It be only bolted. On your side, of course.'

'Is that so?' said Mudge, stepping back to examine the door. The two bolts were easy to find, and looked well-oiled. He considered the situation for a moment, then drew out his seaman's knife. The honed edge of the blade was a line of fire in the lamplight. He checked the corridor was still empty, and heard muffled cries coming from the cockpit. Good, they may prove useful, he thought. He returned the knife to its sheath, swung the door open and slipped into the cell. He closed the door behind him, and stood with his back against it.

'I bloody knew it were you, Tombstone,' he said. The sailor started at the name, and then peered more closely at his visitor. Mudge hung the lamp from the beam overhead, so that the light shone on his face.

'Well, I'll be damned!' exclaimed the prisoner. 'Being stuck down in this cell must addle the mind, for me not to have marked that voice! Jack bleeding Broadbent, if I ain't mistaken. How come you ain't long gone, away to the South Seas on one of them Yankee whalers you was always banging on about? You been pressed?'

'Nah, I went an' volunteered.'

'You did what? After all we done! Have you gone an' lost your bleeding mind?'

'Steady there, Tombstone, an' I'll have less of that "we". I never did more than strike down Daniels.'

'Oh, is that all?' scoffed the prisoner. 'Well, you be sure to tell the hangman that, when he comes for you. He'll be all ears. So when did you join this here barky?'

'Back home, like,' explained Mudge. 'Found me a nice little berth, with a captain as treats his people fair. Course I had no notion as to where the *Griffin* were bound. They was just back from foreign parts, so I reckoned she were due a nice quiet year in the Channel Fleet, or maybe a run to the Med. Enough time for word to blow over, any road. I damned near soiled myself when I found that I had picked the one ship as was to be sent straight back here, hunting after the old *Peregrine*.'

'But what possessed you join the bleeding navy, for all love!'

'I held it the last place the buggers would look for me,' he explained.

'Is that right,' marvelled the prisoner. 'You was always a deep one, but I never held you to have the pluck for that, Jack Broadbent.'

'I left that name on the quayside, Tombstone. I be Larcum now. Larcum Mudge.'

His companion roared with laughter. 'Larcum, bleeding Mudge!' he spluttered. 'What kind of name be that?'

'A right good one, I think you'll find,' said Mudge. 'You still go by John Graves?'

The prisoner spat to one side before answering. 'I ain't given the traps no names, nor aught else besides. You be the only man on board as knows me, not that that will serve me any.' He raised a hand to his scar. 'A cut like this marks a man plain enough, whatever daft name he might choose to hide behind.'

Mudge nodded at this, and there was quiet between the two men. The noise of the sea sloshing past the hull sounded from beyond the curved outer wall of the cell. From somewhere forward of them came the thump of the bow chasers firing.

'Nice of 'ee to find the time to come an' call on an old mate,' said Graves. 'What with a battle raging an' all. Or were there some purpose behind it?' Mudge watched the mutineer. The prisoner's hard face was cross-lit by the glow of the lamp, making the puckered scar seem deeper. The eyes that looked back at him were every bit as fierce as he remembered them from that night in the Mona Passage. Fierce, but also holding a note of calculation in them, he decided. He inched his hand behind him, feeling for the reassurance of the knife that hung from his belt. Graves's eyes flickered towards the movement, and a faint smile crossed his lips.

'Ah, so we comes to it, at last,' he said. 'Not just a social call on poor old Tombstone, then, left down on the orlop with aught but rats for company. Why, I'd be kicking my heels, if they wasn't clamped down so bleeding well. Go on then, Jack, or Larcum, or whatever. What were it as truly brought you here?'

'Did you enjoy that night?' demanded Mudge.

'The one we killed that shit Daniels, you mean?'

'I don't give a damn for that one!' snarled Mudge. 'But what of the others? The nippers and the sick? Them Lobsters and the loyal hands as had done us no ill?'

'I just done what needed doing,' shrugged Graves. 'We

all swore to it.'

'I never did.'

'Aye, that's right,' said the prisoner, pointing at him. 'You was too high and mighty to join hands with your shipmates. Or too shy, more like.'

'That were because of all the other slaughter,' snapped Mudge, his face growing red. 'I wasn't having no part of killing nippers, and the like.'

'That be you all over, Jack Broadbent,' scoffed Graves. 'Happy to share in the feast, but having no truck with sweeping the tavern floor after!'

Mudge ripped his knife out, and leant over the prisoner, the blade glittering in the lamplight. 'Just you listen here,' he growled. 'I shot that snivelling little shit O'Connell, for no more than looking like he were going to blab on me.'

'That bleeding Irish fool!' laughed Graves. 'Where did you chance to come across him? On that Frog privateer he was idiot enough to join? You'll find me a harder man to do over, damn your eyes!'

'I can kill you, Graves, easy, for what you did that night. Right now!' Mudge, stepping behind his victim, and hauled his head back by its pigtail.

'I dare say you could, me being shackled and you with your blade an' all, but it'll be me as will be having the last laugh, in hell, where I'll be waiting for you, Broadbent!'

'How'd you figure that, then?'

'I'm already a dead man!' sneered Graves, looking up into his killer's eyes, his throat exposed. 'I been caught, you fool! Ain't no ways as I be getting out of this. Go ahead! Save the hangman the bother. But you'll be swinging straight ways after.'

'Aye, 'cause you will fucking tell them about me if I

don't stick you, you bastard!'

'No, that ain't it,' said Graves, the smile still playing on his lips. 'Didn't you say how a Lobster stopped you coming down here, with some nipper as had copped it?'

'What of it?' snarled Mudge.

'Only I daresay he might recall you, when I be found murdered, and his Grunter wants to know who he let pass.' Mudge released the pigtail, and stepped away in confusion, breathing heavily. He had screwed himself up to kill, and his pulse was still banging in his head as he pulled himself back from the ragged edge of violence. He looked at his knife and found the blade was trembling in the lamplight.

'You are a stupid bleeding arse, Broadbent,' said Graves, rubbing his throat. 'Now fuck off back to your little battle, before they string you up for desertion.'

Mudge nodded weakly, and then stumbled from the cell.

'Don't forget to hang that light back up, and see you bolt me back in, good and proper,' sneered the prisoner.

When the door was secured once more, Mudge looked back through the bars. 'Ain't you going to ask me to let you go free, or something,' he said weakly.

'Don't you go fretting on my account,' said Graves, tapping one temple with his forefinger. 'I got my escape all worked out.'

'How you going to do that then?'

'Why, I shall be set free presently, by my new friends. You doesn't really think this little ship has the beating of that Frog monster you be milling with?'

Chapter 11
Battle

Larcum Mudge came back up onto the main deck just as a shot from the *Centaure*'s stern chasers passed overhead with a sound like ripping canvas. He ducked down with his hands protecting his head as a severed line rattled down from above, coiling into a heap on the deck beside him. When he looked back up, he saw O'Malley waving him across, and he hurried over to take his place among the crew of the eighteen-pounder.

'Where the feck have you been?' demanded the Irishman. 'Fletcher's been raging fit to burst.'

'I … I only took Charlie down to the sawbones,' said Mudge, forcing himself to think clearly.

'Aye, but that was last fecking week!' exclaimed O'Malley.

'You be alright, Larcum mate?' asked Trevan. 'You looks all pale, like.'

'Watch it lads,' hissed Evans. 'Here comes trouble.'

'Good of you to bleeding join us, Admiral Mudge!' roared the red-faced petty officer. 'Has his lordship enjoyed a diverting turn around the lower deck?'

'Sorry Mr Fletcher, only Mr Corbett needed me to help hold the lad down …'

'Don't you play me for a bleeding fool,' warned Fletcher, leaning close. 'You telling me that a sawbones with three assistants couldn't tend to one nipper without you? You're in a world of shit, once this is over. Deserting your post in the face of the enemy, that's what you gone and done! Now get back to your station, and bleeding well stay there!'

'Aye aye, sir,' said Mudge, his face contrite.

Clay had watched the sailor's return, and the petty officer's burst of rage that accompanied it, from his place at the rail. There he stood, aloof from the hurly-burly of the crowded main deck beneath him, watching on with Olympian detachment. He pondered the incident he had witnessed, wondering what had caused it, and then pushed it to the back of his mind. There would be time for such matters later, he told himself. He had quite enough to deal with staying clear of the dangerous opponent sailing a few cable lengths off the bow.

The chase had resumed while Mudge had been away. The *Centaure* was moving appreciably slower now. She had just lost the topgallant sail on her main mast, thanks to an astonishingly fortunate direct hit from one of the bow chasers. It had smashed clean through the yard, breaking a ten-foot length off from one side. Clay could see a cluster of men working aloft, trying to secure the broken yard as it thrashed around, causing yet more damage to the rigging. The sails beneath that one and on the foremast were all still drawing, but wherever he looked he saw trailing cables and ragged holes punched through canvas. Her mizzen was reduced to just the thick lower section, with a jutting stump marking where the upper mast had once been. The wreck of that had been cut free some time ago, falling in an avalanche of debris into the sea alongside. Looking behind him he could see the mass of flotsam bobbing in the *Griffin*'s wake. Just beyond that was the *Stirling* and the *Daring*. Both ships were hull up, with every sail set as they thrashed along. The distance between them and the *Griffin* was shrinking all the time.

'Sir! Sir!' warned Armstrong beside him. 'Mr Preston is signalling.'

Clay spun around and saw the lieutenant standing at his post on the forecastle. This time he was waving his hat to the left. Clay focused beyond the frigate's bowsprit at the battered stern of the French ship. The rudder was only slightly over, pushing the *Centaure* into a long, gentle curve. As he watched, the Frenchman's stern chasers fired again, and a fresh hole appeared in the frigate's foretopsail.

'What are they about, I wonder,' mused Clay. 'Not seeking to bringing us under their guns, I think, with such a leisurely turn. We had best follow them around, Mr Armstrong.'

'I declare they may be making for Pointe-à-Pitre, sir,' said the ship's sailing master. 'Returning to port to effect repairs, perhaps? You can mark where the island lies, over there.'

Nothing could be seen of Guadeloupe itself this far out to sea, but a cluster of white clouds on the far horizon marked where the island lay. The sweeping turn ended with the Frenchman's bow pointing directly towards the clouds. The *Griffin*'s bow chasers fired once more, and Clay watched as one of the French sailors working aloft was knocked from his hold by the passage of the shot. The tiny figure tumbled through the air as he sped towards the stone-hard deck beneath, thrown this way and that by the rigging before vanishing behind a tattered sail.

'Heading home, with their tail between their legs, you think Jacob?' resumed Clay, wrenching his gaze away from the place where the poor seaman had vanished.

'Yes, sir. Can you blame them?'

'How far off is Guadeloupe?' he asked.

'Every part of thirty miles, sir,' replied Armstrong. 'It will be after sunset by the time they reach it.'

The two men turned to look at the chasing ships behind them, estimating the distance.

'Three hours?' suggested Clay. The American rubbed his chin thoughtfully.

'A little less, I should say,' he offered. 'Especially as we should be able to wound the enemy's rigging further.'

'Time enough for us to let the gun crews stand down for a while and have a bite to eat,' said Clay. 'No question of lighting the galley, while French shot continues to arrive on board. Some cheese and ship's biscuit will have to answer.' He turned and beckoned over one of the midshipmen standing by the wheel.

*****

By the time that the last of the gun crews had returned to their posts, wiping their mouths as they crossed the deck, the tropical sun was past its zenith and had begun its long descent into the west. It still shone fiercely on the crew, who had been active since just after dawn. They had spent long hours manoeuvring their frigate across the azure water, hitting their opponent again and again. There had been lengthy queues at the scuttlebutts as the men had drunk their fill, and Clay had been surprised how thirsty he was, draining the jug of watered wine that Harte had brought for him in moments. He felt weary with the tension of the day, but he steeled himself for one more effort.

The crews of the two bow chasers had just been

changed, and the rate of their steady bombardment of the *Centaure* had picked up. They fired again as he looked, sending another pair of little nine-pounder balls fluttering through the tattered rigging of their opponent. They were tiny spheres when compared with the frigate's main armament, or the huge shot spat out by the big carronades that lined the sides of the quarterdeck, but little by little, remorseless hour after remorseless hour, they had done as much damage as the half dozen broadsides that Blake's crews had managed to fire. High in the French ship's masts there was a splintering crack, and another yard hung down, the sail it supported blowing free.

But the wreck of the French ship's sails had come at some cost to the frigate. While the enemy's fire had been far less effective, over time it too was starting to tell. The frigate's big foretopsail had half a dozen ragged holes in it, and Harrison's men were all aloft repairing cut lines. The *Griffin*'s bow was scarred and battered, and the bowsprit bore a strip of naked wood where a glancing blow had torn away a large section. The surgeon had treated several casualties, but on the whole Clay was content. When the time came to close with the enemy, his ship would be in almost as good a fighting trim as it had been when he had awoken that morning. Then he gulped nervously as he realised that the same would be true of the *Centaure*. Although her masts and rigging were in a shocking state, that huge hull with its double row of massive cannon had been largely untouched by the frigate's fire. As the two bow chasers reloaded, a fountain of water lifted up from just beside the enemy's stern. Clay looked around in confusion.

'The flagship has opened fire, sir,' explained Armstrong. 'With her bow chasers.'

Clay was surprised to see how close the other two ships

had come. He had been focused so intently on the enemy ahead that he had almost forgotten the friendly ships behind. The *Stirling* was leading, a creaming bow wave beneath her beakhead. Her hull was almost as high out of the water as the *Centaure*'s, and she had every one of her double row of cannon run out, but there the comparison ended. The sixty-four was a good third shorter, and her beam was barely wider than the *Griffin*'s. Sir George would need all the help Clay could give him to win this battle.

'The admiral is signalling, sir!' announced Midshipman Russell. A line of flags fluttered out high on the *Stirling*'s mast.

'*Daring*'s number, sir,' reported Russell, coming over with his signalling slate. "Engage enemy from astern".'

'That makes sense, sir,' commented Taylor. 'Those little sloops have hulls like egg shells. She can rake them from athwart her counter, easily enough.'

'*Daring* has acknowledged, sir,' announced the midshipman. The little sloop pulled out from behind the flagship and came on in fine style. Clay could see points of scarlet in the sunshine as some of her marines climbed aloft.

'Our number now, sir!' announced the midshipman, writing quickly. '"Flag to *Griffin*, engage enemy from leeward side".'

'Acknowledge, if you please, Mr Russell,' said Clay. 'Mr Todd. Give Mr Preston my compliments. He is to order his bow chasers to shift their aim to the enemy hull, after which he can re-join me on the quarterdeck.'

'Aye aye, sir,' said the youngster.

'Steer a point off to leeward, if you please, Mr Armstrong.'

'Aye aye, sir.'

Clay next called down onto the main deck. 'Mr Blake?' Along both sides of the ship the gun crews quietly stopped what they were doing.

'Yes, sir,' said the lieutenant, stepping out from beneath the quarterdeck, and looking back up at him, a single face among a sea of listening men.

'We shall presently be going into action proper,' he said. 'Your mark is to be her hull from now. You should be able to land a few broadsides into her quarter as we approach, then we shall range up alongside. Fire swift and true, and all will be well.'

A growl rose up from the crews, and several rammers were brandished aloft.

'Aye aye, sir,' replied Blake, with a grin. 'The men will not be found wanting.'

*****

Guadeloupe had just risen over the horizon, her highest peaks a jagged silhouette, breaking the perfect deep blue line where the sea met the sky. The sun was perhaps halfway to the horizon, low enough to cast black shadows on the water from the four ships as they sailed across it. The *Centaure* led, her huge main and foremasts looking odd and unbalanced compared with the stump of her mizzen. She had given up altogether with trying to manoeuvre. Her tattered sails and creaking rigging were too fragile for anything bold. Safety lay ahead, and she made her way towards it as swiftly as she could. If her pursuers wanted to stop her, they would need to brave the eighty big guns that studded her sides.

Behind her the three British ships were in a ragged line abreast. All were pounding the *Centaure*'s stern with their chase guns, sending a glittering confetti of broken gilding and shards of glass tumbling into her wake, and inflicting further unseen damage on the packed gundecks beyond. All of them, even the portly *Stirling*, were steadily overhauling the Frenchman, their courses diverging like the spokes of a fan. The *Daring* was in the middle, with the flagship easing out to one side, and the *Griffin* pulling away on the other.

Clay was nearer to the *Centaure* than he had been all day. She loomed very close, her enormous hull seeming to fill his view. The elaborate decoration of her stern continued a short way along her side until it blended into the double stripe of her gundecks. He could hear orders being shouted on board, the flap and whip-crack of her torn sails. Faces lined the rail of her poop, staring down at him, while individual crewmen peered out from some of the open gun ports along her side.

'Open fire, as your guns bear, Mr Blake,' ordered Clay.

'Aye, aye, sir,' replied the officer. 'Ready Larboards?' The line of arms rose into the air once more and the crews settled down beside their cannon.

'Luff up a little, Mr Armstrong,' Clay said to the sailing master.

'Point to windward, helmsman,' said the American. The frigate turned a little up into the wind, losing some ground on her opponent, but swinging around until every gun could bear on the French ship's quarter.

'Fire!' yelled Blake, and with a thunderous roar, the frigate poured her broadside into her opponent. For the first time the range was such that even the carronades on the quarterdeck had taken part. A curtain of brown smoke blanketed the target, as the *Griffin* rolled away from her opponent.

'Back on course, Mr Armstrong, if you please,' said

Clay.

'Aye aye, sir.'

All around him the carronade crews flew through their task of reloading, while ship's boys raced away to collect fresh charges the moment they had handed over the ones they held. The frigate sailed on, leaving the bank of smoke she had created and emerging back into sunshine. Clay looked at his opponent. The broadside had been well aimed, striking home along the line of the *Centaure*'s lower deck. Many balls had struck at an oblique angle, leaving long scores and tears in the thick wood, but he could also see where other balls had punched their way through. The perfect symmetry of gun ports was spoilt, with one lid hanging down by a single hinge, and another that had disappeared entirely. All along her side, cannon were trained aft as far as possible, straining to reach the frigate. One of the figures standing at the rail drew his sword, and waved the glittering blade in the sunlight. Clay assumed this was a mark of defiance, but shortly after a thick line of soldiers appeared, almost all of whom were black, and muskets were levelled at the frigate.

'Carronades, load with cannister!' ordered Clay. 'Mr Macpherson, I'll trouble you to clear away those men.'

There was a shouted order, the rail of the French ship disappeared in smoke and the air filled with the crack of passing bullets. It was long range for a musket, but the French soldiers had the advantage of firing down onto their opponent. A sailor manning the nearest carronade spun away, clutching his arm, and a marine toppled backwards onto the deck.

'Marines, line the rail there,' ordered Macpherson, calm as ever as he stepped over the body of the fallen soldier. 'Rapid fire.'

Clay watched as the big copper cylinders were loaded

into the carronades, each one chinking slightly with the mass of balls they contained He was reminded of the improvised vase that Harte had made for his cabin. The gun captain nearest to him adjusted the elevation of his weapon slightly, raising his aim from the side of the *Centaure* to her rail. Another volley of musket fire crashed out from the enemy ship, and Clay felt his hat whisked from the top of his head with a loud smack. When he turned around to look for it, he noticed that one of the quartermasters at the wheel was being carried below.

'Ready to fire, Mr Blake?' he yelled, over the bang of the marines shooting beside him.

'Ready, sir,' came the reply.

Clay watched the two ship's courses with care, judging the right moment.

'Your hat, sir,' said a voice at his elbow.

'Not now, Mr Todd,' snapped Clay, still watching the *Centaure*. 'Luff up again, if you please, Mr Armstrong.'

Once more, the frigate turned a little away from her opponent, and again her broadside roared out. The tone of the carronades on the quarterdeck was subtly different, as they each spat a whining cloud of musket balls towards the enemy. Clay turned to grab his hat from the midshipman with a nod of thanks and clapped it back on his head. A flap of torn felt flopped down over one eye, and he snatched the hat off in irritation and tossed it into the scupper.

'Back on course, Mr Armstrong,' he ordered, continuing to watch their opponent.

'Aye aye, sir,' replied Taylor, giving the order to the wheel. 'Jacob is down, sir,' he added.

Clay spun round to see the big American being helped away by two sailors. With one hand he was clutching at his periwig which was sadly askew, while blood dripped freely from the other.

'Leave me be, darn it!' he protested. 'It is little more than a scratch!'

'Let the doctor be the judge of that,' ordered Clay. 'If he is content, then by all means return to your duties when you have been properly attended to.'

The sailing master continued to grumble as he left the quarterdeck, but Clay had no more time for him. Once more the *Griffin* emerged from her gun smoke, level with the stern quarter of the French ship. The line of soldiers was much thinner, and several sections of the rail had been torn loose. But puffs of smoke blossomed briefly into view before the wind took them away, to mark where the survivors kept up a brisk exchange of fire with Macpherson's marines. More damage was evident lower down on the hull, where the frigate's eighteen-pounders had struck home. At this range, even the heavy timbers of an eighty-gun ship of the line could not keep them out. In addition to the holes that had been torn in the side, one of the lower deck guns pointed upwards at an impossible angle, a scar of bright silver on the barrel showing where it had been struck.

After hours of patient chasing, things began to move swiftly. Swarms of French sailors appeared, racing up the two remaining masts to take in much of the sail. With a desperate fight inevitable, her captain wanted to preserve her surviving rigging for the battle ahead. On the far side of the *Centaure*, Clay saw the topsails of the undamaged *Stirling* as she arrived alongside at last. For a moment he could still see the blue sky of a late Caribbean afternoon behind her. Then there was a deafening roar as the two ships exchanged broadsides. A colossal wall of smoke billowed up, replacing sky with the choking fume of a furnace. Behind the slowing French ship the *Daring* was turning broadside on, ready to add her puny contribution to the fight. Clay looked around his ship with pride, noticing the calm efficiency all about him as his gun crews completed their reloading.

'It is time to get this done, Mr Taylor,' he said to his first lieutenant. 'Lay us alongside the enemy. Half-pistol shot, if you please. And may God grant us victory this day, or have mercy on our souls.'

*****

Down on the main gundeck, the crew of Shango were so busy reloading their eighteen-pounder that they were oblivious to the subtle change in the frigate's course. Outside their little world, the side of the French ship grew ever closer, rising above the *Griffin* like a sea cliff. Trevan had just thrust the latest powder charge into the barrel, pushing his arm deep into the muzzle, and Evans was poised to ram it home, when a huge fountain sprang up close alongside. Moments later water cascaded onto the gangway above their heads, and dripped down around them.

'Where did that fecking come from?' demanded O'Malley, cupping his hands protectively over the touch hole. Before anyone could reply there was a splintering crash from the bow, and they all felt the deck tremble beneath their feet. Trevan peered through the gun port, noticing for the first time that the frigate had now reached a point in overhauling their enemy where they were advancing into range of the main battery.

'What the hell's going on?' demanded Fletcher, from behind them. 'Quit gawking and get that gun loaded! It's a bleeding Frog ship, in case you ain't never seen the like. You fires at it, quick as quick until I tell you otherwise!'

As the frigate steadily drew level with the *Centaure*, more and more of the double bank of enemy guns came into action, and the world ran mad around them. The men worked in a choking fog, filled with flame and smoke, until their universe shrank to just a single gun on one strip of deck. Shango had an insatiable hunger for more and more powder and shot, and they, his servants, rushed to feed him. Powder from the magazine, thrust into a barrel that had grown uncomfortably hot to the touch. Heavy iron balls from the shot garlands, each one brought from farther away as the line of spheres shrank. Evans hauled the rammer clear once more, the sweat that poured from him cutting fresh pink rivulets across his blackened chest.

'Loaded!' he croaked, stepping back to let the crew run the gun up. A cannon ball from the upper gundeck of the *Centaure* howled overhead, causing him to flinch and duck. The gun crew heaved back on the tackles, driving the big cannon forwards, and O'Malley crouched over the touchhole, stabbing his barbed rod through into the serge charge bag, and then pouring fine powder into the hole. When it reached the top, he snapped back the lock, grabbed the lanyard and stepped out of the path of the recoil.

'Clear!' he yelled, checking both sides of the gun carriage, before he jerked on the line. A white spark in the gloom, a bright glow of flame, the gun roared back across the deck, and the weary crew stepped forward again.

The two ships were separated by fifty yards of water, a ravine of fire and smoke between their hulls. Forcing the *Centaure* to fight on both sides had stretched the French crew's ability to man all her guns. Those who faced the frigate were barely achieving half the rate of fire of the men of the *Griffin*, but each huge ball dealt a hammer blow that rocked the whole ship. Her scantlings were made from over a foot of cured oak, but the iron shot smashed through them as if they were little more than damp card. One struck the carriage of an eighteen-pounder, tossing the barrel onto the line of crewmen that stood braced against its gun tackle. Another took the bow clean off the frigate's longboat, sending splinters flying across the deck. As the crew of Shango worked on and on, the carnage mounted around them. A steady procession of sailors emerged from the smoke, bearing the wounded down to the surgeon, and the row of dead that lay along the centre line of the main deck began to lengthen.

Evans dipped the swab end of his rammer into the bucket, and thrust it down the barrel. Water hissed and jumped from the scalding metal. 'Clean,' he croaked, pulling it free, and another charge was pushed down the gun. More work ramming the charge home, then the ball, then the wad. The sweat in his eyes made him almost blind, and he felt leaden with weariness. In his mind, he was back in the prize ring once more, toeing the scratch, unable to remember which round he was fighting. Every muscle was aflame, and nothing but his will not to step back was keeping him in the fight.

'Clear,' yelled O'Malley, the eighteen-pounder roared out again, and another round began for the exhausted Londoner.

Above it all, on his quarterdeck, stood Clay, aloof from the battle going on around him. He was still hatless, and now had his left hand bandaged with his handkerchief. It was nothing more than a nasty cut caused by a fragment of musket ball as it ricocheted off the barrel of nearby carronade. He was trying to stand back from the fray, balancing what he knew was happening on his own ship with what he felt was happening on the *Centaure*.

'The carpenter reports a foot in the well and gaining, sir,' said Preston. 'We have been struck twice between wind and water. One hole he has plugged, but he has yet to attend the second.'

'My thanks to Mr Kennedy, and tell him to have the starboard pump manned,' replied Clay. A gust of wind tore a rent in the smoke that blanketed the ships, and for a moment Clay could see the upper masts of his French opponent. Her foremast stood defiant, rising up like a forest giant, but her main topmast was down, the wreckage festooned across her deck.

'Mr Blake has sent word that four of his guns are unserviceable, sir,' said the first lieutenant, arriving from the other side. He glanced up as something caught his attention. 'Have a care!' he yelled, and shouldered his captain to one side. A wooden block smashed onto the deck beside them, followed by a hissing tail of rope.

'My thanks to you, Mr Taylor,' said Clay, pulling his coat straight and checking aloft for any more falling debris. 'You were telling me of the state of our guns?'

'Indeed, four cannot fire, but the rest are all in action, although the crews begin to grow weary.'

'They shall have to endure that,' said Clay. 'We cannot pause before the enemy does.'

'Indeed, sir.'

'Thank you, Mr Taylor.' The older man touched his hat, and Clay was most of the way to responding to the salute before he realised that his own headgear was a crumpled wreck lying somewhere on the quarterdeck.

'Mr Hutchinson's compliments sir, and the end of the

bowsprit has been shot away,' said a breathless sailor, who had run the length of the ship.

'Does the forestay yet hold, Stevens?' asked Clay.

'Aye, for now, sir,' said the messenger.

'Thank the boatswain for me, and tell him …' but the man was gone, falling to the deck with a thump at his feet. Clay dropped down beside him, but the musket ball from the *Centaure* had killed him instantly. Lifeless eyes stared towards the mizzen top, and a dark mass stained his blond hair just above his ear.

'Get him moved away, Mr Preston,' ordered Clay, letting the body slide back down onto the planking. The carronade next to him roared out, sending tendrils of smoke snaking around him. He closed his eyes, partly to blank out the crumpled figure at his feet and partly to concentrate on the battle. Listen, he urged himself. What is really going on?

For a moment he could only hear the noise that was close to him. The bark of orders from the carronade's gun captain, urging his crew on. The bang of muskets from the marines. The splintering blow as the enemy sent another huge cannon ball deep into his ship. The pitiful cries of the wounded, desperate for relief, and yet fearful of what horrors awaited them in the cockpit below. Then he groped beyond that. The sharper bark of the *Daring*'s little cannon from someway close, still firing into what remained of that gilded stern. His own guns, a steady, rumbling roar, moving up and down the main deck of the frigate. And the enemy, barely firing at all. That should be a sign of victory, he pondered, and yet it felt wrong. Worryingly wrong. He opened his eyes wide, and the battle rushed back in, close on every side.

'Mr Taylor!' he yelled. 'Can you hear the flagship firing?'

The older man paused, his head on one side, like a terrier in a barn. 'Can't say as I can, sir.'

'Mr Preston!' he called. 'You have young ears.'

'No, sir,' he confirmed. 'The French are barely firing either, but I can still hear a deal of noise from the *Centaure*.'

'Yelling and the like?' queried his captain.

'Aye, that might be it, sir.'

'Arm the crew for boarding,' ordered Clay. 'Swiftly now. Mr Macpherson, get your men down from aloft, and assemble them here on the quarterdeck.'

'Aye aye, sir.'

'Mr Preston, start to edge us in alongside the enemy, if you please.'

'Aye aye, sir.'

'Mr Todd, run down and find Mr Blake. Tell him he is to secure the guns, and bring his crews up on to the gangways.'

While Clay watched the youngster dash away, Taylor came over to stand beside his captain. 'Those big eighty-gunners carry over seven hundred men, sir,' he said. 'Not to mention any additional soldiers she may have picked up in Guadeloupe. I doubt if we can muster beyond two hundred, all told.'

'Which is why I believe she has opted to try and board the *Stirling*, and win victory at the point of a cutlass, since cannons will not serve,' said Clay. 'We must come to the admiral's aid, and swiftly, if all is not to be lost.' He saw the concern in the older man's eyes, and took him by the arm. 'Trust me on this, George. You forget that she will have suffered cruelly from all our fire. And I doubt she will expect our little crew to dare an assault on such a leviathan. They do say surprise is half the battle.'

Chapter 12
Larcum Mudge

After noise and thunder came calm. The guns down on the main deck stood silent, surrounded by scarred planking strewn with debris. The odd wisp of smoke still curled out from their muzzles, and their bright red carriages were filthy with powder stains, but the crews who had worked them with such fury in the heat and smoke were gone. They had come up from the main deck, dirty and tired, and now thronged the side of the frigate, fingering their weapons. Some of the topmen had climbed a little way up the surviving shrouds, each with a grappling hook dangling from his fist.

In the relative quiet fresh sounds were heard. From deep in the hold came the reverberating beat of hammers as the carpenter and his mates worked in the cramped dark. Somewhere beneath Clay's feet, they would be struggling amid cascades of water. The clank of the pump, sending water gushing into the sea alongside. The sound of sharp pleading from one of the surgeon's patients as he was carried away to be treated.

Clay looked over his battered command and was content with what he saw. To an outsider the shot-torn rigging, shattered side and overturned guns spoke of bare survival, but he knew otherwise. The fighting power of any ship lay in her crew, and he studied his men with care. Although their ranks were thinner than he would have liked, and they looked tired, he could sense there was plenty of fight still left in them. They stood with an arrogant swagger, calmly checking over their weapons, or exchanging nods of recognition with fellow survivors.

Compared with the perfectly aligned ranks of Macpherson's marines on the quarterdeck, the sailors appeared to be little more than a jostling crowd, but he could see the underlying organisation. Preston and Hutchinson stood on the forecastle at the head of their men. The lieutenant was pulling his sword part-way out from its scabbard, to check it was free, while a hefty axe dangled from the boatswain's fist. Blake's gun crews were arranged in their divisions, each gathered around their petty officers, armed and ready. He could see the huge figure of Evans, who had pulled himself up into the main chains and was flexing a cutlass in an arc of silver to test the blade. Beside him was Mudge, looking more like a pirate than a Royal Navy sailor with two pistols stuffed into his waistband and the gold hoop in his ear catching the sun as the last of the smoke rolled clear.

With torn canvas flapping and a troubled bow wave gurgling and fretting around the trailing remains of her bowsprit, the *Griffin* eased across towards the *Centaure*. The French ship was in a dreadful state. The top of her foremast had been torn free, leaving only her long bowsprit untouched by the fight. The white strakes on her side were grey with powder stains, and punched full of holes. Several of her guns were missing from the open ports, others hung at drunken angles, but still she fought on. A giant tricolour flapped from the remains of her mizzen mast, the red fly torn in places but the colours bright in the sunshine.

Fifty yards separated the two ships, the strip of sapphire-blue water shrinking all the time. Only the *Daring* continued to fire. She lay across the big ship's stern, apparently undamaged by the battle, still raking her opponent from end to end. Beyond the hull of the French ship, Clay could see the clumped ruins of the *Stirling* rigging. Her main mast had vanished completely, as had much of her fore topmast.

Forty yards to go. A figure appeared at Clay's shoulder, and he felt cold metal pressed into his hand. 'I just been an' renewed the priming, sir,' rumbled a low voice. 'Got the other one for when you have need of it.' Clay hefted the pistol in front of him, checked it was uncocked and then pushed it into the left-hand pocket of his coat.

'Thank you, Sedgwick,' he said, looking around at where his coxswain stood with the rest of Clay's barge crew, massed at his back.

Thirty yards now. The bang and crack of small arms drifted towards them from somewhere out of sight, together with a low grumbling roar, as of a distant crowd.

'Where the devil are the French, sir?' asked Taylor. 'I can hear them, plainly enough.'

'I dare say most will be aboard the *Stirling*,' replied Clay. 'We shall come at them presently.'

'Corporal Edwards, have the men fix bayonets,' ordered Macpherson, somewhere to his left. Edwards yelled the order with unnecessary violence, and the rasp of steel was followed by the double click as they were locked into place.

Twenty yards, and faces appeared on board the enemy, looking down over the rail at them. Alarmed faces, their eyes wide and mouths round as they cried warnings. Scared faces, vanishing as quickly as they appeared. Determined faces, levelling muskets towards the approaching enemy. Several puffs of smoke blossomed, although where the hasty shots went, Clay couldn't tell. The gun ports of the *Centaure*'s upper battery were just below him, and he found his gaze held by a scared-looking ship's boy as he peered back at the approaching frigate.

Ten yards, and a solitary gun bellowed out from low on the *Centaure*'s hull, followed immediately by the crash of the shot striking home.

'Another wee dint for Mr Kennedy to attend to,' muttered Macpherson to Taylor. The rail of the enemy ship was above them and the air filled with snaking lines as grappling hooks were hurled across and then drawn tight. Someone came clattering up the ladderway behind Clay, breathing heavily.

'I trust you're not proposing to board that monster without me, sir,' said Armstrong. Clay looked around and grinned at the sailing master. He wore no coat, and his left arm was bound across his chest in a sling, but he had his sword by his side.

'Make free to join us if you are able to scramble across, Jacob,' said Clay, indicating the difference in height between the two ships. 'Or you can stay here with Mr Taylor?'

'If young Preston can do so with no arm, I daresay I shall manage, sir,' growled the American. 'Perhaps Tom will favour me with a brace of his stouter red coats to hurl me.'

With a squealing judder the hulls came together. Clay grabbed his sword and swept it out. It was a magnificent weapon, given to him after the Battle of the Nile. The pommel was the shape of a snarling lion's head, and the blue steel blade was razor sharp. Then he pulled himself into the mizzen chains, where he was visible to all his men. From that height he could see across to the *Stirling*. She too was close against the other side, locked to the *Centaure* by the tangled mass of her fallen main mast that lay across the two ships. On the British ship's upper deck, a fierce fight raged. Puffs of gun smoke rose above the struggling melee, and steel flashed in the sunshine.

'Away Griffins!' he yelled. 'Make her ours, lads!' Then he flung himself across the gap between the ships and scrambled on board. With a roar, his men followed at his heels, in a wave of fury.

*****

Evans was one of the first to follow his captain across, but he had underestimated how tired he was. His leap only just reached the lip of the *Centaure*'s main chains, and he barked his shin painfully against one of the deadeyes. For an endless moment, he thought he would fall down into the trench between the hulls. Two French sailors were on the deck below him, one looking aghast, the other scrabbling to pull out his pistol. Evans felt his flailing left arm latch onto one of the shrouds, and he heaved his bodyweight forwards. Then he was on them. He led with his cutlass, holding it stiffly ahead, like a lance, aimed at the man with the pistol. He felt his arm jar as the tip struck deep, knocking the Frenchman backwards. Evans swept the blade out and rounded on the other sailor, but he was already down, with Mudge standing over the body, a smoking pistol in his hand. The rush of men following them swept past, quickly overwhelming the few opponents who remained on the abandoned gangway.

'Give me a fecking hand there!' demanded O'Malley's voice from behind them. Evans peered over the rail, and saw the Irishman clinging to the outside of the ship. Evans and Mudge leant over, each grabbing a fistful of their shipmate's trousers, and dragged him unceremoniously on board. 'Cheers lads,' he gasped, as Trevan helped him to his feet. 'I was that bushed, I missed my fecking leap.'

The jostling crowd of sailors dithered, wondering what to do next. They had been keyed up to a high pitch of ferocity as their frigate ground alongside the enemy, and they now sought for an outlet. Boarding an enemy ship normally meant a fierce battle, desperate resistance, and finally the surrender of the overwhelmed enemy. But this attack had been all too easy. The few dozen opponents manning the side had been swept away in an instant, leaving the victors milling in confusion.

Evans stooped to peer down onto the upper gundeck, searching for the enemy, but could only see lines of abandoned guns, with fallen bodies lying among the debris.

'Where has all the bleeding Frogs gone!' he exclaimed.

'Some of the feckers are up in the bow,' said O'Malley, pointing to where Preston's men were driving the enemy back across the forecastle. The boatswain was leading, swinging his axe around him, endangering friends almost as readily as he was dispatching foes.

'Nar!' exclaimed Trevan. 'That mill be all but over. The Frenchie hasn't been born as can stand up to old Hutchinson in a passion.'

'This way, Griffins,' called the voice of Blake, pushing his way through the crowd. 'Follow me!'

The men surged along the gangway after him and fanned out onto the broad quarterdeck of the *Centaure*. Here the afterguard was battling a much larger crowd of French sailors gathered around the wheel. A young officer with a thin black moustache was locked in a fight with Clay, their swords clashing and flickering, while Armstrong laid about him in a strange, one-armed fashion. Farther back was Macpherson at the head of his marines, trying to force their way up the narrow ladderway to the elevated poop deck at the stern of the ship. A line of his men busily fired up at the mass of French marines who defended the top of the steps. Over the poop floated the enormous tricolour.

'Here we bleeding go!' exclaimed Evans, racing forward to loom over the nearest French sailor, a thin man with bright red hair who was holding his own against Midshipman Russell. Suddenly faced with two opponents, he tried to jump clear, but the Londoner's reach was too long for him. He lunged across the deck, landing a savage cutlass blow, and the man went down with a cry of pain. More and more British sailors were pouring across the deck and falling on the group by the wheel. For an instant the French line held, but then the sheer weight of opponents overwhelmed them. Several were killed or wounded, and the rest fell back.

Off to Evans's right, the French officer fighting Clay sprang back from his opponent and placed his sword down on the planking.

'*Je me rends*,' he cried out, his voice choked, holding both hands out in token of surrender. Tears streamed down the youngster's cheeks. The silence that followed was ended by a prolonged clatter as the French sailors around him dropped their weapons. Sedgwick darted past his captain to recover the sword and brought it back to him.

'Do you surrender the ship, sir?' demanded Clay.

'*Non, monsieur*,' said the young man, wiping his eyes on his sleeve. 'I cannot. I only *Enseigne*.'

'I understand,' said Clay quietly. He held out a hand and touched the Frenchman's sleeve, but the officer pulled away. 'Where is your captain?' he continued.

'He dies,' said the officer, sadly. 'When first your big ship shoot at us. First Lieutenant Senard captain, now.' The officer jerked a thumb towards the ongoing melee on the *Stirling*.

'Mr Armstrong, take command, if you please. Kindly secure these prisoners,' ordered Clay. 'And send Macpherson and his marines after us once he has taken the poop. The rest of you, come with me.'

'Aye aye, sir,' said the American.

The tears of the young officer seemed to have calmed the men of the *Griffin*, as they followed their tall captain across to the far side of the deck. Here the damage to the French ship was colossal. The *Stirling* had hammered her opponent from very close range, and the men picked their way across planking strewn with splinters and fragments of oak, discarded equipment, fallen blocks and lines from above and the bodies of the slain. The main mast of the *Stirling* lay at an angle across the whole, festooned with shattered spars, torn sail and a spider's web of cables. Evans hesitated as he found his way blocked by the enormous column, groaning and creaking as the two hulls rocked beneath it.

'Move yer fecking arse, Sam,' said O'Malley, as the men backed up behind the big Londoner.

'Look lively there, Evans,' ordered his petty officer.

'It don't seem quite safe, Mr Fletcher,' said the sailor. He rested one hand on the mast, and felt a trembling as it shifted under his hand.

'If it was safe you was after, you've chosen the wrong bleeding calling. Now shift yourself!'

'It be fine, Sam, lad,' said Trevan, pushing past him. 'Just you follow close astern.' The sailor ducked down beneath the massive pillar, and crawled away out of sight. After a hesitation, Evans followed him. For a long moment the mast was above him, and he could sense its colossal, crushing weight. Then he was through.

'Bleeding hell, that were passing strange,' he said, wiping the sweat from his brow. 'A deck full of murderous Frogs don't see to trouble me, but that piece of lumber gave me a proper turn.'

One by one, the men filtered through the wreckage of the fallen mast to join their captain on the far side of the French ship. Here they found themselves staring across at a vicious fight that ebbed and flowed over the deck of the *Stirling*. The British flagship lay close alongside. Its hull was almost the same height as the *Centaure*, with only the curved tumblehome of the two vessels creating a gap the width of a modest ditch. Like the occupants of a neighbouring field, they looked over the rail at the packed crowd of struggling bodies. The first to arrive began to pull themselves up onto the thwarts, eager to press on, but Clay held them back.

'Steady there, lads!' he ordered. 'Belay that! Wait until we have the numbers to answer.' Just in front of them, a red-coated marine was stabbing at a French sailor with his bayonet, only for each thrust to be knocked aside by the man's cutlass. Beside him another sailor turned to hack at the British soldier, but before he could land his blow a pistol cracked out from further back in the melee, and he fell to the deck. Then the nearest French sailors were starting to look around at the new arrivals. One shouted a warning, and another tried to disentangled himself from an opponent so he could turn and fire his pistol in their direction.

More and more Griffins came streaming through, but their captain continued to hold them back. The fight ahead seemed finely poised. Black French soldiers struggled with marines, cutlasses flashed in the low shafts of light from the dropping sun that penetrated through the smoke and battered rigging. Just beside Clay two sailors broke out from the throng, one wrestling around the other, each with a hand locked about the wrist of their opponent's sword arm. Up on the flagship's lofty poop, Montague could be seen, surrounded by his staff, barking instructions to the men beneath him. The waiting sailors shifted uncomfortably from foot to foot.

'Steady, lads,' repeated Clay, as more and more men joined them. 'Ah, Mr Preston,' he called. 'You and Mr Hutchinson, take your men forward. But wait for my signal.'

The sailors were spreading out along the rail, two and three deep, and still Clay held them back. More faces were turning towards them from on board the *Stirling*. A black corporal barked an instruction and a ragged line of soldiers began to form facing towards them. Close to the ship's wheel, Clay could see Captain Thompson, sword aloft, leading a counterattack of sailors, all armed with boarding pikes. Pistols banged towards them, and a sailor near to Evans fell back.

'Hold fast, Griffins,' urged Clay, his voice firm.

Then something changed, behind them. More light seemed to be falling on the deck, and many more of those on board the flagship were looking towards them. No, not at them, Evans decided, but above them. There was despair on some of the faces, and jubilation on others.

'What the feck are we waiting for?' protested O'Malley.

'Look! Over there,' said Evans, pointing.

The *Centaure*'s enormous tricolour gave a last, languid flap as it came tumbling down the broken mizzen, and settled in huge folds across the poop deck. One third of it was as deep a blue as the sea around them, while the white and red parts were a match for the coats and cross belts of the line of marines who tailed on the halliard, hauling the flag down. The collective groan that arose from the French boarders on the *Stirling* was quickly drowned by the renewed cheers of the defenders. Macpherson stood on the high poop deck and swept his sword up in front of his face in a salute towards Clay, who turned back to his men.

'Now is your time, Griffins! Boarders away!' he yelled, and the men of the frigate swept across onto the flagship, driving the surviving crew of the *Centaure* before them.

*****

The following day, the great cabin of the *Griffin* had been reassembled around Clay, with all his familiar furniture back in the usual places. His desk was positioned just where he liked it, with the light from the cabin windows falling across the surface. From his chair he had only to glance up to see the full-length portrait of Lydia hanging once more on the bulkhead opposite.

Much had also changed, however. The light flooding in was less than before, with three of the seven windows that ran across the stern of the frigate boarded up; and the paintwork around the cabin's two eighteen-pounders was smudged grey from gun smoke. Crude squares of lead sheeting had been nailed to the far cabin wall to cover the jagged holes punched through the ship's side by French cannon. One of the shots had scored a path across the deck, ending close to a dark stain on the planking that must mark where one of his crew had died.

Clay picked up the report of casualties supplied to him by the surgeon and ran a finger down the list, recalling to mind the face behind each name picked out in Corbett's crabbed hand. He paused at one, David O'Brien, gun captain. He would have been standing in just that spot, manning the aftmost eighteen-pounder when they drew alongside the enemy.

He rose from behind his desk, remembering the cheerful Irish sailor, and stared out on the frigate's wake. It was a gentle stream, as the line of ships moved towards Antigua at the speed of the most battered. His vision was filled by the spreading bow of the *Centaure* once more, the one part that had survived relatively unscathed. The elegant sweep of the headrails curved towards him, meeting just behind the tall, rearing figurehead, all glaring eyes and curling beard. High up in the foremast, the ship's big tricolour was back, this time streaming beneath a Royal Navy ensign. A long, shuddering pulse of silver splashed out from the side, where her pumps struggled to hold back the water flooding on board. From somewhere behind him he could hear the mournful clank of his own ship's chain pump. Not long to go, he reminded himself. They should make English Harbour shortly after dawn tomorrow, even at this pace. Thoughts of Antigua reminded him of other matters he needed to resolve on board. He turned from the stern windows.

'Harte!' he called.

'Yes, sir,' said his steward, coming through from the coach.

'My compliments to Mr Taylor, and would he send Larcum Mudge to me.'

'Mudge, sir?' queried Harte. 'What, that lanky bloke, in the larboard watch?'

Larcum Mudge

'I can't believe we can possibly have more than one man of that name on the ship,' said his captain.

'Eh, no, that's for certain, sir,' said the steward. 'Will you be wanting his divisional officer an' all?'

'No need to trouble Mr Todd. Just send for him, if you please.'

'Aye aye, sir.'

When Harte left the cabin, Clay opened the bottom drawer of his desk and took out a flat case of polished mahogany. He opened the lid and removed one of the two pistols it contained from its velvet-lined recess. He checked the priming, slid the weapon into the pocket of his coat, and returned the box to the drawer. Then he tidied away his report to Rear Admiral Montague. It was almost complete, save for a couple of details. The next few days will serve to resolve those, he told himself. He paused to glance over Corbett's casualty list for a moment, before replacing it with another, much longer list.

The rap at the cabin door was faint and hesitant when it came. 'Come in!' he ordered.

The softness of the knock was matched by the guarded expression on Mudge's face. He came in and stood in front of the desk, looking past his captain's shoulder towards the bow of the *Centaure*.

'She is a fine prize, is she not?' said Clay, following his gaze. 'The Admiralty will buy her for certain, and even split three ways, our share will be healthy.'

'Aye, sir,' agreed the sailor.

'You played your part in her capture, I understand,' continued Clay. 'Mr Blake tells me that you and Samuel Evans were among the first to board.'

'That we were. Thank'ee kindly, sir,' agreed Mudge,

relaxing a little.

'Of course, there was the matter of you disappearing to go below, without your petty officer's permission,' said Clay. 'Mr Fletcher was quite vexed, but I think I can afford to be generous in that regard, given your later contribution to the victory.'

'I take that most kindly, sir.'

'Yes, you have done well,' continued his captain. 'Rated able so soon after joining the ship, all the reports I hear from your officers are satisfactory, and Mr Russell speaks very highly of the manner in which you conducted yourself during the attack on the *Peregrine*.'

'Thank you, sir,' said the sailor, the ghost of a grin appearing on his face. 'I were only doin' me duty, like.'

'Quite so,' agreed the captain. 'Of course, in his enthusiasm to praise your actions, he never thought to ponder how exactly it was that you were able to navigate your way in the dark, from out of a burning ship that you were wholly unfamiliar with.'

The grin vanished as quickly as it had appeared. The sharp features, side-lit by the bright sunlight from outside remained, the dark eyes wary.

'But perhaps you knew the layout perfectly well,' continued Clay, his eyes watching the sailor closely.

'Them little sloops of war be built much the same, sir,' offered Mudge.

'Really?' queried Clay. 'My first command was another sloop, you know, named *Rush*. Sedgwick, O'Malley and Evans all served with me on her, and yet that experience doesn't seem to have been of any assistance to them. Only you knew the way to safety. What do you suppose accounts for that, pray?'

Larcum Mudge

Trapped at last, thought Mudge to himself. The sound of the ship's bell from elsewhere in the *Griffin* had a funereal air, and the oak walls of the cabin seemed closer about him than earlier. He looked outside, where the sunlight glittered on a sea of impossible blue, and realised how fervently he wanted to live. He found himself taken back to a similar, earlier occasion. The sea had been lovely that evening too, up on the *Griffin*'s forecastle, as the chime of the bell had signalled the changing of the watch. He remembered Sedgwick, leaning close amid the confusion, urging him to have a better explanation ready when next asked about that night of fire and terror. But somehow, under the remorseless gaze of those cold, stone-grey eyes, nothing came to him. All he could manage was a shrug.

'Come, let us be frank with one another,' urged Clay. 'It is plain that you knew the *Peregrine* because you have recently served on her. You are one of those damned mutineers! It explains much, not least why you spent so long below deck during our chase of the *Centaure*. Conspiring on the orlop with your fellow rebel, perhaps?'

'Has that bastard Tombstone been a squealing?' he demanded. 'I knew I should have stuck him when I had the chance.'

'Ah, now we see your true character, Mudge,' said Clay, slipping a hand into his coat pocket. 'The red-handed mutineer! No word of remorse for the slaughter you took part in? Your only regret that you failed to claim another victim when you had the chance!'

'It weren't like that, sir!' pleaded the sailor. 'Least ways, not my part in it, whatever Tombstone's been saying.'

'Actually, he has not breathed a word, but thank you for confirming that you are acquainted with him.' Clay picked up the list from his desk. 'This is a copy of the *Peregrine*'s muster book, issued to all ships by the Admiralty. Tombstone, Tombstone … Ah, I have him. John Graves, forecastle man. One of the uprising's leaders, I believe.'

The grey eyes were back on him again, penetrating and hostile.

'So what was your part in these revolting events, I wonder?' continued Clay. 'Did you kill the fourteen-year old midshipman?

'No, sir!' exclaimed the sailor.

'Really? Then perhaps it was you who struck down Lieutenant MacDonald, as he lay unconscious with the Yellow Jack?'

'No! I never touched him!'

'How curious,' sneered Clay. 'A mutineer as mild as any Quaker!' He spun the paper around on his desk and prodded it towards the sailor. 'There is the watch list. Tell me who it was you killed?'

Mudge stared at the paper, his head bowed, sweat beading on his forehead. 'I … I ain't got me letters, sir,' he said.

'Give me a name,' growled Clay, his face cold with suppressed fury.

'Daniels,' muttered Mudge. 'I killed that bastard Daniels, sir.' Then he looked up, and held Clay's eye. 'And I ain't sorry for it, neither. He were the only one that I done for that night, an' that be the honest truth. I'll go to my grave sorry I did nothing to check the slaughter that followed, but I ain't never going to say sorry for that man's passing.'

Clay watched the play of emotions on the sailor's face. Fear, for the most part, blended with defiance. But also truth, if he was any judge of a seaman's character. 'Let me give you some advice, Mudge, or whatever your name truly is,' he said. 'This mutiny has run its course. Those responsible will be found and punished, however they twist or turn. Cooperate with me now, and it will stand in your favour when you come to trial.'

He waited in silence for an answer, letting other shipboard sounds fill the void. The creak of the rudder, louder than normal through the broken windows. Midshipmen Todd and Russell sharing a joke, somewhere on the quarterdeck above them, and the sound or Blake reprimanding them for doing so on duty. The continuing clank of the ship's pumps. The distant thump of hammers as the work of repairing the frigate went on.

'It be Broadbent, sir,' said Mudge at last. 'Jack Broadbent.'

'Broadbent … yes I have you set down here,' said Clay. He replaced the list in front of him, and returned his attention to the mutineer. 'What occasioned you to select such an unusual alias? Most sailors in my experience are content with Brown or Smith.'

'I borrowed it from the parson back in my village in Suffolk, like, sir,' said Broadbent. 'He were a proper whining, stuck-up arse, beggin' your pardon. In truth, I chose his name for the sport if he ever heard tell as I were using it.'

'I can well picture the Reverend Mudge's annoyance,' said Clay. 'How long were you in Guadeloupe, after the mutiny?'

'Maybe two-month, sir,' said Broadbent. 'The Frogs looked after us well enough, but it didn't feel right, staying on in an enemy port, like. So I got myself smuggled out sharpish, on a schooner bound for St Croix. From there I worked a passage home on a Danish brig. No word of the mutiny had broke then, so 'twas easy enough.'

'Did you see much activity while you were in Pointe-à-Pitre?' asked Clay. 'Shipping movements, for example?'

'Oh aye, that I did, sir. Not at first, mind, it being the hurricane season an' all. But once that had passed, them little schooners was a comin' and going like bees from a hive.'

'That is interesting. If I asked you to sit down with my clerk, and furnish him with particulars, would you give them to him? It could help at your trial.'

'Aye, I reckon I could do that, sir,' confirmed the sailor.

'Thank you,' said Clay. 'Let us come to the part that I find truly peculiar. What was it that persuaded you to re-join the navy? Were you not fearful of being caught?'

'Tombstone reckoned how word of the mutiny would stay quiet, but I were certain it would come out, sir,' explained Broadbent. 'The Caribee ain't like the South Seas. It only needs one drunken fool to talk when he shouldn't, and we had no shortage of them on the old *Peregrine*. I had thought to join a merchant ship, but that were too obvious a place to hide. Then I chanced to be in Tavistock one market day, and caught sight of some jacks by a poster on the side of an alehouse. Why not join the navy once more, I was thinking? Surely that'll be the last place as folk would come a looking for me. So I went an' got myself signed up, there and then by Mr Macpherson. Besides …' The sailor broke off.

'Besides …' prompted Clay.

'I don't want to rattle on, over much, but it … it felt right, sir,' he said. 'Serving the king, like, ag'in them Frogs. Under that bastard Daniels, we was just staying hid, to be clear of the next flogging. Them four outside that tavern seemed right proud of their barky, and maybe I just wanted a taste of how that felt, for once.'

Clay felt shame. Shame as no captain should of his navy, and shame that he had thought to place a loaded pistol in his pocket. The competing emotions within him made his voice unusually harsh and grating as he called towards the cabin door. 'Harte!' he yelled.

'Yes, sir,' said the steward, coming in after a pause that was just sufficient to suggest that he had not been listening at the door the whole time.

'Kindly ask the master at arms to step this way,' ordered Clay.

'Aye aye, sir.'

'Am I to be arrested, sir?' asked the sailor.

'I am afraid so, Broadbent,' said his captain, 'and you will be tried for mutiny.'

He bowed his head at this. 'Will I swing for it, sir?' he asked.

'You must reconcile yourself to that probability,' said Clay. 'The rising was of such uncommon violence that I would not be expecting mercy if I stood in your place. And you did kill your captain, which is like to go ill with judges drawn from his fellows.'

Broadbent raised his pale face towards Clay. He seemed about to say something more, but no words came.

'Perhaps I can offer you a little comfort,' continued his captain. 'It may not suffice, but I am minded to speak in your favour at that trial. Whatever you have done in the past, your service to this ship deserves to be considered.'

Chapter 13
Antigua

The sun had cleared the eastern horizon, and another day was well underway in Antigua when the squadron limped into English Harbour. To the triumphant clatter of the bell in the dockyard chapel, the French crew of the *Centaure* were taken ashore and handed over to a detachment of the West Indian Regiment who lined the quayside to receive them. Her surviving upper masts were all then struck down on deck, and the great ship was beached to prevent her sinking. She would have to wait, while the dockyard concentrated on repairing the British ships.

Of these, the *Daring* had survived almost unscathed. The *Centaure*'s stern chasers had been abandoned during the heat of battle, as their crews had been urgently redeployed to man the guns facing the larger opponents. This had left the little sloop to pour her stream of broadsides into the enemy's stern unopposed. In her own noise and fume, she had been largely oblivious to the ferocious hand-to-hand fighting taking place close to her. It was only when the French ship's tricolour had come down and the clouds of smoke had parted that Camelford had become aware of how fierce the fight had been aboard his admiral's flagship.

The *Stirling* was in the worst state. As the *Centaure*'s largest and most dangerous opponent, the French had concentrated their attention on trying to defeat her. Her starboard side was beaten full of shot holes. Port lids had been ripped away, and her paintwork was scorched by the flame of her enemy's guns. A mournful precession of boats ferried her wounded across to the hospital ashore, before she was handed over to the dockyard for urgent repair.

'All in all, we may count ourselves fortunate to have come through such a battle in the state we have,' said Clay to his first lieutenant, as another boat full of the *Stirling*'s wounded passed under the stern windows of the frigate, and headed for the shore.

'Indeed, it only needed three trips with the launch for Mr Corbett to take our worst cases across,' confirmed Taylor from the far side of Clay's desk. 'Twenty-four dead, and forty wounded, of which the surgeon believes all bar a dozen will make a full recovery. Many of the lightly hurt have asked to stay on board.'

'Very wise,' observed Clay. 'I fear the dockyard hospital won't have had this much to do since Hood bested De Grasse. I shall go across later to visit our people, but I do fear what sights will greet me. The *Centaure* had close to three hundred wounded alone.' He let out an involuntary shudder and the scar on his shoulder ached in sympathy. It was just over five years since another naval surgeon had dug a musket ball out, while Clay wrestled against the straps that held him down, with only a hasty mouthful of rum to dull the pain.

'How is the ship?' he asked, driving back the memory of that dark time.

'The dockyard can only spare us a dozen men for now, while they yet battle to keep the poor *Stirling* afloat,' said Taylor. 'We will be warped across there sometime tomorrow.'

'Will it answer?' asked Clay.

'They have all the materials that we need, sir. We shall

just have to make shift with what we have. Mr Kennedy and the boatswain know what they are about, and we have our crew for the less skilled work.'

'And what of the mutineers?' asked Clay.

'Both handed over an hour back, sir,' said the first lieutenant. 'I still cannot believe Mudge to have been responsible for such wickedness. All his officers spoke so highly of him.'

'According to Captain Sutton, Daniels was quite the tartar,' said Clay. 'It was probably only a matter of time before his men rose against him. I have said that I will speak up for him, when he comes to trial.'

'Is that wise, sir?' queried Taylor. 'To defend a known mutineer?'

'No, George, not if I value my progress in the service,' said Clay. 'But I have said that I would do so, now. I cannot but think that if he had served with us instead of on the *Peregrine*, he would have made an exemplary shipmate.'

The two men were quiet for a moment, and then Clay picked up an open letter that lay on his desk. 'Would you care for some more pleasant tidings, George?' he asked.

'I would like that above all things, sir.'

'We have been invited to a reception this evening, hosted by the admiral in his residence ashore,' announced Clay. 'To celebrate our victory over the *Centaure*. I had best get Harte to give my shoes an extra polish.'

'Really?' queried Taylor, running a hand through his hair. 'I am not sure those are welcome tidings, sir. As if we did not have sufficient to attend to with setting the ship to rights.'

'Cheer up, George,' said his captain. 'I am sure it will be a most pleasant distraction. Besides, there is someone I particularly wish to speak with who will be present.'

Larcum Mudge

*****

It was evening when the officers of the *Griffin* climbed down the battered side of their ship and into the waiting launch. The calm water of English Harbour was turning to the palest of blue in the fading light, and the first lamps were being lit in houses high on the slopes around them. The commissioning pennant of the frigate fluttered and cracked in the sea breeze high above their heads, but down on the surface of the sheltered inlet lay a blanket of warm, still air. All around them were scrub-covered hills, like the walls of a crater. To add to their discomfort, the officers were wearing their heavy dress-coats, and were packed uncomfortably close in the boat.

'Apologies for the tightness of the accommodation, gentlemen,' said Clay, resisting the urge to run a finger around his neckcloth. 'Blame the French, if you will, for knocking the bow off our poor longboat. Fortunately, the journey is but a short one. Carry on, Sedgwick.'

'Aye, aye, sir,' said the coxswain, and then, rather more loudly, 'Shove off in the bow, there! Larboard side, take a stroke. Handsomely now!'

The launch gathered way, while the sweating officers looked on enviously at the open shirts and bare arms of the rowers. They headed across English Harbour towards a little stone jetty a few hundred yards away, where the cutter from the *Daring* was unloading its guests. The clatter of a dropped oar was followed by a shouted oath from Camelford directed towards the unfortunate sailor.

'Goodness, the prize is attracting quite a crowd, sir,' commented Taylor. 'Why, half the island must have come to gawk. The Gordon riots ain't in it!' Clay looked towards the beach where the *Centaure* lay like a huge stranded whale. She was surrounded by a ring of red-coated soldiers from the garrison, who were struggling to hold back a mass of sightseers. The lane that ran along the top of the shore was thronged with carriages and traps.

'It's rather a sad position, for such a such a proud ship, sir,' commented Preston. 'Being reduced to a spectacle for the diversion of the mob.'

'Easy there!' barked Sedgwick. 'Oars in!'

The launch swept smartly up against the jetty, and the officers began to disembark. There was a party of marines guarding it, and they ushered them towards a path that cut its way up the hillside. Above them was a large square house ablaze with light on the summit of the headland. As the officers followed their guide, they were relieved to find the temperature dropping steadily as they climbed into fresher air, blowing in from the sea.

The path was lit by lanterns hanging from metal rods driven into the bank, and as it wound its way upwards the scrub on the lower slopes steadily gave way to trees, bushes and flowers until, almost without noticing the transition, they arrived at the top in the midst a tropical garden. An expanse of manicured lawn ran away from them towards the square house. In the evening light they could see it had pale yellow walls and a broad, pitched roof. This extended out to cover a veranda that surrounded the building, lined with white classical columns. The doors facing towards the garden were thrown open, and from within came the buzz of animated conversation.

'What a fine dwelling Sir George has the benefit of,' exclaimed Faulkner. 'What, pray, is the name of this place, Corporal?'

Larcum Mudge

'Clarence House, sir,' barked the soldier who had led them up the hill.

'Clarence House,' repeated Faulkner, eyeing the building with renewed interest. 'Would there be some association with His Royal Highness?'

'What, with Sailor Bill?' queried Blake.

'He is a prince, not a petty officer, John,' corrected the purser with a sniff. 'Sailor Bill, indeed!'

'Aye, the house were built for him, sir,' continued the marine. 'Back afore the war, like, when he were captain of the *Pègasus* and stationed in these parts. Now the admiral has use of it.'

'Not a bad wee life, is it?' said Macpherson, 'being an admiral on a foreign station.'

'Nor being a captain with a king for a father,' added Clay.

'If you will excuse me, sir, I needs to return to my duties,' said the marine. 'One of them flunkies will attend to you,' he added, pointing to a pair of black footmen who stood nearby, beneath a palm tree. With a bow and an extended arm, the officers were shown across the darkening garden into the well-lit interior of the house.

The room they entered was big, stretching across the whole rear of the house. On the walls hung portraits of various naval officers, some with hands resting across globes, others lounging against conveniently placed anchors. The light of numerous candles was caught in the richly polished wooden floor underfoot. Although the Griffins were on time, as the chimes from a tall clock that stood against one wall confirmed, they found that many of the guests were already there. Scarlet-coated officers from the garrison or the marines were mixed with the blue of the navy. Dotted among them were a few dark-coated civilians, each paired with a white-gloved wife.

'Ah welcome, Captain Clay,' beamed Montague, resplendent in his rear admiral's uniform.

'Thank you for inviting us, Sir George,' said Clay. 'May I reacquaint you with my officers? Most you will remember from our time together in the Indian Ocean.' He was quite certain that a man as aloof as the admiral would have remembered none of them, so he introduced them each by name.

'Splendid, gentlemen,' said Montague. 'You have my sincerest gratitude for coming to the assistance of the poor old *Stirling*, in such a timely fashion. Another five minutes, and she might have needed a new commander.' He drew Captain William Thompson forward, his bald pate glowing red in the warmth of the room, and his left arm pinned across him in a sling.

'My dear sir, I had no notion you had been hurt?' exclaimed Clay.

'Nothing more than a scratch, I assure you,' he replied. 'The last Frenchman I fought had some skill with the small sword.' He indicated the sailing master's matching sling. 'I see that Mr Armstrong may have come across the same cove.'

'A glass of wine, sir,' murmured a footman, holding a laden tray towards the new arrivals. Other servants converged on the group, some bearing drink, others plates of food.

'May I leave you in Thompson's company, Captain,' said Montague. 'My duty as host summons me away.' He indicated a new arrival, a large florid man in a heavily decorated red coat.

'Of course, Sir George.'

'Were you injured badly, Captain?' asked Thompson, noticing the dressing around the hand that held the wine glass.

'A small cut, no more than that,' said Clay. 'Alas, the same cannot be said for my best scrapper. It was shot through by a musket ball. That is another four guineas Boney owes me for its replacement. I trust our peace negotiators are battling hard on my part.'

The group laughed at this, just after Preston had accepted some food proffered to him by one of the servants. He filled his lungs to join in the laughter, and felt a morsel lock into the top of his wind pipe.

'Something deuced similar happened to poor Lieutenant Spotswood, over there,' explained the captain of the *Stirling*. The officers of the *Griffin* turned to look at the tall, thin officer on the far side of the room, and away from Preston, who was gaping wide as he tried to dislodge the blockage. In his mind he was calling for help, but as in a nightmare, no sound came from his mouth.

'What happened to him?' asked Taylor.

The noise in the room was growing to a steady roar in Preston's ears, and colours were becoming brighter. The back of Macpherson's tunic glowed like a fire as he stumbled towards him. He found himself wondering if a hanged man saw the world like this, in the moments before his neck snapped.

'He was struck in the throat by a pistol ball during the battle,' continued Thompson. 'Fortunately, it was spent when it reached him, having come from some distance. The broadcloth of his coat took much of the impact, and his neckcloth the rest, but the poor man still lost the power of speech for a good while. Even now, he has a curiously distorted address. I dare say it will pass.'

The others were all busy commenting on this, while Preston grabbed at Macpherson's arm, spilling the marine's drink as he desperately sought help. He pointed with his lone hand towards his throat, and directed a look of wide-eyed panic at his fellow officers.

'By Jove!' laughed Thompson, pointing at him. 'That is exactly it! Bravo, sir. Why, it is as if you were Spotswood himself!'

Fortunately, the noisy levity of the group had attracted the attention of others. This included the recently arrived surgeon of the *Griffin*, who had come directly from the dockyard hospital, where he had been helping tend to the wounded. He took in the blue lips and desperate gaze, and hurried across the room.

'Upon my word, what are you all about?' demanded Corbett, moving beside the stricken lieutenant, and gesturing for him to lean forward. 'Can you not see this man is expiring before you for want of air?' He struck him fiercely between the shoulder blades with his balled fist, and with the third blow, a piece of something flew out of his mouth. With a gasp like a surfacing diver, Preston stood back upright and colour flooded his face.

'What must you think of me, Mr Preston,' exclaimed the *Stirling*'s captain. 'Rattling away like that, while you were in such distress. Can you ever forgive me?'

'Pray do not mention it,' said Preston, more embarrassed than harmed now that he could breathe again.

'Bring a chair!' Blake ordered to one of the footmen.

'Should Mr Preston not return to the ship?' asked Clay, a hand on the lieutenant's arm.

'I am quite recovered, sir,' insisted the young officer.

'Just as well,' scolded Macpherson. 'Consider your intended, awaiting your return? I struggle to conceive how we would have explained your demise to wee Miss Hockley.' He pantomimed the scene for the benefit of the others. 'Eh, no, it was not at the hands of the wicked French that he succumbed, but rather to vittles, consumed with injudicious haste.'

'Do not fuss, gentlemen, and kindly take away the chair,' said Corbett. 'Distressing as a blockage to the trachea can be, recovery is swift, once access to life-giving air is restored. Eat no more tonight, Mr Preston, and be moderate in the matter of drink, and I see no reason why you should not remain as one of the party.'

Once it was clear that Preston was feeling better, the officers in the group began to disperse into the room. Macpherson was called over by his fellow marine commanders of the *Daring* and *Stirling* to discuss the battle. Armstrong took Taylor, Blake and Preston away to introduce them to an acquaintance he had spotted, and Faulkner and Corbett excused themselves from the two captains' company.

'How is your ship, Captain?' asked Clay.

'William, please,' corrected Thompson. 'Now we have fought together, there is surely no need for formality. Would you find it presumptuous of me to call you Alexander?'

'By no means. So how then is your ship, William.'

'Sadly buffeted,' reported its captain. 'Several frames have been shot through. The dockyard declares the best they can manage is to patch the poor girl up so we can sail for Jamaica. They have a dry dock there. And yours?'

'Much less gravely wounded,' said Clay. 'I fear the *Centaure* reserved her fullest attention for the *Stirling*.'

'While but for a few powder smudges, young Camelford's *Daring* might not have been there at all,' said Thompson.

'Where is Captain Camelford?' asked Clay. 'He arrived at the jetty ahead of me, yet I cannot see him anywhere.

I have something urgent to discuss with that young man.'

'He is sulking,' said his companion. 'I am afraid that is my fault, Alexander. I sought to make game of him, saying how refreshing it was to see him arriving ahead of time, for once. Sir George gave him a roasting for his failure to come to the aid of the *Stirling* when we were boarded.'

'Perhaps he was unaware of the gravity of the situation?'

'Too dull to realise, more like,' scoffed Thompson. 'You detected our urgent need, with a whole deuced ship of the line betwixt us. The *Daring* was a biscuit toss off our stern!'

'Perhaps that was ill done,' conceded Clay. 'So where do you suppose him to have gone? He surely will not risk further censure from Sir George by abandoning his gathering altogether?'

'I have no notion. He simply stormed off when others laughed at my jest.'

Clay waved over one of the footmen.

'Yes sir,' enquired the servant.

'Tell me, does Clarence House have a library?'

'Indeed it does, sir. A very fine one. It lies through that door and at the far end of the corridor. Was it a particular volume you wanted to see?'

'No, I seek another guest,' said Clay. 'Would you excuse me, William? I believe I know where he may be found.'

One of the library's double doors stood ajar, a bar of darkness at the end of the lamp-lit passage. Clay stepped through the gap into the room beyond, closing the door behind him. The distant chatter of voices from the back of the house vanished as the heavy wood swung into place. In the dimly lit room, Clay could see that books lined all the walls, while the centre of the library was scattered with comfortable-looking chairs and a small table. A glow of flickering light came from off to one side, where the figure of Camelford stood close to a wall of leather-bound spines, with a branched candelabra in his fist.

'Who is there?' demanded the *Daring*'s captain, turning from the shelves. The flat glow of the candlelight could not disguise the look of annoyance on his face.

'It is me, Captain,' replied Clay. 'I thought I might find you in here.'

'I came to escape that bore Thompson, and his damned insinuations, sir,' said Camelford, coming over. 'Cleland's *Memoirs of a Coxcomb*,' he explained, hefting the book he carried. 'You can tell a lot about a man from his taste in literature, I always hold. This seems decidedly racy for old Sir George. I would have said dusty old Gibbon was more his style, but perhaps I have misjudged the hound, what?' He placed the candelabra down on the table, and turned to face Clay. 'Why were you looking for me, sir?'

'I shall be returning to England soon, Captain, and there is a matter I need to discuss with you before I depart,' said Clay, sitting down in one of the chairs.

'You go so soon?'

'I shall, once the *Griffin* has been repaired. With the *Peregrine* destroyed, the orders that brought me to the Leeward Islands have been fulfilled.'

'Your friend Sutton will be disappointed to find you absent when he returns from patrol, sir.'

'Indeed,' said Clay. 'But perhaps with all this talk of peace, I will soon have the leisure to enjoy more of his society.'

'I dare say that is so, sir,' said Camelford, taking the chair opposite. 'Was it something in particular you wished to discuss?' The flickering light made his expression hard to read, but the younger man sat very upright in his chair, with both arms folded.

'I have completed most of my report for Sir George,' continued Clay, 'but I have some supplementary observations I intend to include. I wanted to give you the opportunity to comment on them.'

'How intriguing! And what do they chiefly relate to, sir?'

'Sugar, for the most part.'

'Sugar!' exclaimed Camelford. 'I am not sure that I have the pleasure of following you, sir. What concern might that be of mine?'

'Let me share my observations with you, and perhaps matters will become clearer,' said Clay, watching the other man's face with care. 'They name it "white gold" in these parts, do they not? Antigua produces it, of course, although not in as impressive a quantity as Guadeloupe. I have heard that many of the planters on that island made considerable fortunes for themselves. But that was before revolution in France, and war with Britain. Suddenly they must have found themselves with no end of the stuff, and few means to get it off their island.'

'Serves the Frogs back for the aid they gave to those damned rebellious Yankees,' commented Camelford. 'Was that what you wished to tell me, sir?'

'No, I wanted your assistance with a few matters that I find hard to explain,' said Clay. 'They relate to when we were both off Pointe-à-Pitre.'

'I will do my best, sir. Such as what?'

'Such as why, when we first approached that port in the *Daring*, I could clearly see men engaged in cutting cane in the fields. I believe I pointed it out to you at the time. To what end do you think French plantation owners would still be harvesting sugar, on an island unable to export its product?'

'Perhaps they are preparing for the peace that all speak of, and the resumption in trade that must follow, sir.'

'Maybe, Captain, although that does not explain the very illuminating revelation of your two young midshipmen when they came down from the masthead.'

'Yes, the presence of a ship of the line was quite a shock, sir.'

'It was,' agreed Clay, 'but I was more interested in their description of the port itself. I have the note Mr Thorne wrote for me on that day here with me.' He pushed a hand into the inner pocket of his coat and pulled out a folded sheet. 'Let me see now. Yes, here is the passage. "*Five sail of schooners and a brig, all warped in close to the quayside*." And a little latter, "*plenty of activity there*". Plenty of activity,' repeated Clay. 'Does that not strike you as strange, for a place that has been under Royal Navy blockade for some years?'

'Frankly, sir, I don't have an opinion on the matter,' said Camelford. 'How the dashed Frogs chose to waste their time, is surely their affair.'

'Unless they were not wasting their time.' Clay held Camelford's gaze for a moment. The light of the candles threw a huge shadow of his hunched form onto the wall behind him. Even in their flickering glow he could sense the other man's face colour.

'What are you damned well implying, sir?' he demanded.

'Why were you so determined that the *Peregrine*

would not be found in Pointe-à-Pitre when we first met?' asked Clay.

'To save you from what I thought would be a damned fool's errand, sir!' Camelford rose to his feet. He slammed down the book he had taken from the shelf, setting the candle flames to dance.

'And yet there she was, not so concealed that a man who knew his duty would not have seen her,' said Clay. 'Which got me pondering if the true reason you want me to stay away had nothing to do with the *Peregrine*, and everything to do with what else I might discover.'

'Have a care!' warned Camelford, wagging a finger towards him. 'I have killed a man for saying less!'

'The game is up, Captain,' continued Clay. 'The owner of that French schooner we captured was good enough to explain the whole arrangement to me. For a suitable cut of the profits, you have permitted ships like the *Saint Christopher* to bring French sugar into Antigua, where it is sold on as the product of this island. You have neglected your duty to your king. Why, you are little more than a damned smuggler!'

'I shall want satisfaction for that!' spat Camelford, both his fists clenched in fury.

'Satisfaction!' exclaimed Clay. 'Pray don't be so ridiculous. Sit down man, I am not going to fight you. A duel implies a meeting between men of honour. It is a privilege you put aside when you chose to line your pockets with the enemy's coin. I would also warn you that the Articles of War are quite clear on challenging a superior officer, as you have just done. It is a court martial offence, punishable by death.'

'Hah! I might have expected you to hide behind the King's Regulations! But then you're no gentleman, Clay! You're little more than the mewling brat of a country parson!'

'Mewling brat of a country parson, *sir*, if you please, Captain,' said Clay rising to his feet to confront the furious officer. 'I wanted to grant you the opportunity to explain your conduct, before I lay the matter before Sir George. Now that I have done so, my duty is clear. I shall expose you for the traitor that you are. Good evening to you.'

Clay was braced for a blow, but instead a smile spread across Camelford's bulging red face. 'Best of luck with that, *sir*! In all your damned interfering, did you ever stop to consider why it was always my *Daring* that was stationed off Guadeloupe, and never that choirboy Sutton?'

*****

The *Griffin* was brought alongside the dockyard wharf early the following morning. Then the boatswain's calls echoed through her decks, summoning her crew for a day of toil under the hot Antiguan sun. Before the frigate could be repaired, she had to first be stripped of everything she had on board. Lines of men heaved away on blocks and tackles, swaying each ponderous gun or huge barrel from out of her cavernous hold. More modest items were carried down the gangplanks by relays of ship's boys, each holding a single cannon ball or a mess stool. The warehouses that lined the quayside began to fill with weapons and tools, barrels and boxes, sails and coils of rope, each item carefully recorded by the anxious officer responsible for that part of the ship. Steadily, as the men toiled away, the frigate's hull rose from out of the sapphire-blue water, exposing a broad stripe of gleaming copper and the crudely filled holes smashed into her by the *Centaure*. By evening, the task was complete and the exhausted men stared in disbelief at the mounds of gear they had created, wondering how such a vast amount had ever been able to fit into a single frigate.

Antigua was a small island, the crew of the *Griffin* were a settled company, and all of them were owed a considerable sum of prize money from the capture of the *Centaure*. These were factors that reduced the risk of her sailors deserting to close to nil. Having weighed all this up with the caution for which he was known, Lieutenant Taylor decided to grant shore leave, for once, to any who asked. As it transpired, there were only a few who still had the energy to venture out of the walled dockyard to explore what delights English Harbour had to offer. Most were content to find the nearest grogshop, but a more determined party set off in the opposite direction, taking a road coated in silver dust that wound its way out of town. On one side it was overshadowed by palm trees, their roughened trunks curving in gentle arcs against the evening sky; and on the other side by a patchwork of small fields and allotments.

'How far is this place, Sean?' demanded Evans, who was trailing behind the others. 'Coz I'm bleeding knackered, and me throat's drier than a Turk's sandal.'

'Then you'll like Brannigan's Puncheon House all the more,' said the Irishman. ''Tis just ahead, in Cobbs Cross. There's no fecking grog to match a mug of punch, after a day of thirsting as we've just had.'

'What manner of draft be this punch, then?' asked Trevan.

'Rum, for the most part, cut with sugar and juice and the like,' explained O'Malley. 'Each tavern mixes their own, and guards the fecking secret like a brooding hen, but none is as fine as Brannigan's.'

Their path bent inland for a stretch, towards a

collection of low wooden buildings with thatched roofs. At the heart of the settlement, where the road they followed was crossed by another, stood a shed-like building. A wooden hitching post had been set up outside, at which a pair of horses were tethered. Lamplight spilt out through the open door, together with the buzz of talk and tendrils of tobacco smoke. At these encouraging signs, the sailors hurried towards the entrance.

Inside was a single room, filled with tables and benches. Perhaps a dozen rough-looking men sat in various groups. Close by the entrance, a lively game of cards was in progress, each player with a pile of coins before him. At the next table sat a pair of customers dressed in the leather aprons of smiths, quietly talking with an earthenware jug and two mugs before them. Through the haze of tobacco smoke other groups could be seen, deeper into the room, while opposite the entrance stood the establishment's owner, a florid man with a pair of bushy sideburns framing an almost entirely bald head. The level of sound dropped as the sailors appeared at the door and customers turned to stare at the new arrivals. It vanished altogether as Sedgwick stepped in.

'God bless every fecker under this roof,' said O'Malley, in the resulting silence.

Only the tavernkeeper seemed to react, with a broad smile spreading across his face. 'Why, that's a Leinster greeting, so it is, or I've never fecking heard one!' he exclaimed, coming over and grasping O'Malley's hand.

'You'll not be remembering me, Mr Brannigan, but I was out here some years back, on the old *Mars*. I certainly remember your punch, well enough, and how it can ease a terrible thirst.'

'You remembers it?' queried his fellow Irishman.

'Sure, I must have been going easy on the rum that day. Will you take one of the tables there, and I'll bring you over a jug?'

'Are you serving bleeding negros now, Brannigan?' demanded a voice from deeper in the room. 'I didn't have you down as a damned Abolitionist.' The speaker was one of three wiry-looking men with heavily tanned faces.

'Hush your noise now, Rob Buckley,' said Brannigan. 'Your man's not one of them fecking slaves on that plantation of yours. Can't you see how he's just a regular jack, at all?'

'I'm happy to talk with any bleeder as don't want my shipmate drinking here,' said Evans, glowering around the room. 'Outside, like.' The overseer called Buckley looked at the huge sailor for a moment, and then returned to his drink. Evans re-joined his friends.

'There we go, lads,' said Brannigan, bustling over with a laden tray. 'I'll give them three a little shot on the house. There's no call for a fecking riot, on a hot night like this.'

Slowly the noise level increased as the card game resumed, and the locals returned to their conversations.

'It ain't quite as satisfying as a draft of proper ale,' commented Evans, after he had drained his first mug, 'but that weren't half bad.'

'Wasn't I after telling yous, it was worth the fecking stroll?' said O'Malley, wiping his mouth on a sleeve. 'Best punch in the Caribee.'

'Shame Larcum ain't with us to try it, mind,' said Trevan, lighting his pipe from the lamp. 'Or be his name Jack now? I still ain't entirely certain.'

'No more than a mug of water for him this night, and a longer neck tomorrow, poor fecker,' said O'Malley. 'That's English justice for yous.'

'Mind, he did go and join a mutiny, the stupid arse,'

said Evans.

'And wouldn't you, with a brute for a captain, and a certain flogging for every fecking error?' said O'Malley. 'I hear that *Peregrine* was a cursed, shot-rolling ship.'

'Rising up's one thing,' said Evans, folding his arms. 'But then they gone and done all manner of stuff, from what I heard. Murdering nippers and the like. That ain't right.'

'Aye, but you reckon our Larcum would have done any of that?' queried Trevan. 'He don't seem the type, to me. Remember how upset he were, when the sawbones cut away young Charlie's leg? He probably saved that lad's life, an' copped it from Fletcher for his pains.'

'True, but he shot that fecker on the prize we took, swift enough,' said O'Malley. 'Back when we was coming out here.'

'That's right, the bastard!' exclaimed Evans. 'On the bleeding *Happy Maggie*! Deserter, wasn't he?'

'Or a fellow mutineer, about to grass on him,' offered Sedgwick. The others all stared at him. 'It makes sense, if you think upon it,' he continued.

'Bleeding hell, you're right!' said the Londoner. 'Weren't the prize crew from a privateer out of Pointy Point? That turncoat must have skipped off the *Peregrine*, and taken up with the Frogs, in which case the filthy bastard had it coming!'

'Right. So now you're not after stringing Larcum up?' queried O'Malley. 'Is that it?'

'Eh, well … No, least ways …' stuttered Evans. 'Oh, I don't bleeding know.'

'Harte were saying as how Pipe were going to stand by Larcum,' offered Sedgwick.

'Is he now?' marvelled Trevan. 'Maybe that, and the

peace as all say be in the offing, will save him. I does hope so.' The sailors were all quiet for a moment, contemplating an alien future without war.

'Bleeding peace!' marvelled Evans. 'I wonder what that'll be like? We been fighting them Frogs since I were a nipper. What do you reckon you lads will do, when we all gets paid off, like?'

'Back to my Molly and baby Kate,' said Trevan. 'I never knew my lad Sam afore the pox took him, what with being away whaling, and then the war an' all. Be right good to spend some time with them. Maybe take up fishing. The sea be all I rightly know, but least that be a calling as has you home most nights. What about you, Sean? Didn't you have some wench as you was sweet on, in Ireland like?'

'Aye, back when we was on the old *Titan*,' he snorted. 'I doubt if she'll have waited, an' her Pa was a mean old fecker. He was after breaking my crown with a cudgel, last time I was there.'

'Only after he found you and his daughter in the hay!' exclaimed Trevan.

'True enough,' conceded the Irishman. 'Perhaps it'll be safer to stay as a sailor.'

'I ain't got a clue as to what I'll be doing,' said Evans. 'Clobbering folk is what I chiefly know, but I daresay I'm too bleeding old for the ring now. Besides, getting what wits I has left punched out ain't much of a life. How about you, Able?'

'Have no fear on his part,' offered O'Malley. 'A fecking scholar with his letters, and that book he wrote, an' all. He'll be doing the best of us all!'

'I ain't so sure about that, Sean,' said the coxswain. 'Least you all has places to return to. What have I got? My home has long since gone. Since I cut free from that damned plantation, the only place I've truly known has been the navy. Only now they won't be wanting the like of me.'

Chapter 14
Home

This time the clatter from the dockyard chapel's bell was joined by more distant ones, in the parish churches of Falmouth and Liberta, lost among the rolling hills of Antigua. They had been ringing for a good half an hour, and showed no sign of stopping. Clay clambered up from the stern sheets of the *Griffin*'s cutter and onto the little jetty that served Clarence House. He paused for a moment, taking in the grinning sailors manning the oars, and the signs of jubilation on board the *Daring*, moored farther out in English Harbour. Many of her crew had climbed part-way into her rigging, and were waving hats and neckcloths towards the crowds that thronged the quayside.

'Good morning, sir,' said the same marine who had greeted him on his last visit. 'I give you joy of the peace.'

'Thank you, Corporal,' said Clay, returning his salute. 'It is indeed most welcome. Sir George should be expecting me.'

'Yes, sir,' replied the soldier. 'Would you care to follow me?'

The path that looped its way up the hillside was different in the fierce tropical sun. The surface glared white, forcing Clay to narrow his eyes, and the bushes on either side throbbed with the drone of insects. It was a relief to step onto the veranda and enter the cool interior of the building after his hot climb. An orderly was waiting to take over from the marine; he took Clay's second-best hat from him and then led him towards a polished door close to the library.

He knocked, and then went in without waiting for an answer. 'Captain Clay is here to see you, Sir George,' he announced.

The room was cool and shady. Wooden slatted blinds had been fixed across the open windows, allowing the sea breeze and a few lines of sunlight to enter. The clang of pealing bells filtered in, together with the sound of birdsong from the garden.

The admiral rose from behind his desk to shake Clay's hand. 'Delighted to see you, Captain, on this most propitious of days,' he said with a smile. 'Would you care for a glass of madeira to celebrate?'

'Thank you, Sir George. That would be most welcome.' The admiral waved his visitor to his seat, while the orderly brought over the drinks. Clay was surprised to see the glass was beaded with condensation.

'This wine is chilled, Sir George,' he observed.

'My residence has an excellent icehouse in the grounds, and a fresh delivery has arrived from New England,' explained his host. 'Deuced odd to think of it snowing there while we broil down here, what? To the peace, and God bless the king.'

'The king,' echoed Clay, sipping the delightful cool liquid. 'When did word arrive?'

'Just this morning,' said the admiral. 'The peace treaty was signed in Amiens, wherever that may be. It is a damned wretched deal, mind. The Hollanders have the Cape returned to them, Spain gets Menorca, but as far as I can see the only thing the Frogs are giving up is the deuced Papal States.'

'Why did we agree to such poor terms, Sir George?'

'Well, sending that fool Cornwallis to negotiate with a snake like Talleyrand won't have helped,' explained Montague. 'But our hands were cruelly tied. The mob wants peace and the government is broke.'

'A case of the beggar taking what alms are on offer, Sir George?'

'Quite so, Captain,' confirmed Montague. 'Still, it does mean I can send all the prisoners from the *Centaure* packing back to Guadeloupe. Regrettably, that is not the only transfer I am required to do. The first priority of the Admiralty now is urgent economy. Along with intelligence of the peace came a list of ships to be returned home at once and taken out of commission. It includes almost my entire command.'

Clay felt a churn of emotions within him. The dread of what he knew was coming, surrendering his frigate and laying aside the profession that had dominated his life since he was a boy. But also the joy of returning home, to Lydia, young Francis and the unknown baby that should have arrived by now. 'I take it the *Griffin* is among those ships?' he asked.

'I am afraid so, Captain,' Montague confirmed. 'So, this will also be adieu for us. Is she ready to depart?'

'She is not fully repaired yet,' said Clay. 'Perhaps a week more will see her restored, less if you can instruct the dockyard to allocate more workers to the task.'

'I shall see what can be done,' said the admiral, adding a note to a neatly written list by his elbow. He returned his pencil to its place on his ink stand and then adjusted its alignment with the tip of one finger. 'Camelford and the *Daring* will sail first thing tomorrow, so if any of your people wish to write home with word of their return, that will be their opportunity.'

'Thank you, Sir George,' said Clay. 'Might I speak with you with regard to Captain Camelford? In private.'

'As you wish,' said the admiral. 'Leave us please, Sainsbury.'

'Aye aye, sir.'

Clay turned in his chair and waited for the orderly to depart. When the door clicked shut, he began speaking. 'Something has been troubling me for some time, which I thought you might be able to help me with, Sir George.'

'Happy to oblige if I can, Captain.'

'On my way from Plymouth to join your command, I had the good fortune to fall in with a trading brig, outward bound from Antigua with a cargo of sugar,' said Clay. 'She had been taken by a French privateer.'

'Indeed, the *Margaret Harmony*,' said Montague. 'As I recall, you very handsomely recaptured her. I remember my regret that, as you had yet to join my command, I would not receive my admiral's share of the prize money when she was condemned. What of her, Captain?'

'Only that on my arrival in English Harbour, you and every planter I met with told me that the cane fields here had been devastated by a recent hurricane,' said Clay. 'Which set me to wondering where her cargo could have come from, Sir George.'

'Good grief, Captain, I have no damned idea,' protested the admiral. 'The responsibilities of the commander of the Leeward Islands squadron are certainly varied, but they don't extend to the intricacies of the sugar trade, what?'

'True, and it was but a small matter,' said Clay. 'A nagging thought, if you will, at the back of my mind. Perhaps her cargo had come from another of our islands, I told myself, in the schooners that seem to infest these waters.'

'Doubtless that will be the explanation,' said Montague, glancing past him at the case clock that rested against the wall. 'So how, pray, does this relate to Captain Camelford?'

'Because I have subsequently discovered that he has been permitting French sugar to be smuggled into Antigua.'

'I beg your pardon, Captain! What on earth has given you that impression?'

'Oh, it is much more than an impression, Sir George. It first came to my attention during the *Griffin*'s operations against the *Peregrine*. I even had a French sugar planter offer me an inducement to permit the practice to continue. It is quite certain that French sugar has been smuggled from Guadeloupe to Antigua with the connivance of Camelford and the *Daring*. Doubtless it is this contraband that formed the basis of the *Margaret Harmony*'s cargo. I have set down the particulars of the smuggling operation for you in a separate report.' Clay reached into his coat pocket and produced a thick bundle of paper, sealed in a package. He placed it on the desk.

After a pause, Montague leant forward and pulled the letter towards him. 'This is a very grave accusation you make, Captain. Against a brother officer, to boot. I would urge you to consider with care what you say next.'

'I say nothing to you that I have not said directly to Camelford, Sir George. I had the opportunity to lay my charges before him in your library.'

'That was brave,' said the admiral, his eyes watchful. 'I dare say he was furious.'

'He wanted to call me out,' said Clay. 'But he became much more sanguine when I said I would be taking the matter to you. In fact, he found the thought amusing, and implied that you were involved. That you had sanctioned his actions.'

Clay had expected Montague to be angry. To leap from his chair, and demand that Clay retract what he had said. To shout and rant. To pace the room. Instead he calmly picked up the unopened report, tapped it against the palm of one hand, and looked appraisingly at his visitor. In the silence that followed, Clay realised that the bells had stopped outside.

'I don't believe you will be acquainted with my wife, Lady Montague?' asked the admiral, placing the report back in front of him, the long edge square with the rim of the desk.

'Pardon?' queried Clay. 'What the devil has Lady …'

'Indulge me for a moment, I pray,' continued the admiral. 'You have submitted me to a lengthy explanation. Permit me to repay the debt. Marrying Felicity was a considerable coup for my family. The daughter of an earl, with the most advantageous of connections, it has certainly elevated the name of Montague to be one of note in the service, and indeed the land.'

'I give you joy of your marriage, Sir George, but how can this have any bearing on the matter under discussion?'

'Because the daughter of an earl comes with certain obligations,' explained the admiral. 'Her upbringing has equipped her with many virtues, but restraint and economy are not among them. She expects a house in town, in addition to an estate in the country. A coach and four, numerous servants, dresses smuggled from Paris, and to entertain in appropriate style. With the land tax set where it is, and the income tax starting to bite, even the remuneration of a rear admiral can prove inadequate.'

'Are you saying that Camelford is right? That you are involved?' exclaimed Clay. 'You surely cannot seek to excuse your behaviour by blaming a wife on the far side of the Atlantic!'

'Come, Alexander,' urged Montague. 'What ill has been done? The French have always had the largest of the sugar islands. Our blockade means that their warehouses are bursting with the stuff, while thanks to this deuced hurricane, Antigua has none to offer. Meanwhile our former colonies in America and our allies in Europe run short. Who is truly harmed if I have let a little French sugar reach the market, purporting to be from here? Besides, now peace has come, the arrangement is at an end. The damned French can sell their sugar as they choose.'

'But Sir George, the very essence of a naval blockade is that it subdues an opponent by patient strangulation,' protested Clay.

'We are not speaking of warlike stores here,' said the admiral. 'No powder or shot. It is only sugar that has been allowed to pass.'

'At considerable pecuniary gain for yourself and Camelford!'

'Oh dear!' exclaimed Montague. 'Do I detect the same, sanctimonious tone from the perfect Alexander Clay that I found so wearying when I commanded you in the Indian Ocean?'

'It is not just a matter of a bit of contraband! What of the *Centaure*?'

'What of her?' scoffed the admiral. 'She has been heroically defeated in battle, much to the credit of us both.'

'But did you stop to think how such a vessel was able to arrive in Guadeloupe unobserved?' said Clay. 'The French played Camelford for a damned fool! She must have slipped in while they had paid him to turn his back. Had I not arrived and detected her presence, she would have played Old Harry with the Jamaica convoy. No, my duty is clear, Sir George. I shall be obliged to expose your and Camelford's behaviour to the Admiralty.'

'I think not, Clay.' There was steel in Montague's eyes, replacing the bluff and bluster of earlier.

'I beg your pardon, Sir George?'

'Since you have chosen to reject reasoned argument, let us see if I can find something more persuasive,' said the admiral. 'You regard Captain Sutton as more than just a brother by marriage, I collect?'

'Of course,' said Clay. 'He was my closest friend long before he wed my sister.'

'Excellent. And what was his relationship like with the late Captain Windham?'

'Poor, as you well know, Sir George!'

'Very poor,' agreed Montague, 'and Windham's people are most influential. Why, they have even contrived to have an East Indiaman named after him to honour his memory.'

Now it was Clay's turn to be watchful. 'I am not sure I follow where this is leading, Sir George,' he said.

'No, but you shall presently. There was much disquiet in the service when he took his life, an event which, if I recall correctly, I did much to conceal from excessive scrutiny at the time, did I not?'

The admiral opened a drawer in his desk, without waiting for a reply, and pulled out a leather case. He leafed through the various papers it contained, eventually stopping at a small, folded note. The paper was faded, the surface speckled with points of brown.

'For example,' he resumed. 'I have never made public the note he left beside his lifeless body. But I have it still. These marks upon it are Windham's gore.'

'There was a note!' exclaimed Clay.

'Indeed, there was. You know, Clay, strange to tell, I came close to destroying it on several occasions, but something has always stayed my hand. So here we are, all these years later, and I find it has suddenly acquired a value I had never imagined.'

'What does it say?' asked Clay, his throat suddenly dry.

'You will pardon me for not passing it across, I am sure,' said the admiral. 'But I will happily read it to you. Here is set down in his own hand, the following. "*By this, my final act, I bear witness that Commander John Sutton did murder Captain Percy Follett aboard His Majesty's frigate* Agrius, *and furthermore I call on those who come after me to avenge my uncle's death. Signed N P Windham, Master and Commander.*" You and Sutton were both lieutenants on the *Agrius*, were you not, when her captain was killed, back in ninety-six?'

'These are the ramblings of a drunken madman!' exclaimed Clay.

'Are they? I note that your protest does not stretch as far as denying the substance of the accusation.'

'As for that, I was not present when Captain Follett died,' said Clay.

'True, but Sutton was,' said Montague, his gaze remorseless. 'Did you never suspect your friend might have played some part in murder? Deep in your soul? And did you report the matter, so that it could be properly investigated, as a dutiful officer should have done?'

For a moment, Clay was back on the wrecked quarterdeck of the frigate, all those years before. He could almost smell the sulphurous gun smoke as it swirled about him, see the wreck of the fallen mizzen mast, dragging the ship to a halt, and his friend Sutton, drawn sword in hand, peering over the side.

'There was no evidence …' he stuttered.

'Come sir, pray do not give me such damned lawyers' talk. The mask of perfection slips a little from your brow, I think. You're not quite as guiltless as you would have us all believe. Perhaps we are not so very different, you and I?'

'What will you do with that mischievous libel?' demanded Clay.

'That rather depends on whether you still propose to continue with your ridiculous allegations about me.' Montague picked up the note in one hand and the envelope in the other, balancing the two documents, as if testing their weight. 'I propose a simple agreement between two less-than-perfect men, Captain,' he said. 'The war is over. You take your damned report away, I shall keep my note, and both of us pledge to never speak of these matters again.'

Clay rose from his chair and angrily paced the room. Alternate lines of sunlight and shade striped the floor at his feet, like the bars of a cage. Why had Sutton been such a fool, all those years ago, he asked himself, his hands clenching with anger. As he turned, he saw the admiral's face watching him, a faint smile tugging at the corners of his mouth. An urge to wipe that grin away with his fists flashed across his mind, but then vanished as quickly as it came. Montague might have Clay trapped, but he was not without some leverage of his own.

'Distasteful as I find your suggestion, Sir George, I feel minded to accept,' he said, his voice as cold as the wine he had drunk earlier. 'On one condition.'

'I am not sure you are in a position to place any

demands on me,' said Montague. 'Unless you wish to trifle with the life of your friend?'

'A favour, then,' said Clay. 'I take it you will be presiding at the trial of the *Peregrine* mutineers?'

'Of course. Their offence was against one of my ships.'

'When the accused Jack Broadbent comes before you, I would be obliged if you would commute his sentence to flogging. I shall furnish you with a submission as to his good character, and his exemplary conduct in the destruction of his former ship. That should serve as a justification.'

'You ask much of me, Captain,' protested Montague. 'Earl St Vincent will be furious with me for showing such leniency.'

'His lordship's fury will be as nothing to that which would follow the disclosure that one of his admirals has been comforting the enemy,' said Clay. He extended a hand across the desk towards Montague, and, after a moment, it was accepted.

*****

The farm lay a few miles from the village of Drumgallon, surrounded by small fields, each divided from its neighbour by a thorn hedge and a ditch cut into the rich dark earth. Some contained grazing cattle, their heads low as they cropped the lush grass; others formed a patchwork of growing crops. A line of mature alders screened the buildings from the west wind and the steady, falling rain that it brought. The sailor looked around the little farmyard, searching for any changes that might have happened over the years since he had last been there. The reeds that thatched the roofs wore heavier pelts of moss than he remembered, and there were fewer chickens picking over the manure heap in the hope of a worm. But other things seemed unchanged. The tall barn with its quiet, private hayloft looked the same, as did the rusting hand pump beside the stone water trough. Unchanged, too, was the expression of cold fury that settled on the face of the man who opened the door in response to his knock.

'Well met there, Mr Dougherty,' said the sailor with what he hoped was a winning smile. 'Sean O'Malley, back from the wars, an' all.' He politely removed his hat and stood in the rain.

'Mary!' yelled the farmer into the interior. 'Go fetch the blunderbuss! I need to finish what the French ought to have fecking done by now.'

'Steady!' protested the sailor. 'No need for a fecking mill. I'm done with all that fighting. Can't I come in, so we can talk our differences through, civilised like. That's a fine peat fire I can smell, an' I'm awful wet, what with coming all the way from Dunleary.'

Farmer Dougherty barred the door with one arm, his big fist gripping the lintel. 'Is that all that fecking stands between us? Differences, as can be settled over a glass of ale?' roared the farmer. 'Last time you darkened my door, you ravished my daughter, stole my mare and then disappeared, with the help of that fool of a priest.'

'In all fairness, Mr Dougherty, ravishing is coming it a bit strong. T'was no more than a squeeze I gave the colleen, and the only reason I had to borrow your fecking horse was to get clear of you. Hadn't you raised half of Leinster and were you not after breaking my head with a wicked-looking cudgel?'

'You have some courage, O'Malley, showing yer blasted face here, I'll grant yous that,' snarled the farmer.

'Though I see yous had the sense to bring some giant with you, this time,' he added, pointing to where Evans stood, leaning up against the side of an empty wain.

'Morning there, mate,' said the Londoner in response, touching the rim of his hat.

Dougherty ignored him. 'But it'll make no fecking odds,' he continued. 'The longer you wait on my front step, the easier shooting you down shall be.' He turned to yell again over his shoulder. 'Mary, the gun! Swiftly now, wife!'

'Will you not listen to what I am after saying!' protested the sailor. 'I've come to put that all to rights. I'll marry the girl!'

'Marry her!' exclaimed Dougherty. 'Like that could make any difference! When you disappeared, what the feck do you suppose you left behind? Old Father O'Connell told all who would listen that you'd be after coming back for her, and at first that gave the girl hope. For a time, she could bear that all named her a slut and a whore. But year followed year, and still you never fecking came.'

'I thought about it, truly I did, Mr Dougherty, but somehow, what with the war an' all …'

'Holy Mary, save us,' said the farmer. 'Could you not have written?'

'I … I … don't have my letters.'

'Neither do I, you idiot! That's why I get the fecking doctor to write for me, or the priest, or the bailiff of the estate. Are you telling me there's not a man in the whole of King George's navy as can set down two words together?'

'I am sorry, so I am, Mr Dougherty,' said O'Malley, his head bowed. 'But let me set it right. Can I not come in, at all?'

'What for?' said the farmer, calm at last. 'My girl isn't

to be found under this roof! A time came when she could take no more, and who would blame the lamb? The church has her now. She's gone and joined the Sisters of Mercy, over Kerry way. Now, for the love of the Almighty, be gone from my land, before I truly do shoot you down.'

O'Malley stood before the slammed door for a while, the rain soaking his dark pigtail. After a while Evans came over to stand beside his friend. Dimpled puddles spread all around them in the mud.

'Sorry mate,' he said. 'That didn't go so well.'

'It's my own fecking fault, Sam,' sighed the Irishman. 'Let's get away, before he truly does produce a gun.'

The sailors turned away and headed back down the lane, hunching into their coats against the weather. 'Bleeding hell, but ain't it green here abouts,' commented Evans after a while. 'Does it rain all the time?'

'No,' explained his friend. 'Not above eleven months of the fecking year. But the twelfth one brings quite the change.'

'What happens then?'

'That's when it fecking snows.'

Evans chuckled at this, and the two men walked on, observed with suspicion by the grazing cows. After a while the Londoner spoke again.

'You know, Sean, your home don't seem quite as welcoming as I thought it would.'

'Dougherty's a good enough man. No, it's me, with my roving ways as is the fecking problem. Shall we go and see about that London town yous is always rattling on about?'

'If you reckon as that farmer were savage, wait until you meet some of them as are waiting for me.'

'Surely that trouble you was in will have blown over

by now?' queried the Irishman. 'Is it still not fecking safe for you in London, at all?'

'Perhaps, but I reckon it ain't worth the risk of finding out,' said Evans. 'Now I've seen a bit of the world, I can tell that home always were a shithole, even before I fell out with the wrong folk. No, strange to say, it ain't Seven Dials I'm missing, but the sea. An' I never bleeding well thought I'd say that.'

'You have the truth of it there, Sam lad,' said his friend. 'The fecking sea, is it? That was a handsome looking trading brig as was fitting out in Dunleary when we landed. Shall we go an' see if they need a brace of honest jacks?'

'Aye,' agreed the Londoner, 'an' if they can't lay hold of any, they might yet take us.'

*****

The sailors came striding down a winding track bound by old dry-stone walls. In places they were so covered in greenery that they seemed on the point of being absorbed back into the rearing slopes of grass and bushes that rose on either side. From higher up the slope came the plaintive bleat of a lamb, while ahead of them they could hear the raucous cry of gulls. After a while, the rutted earth of the lane gave way to cobbles. Stone cottages appeared on both sides, each with a little tended plot of vegetables beside it. Dark, narrow alleyways twisted away from the main path, leading back up the hillside towards a little church that perched above the hamlet. The larger of the two men looked around him with keen interest in all he saw, while his slighter companion pressed on, as if eager to arrive at their destination.

They turned a corner and saw the sea, a green,

shimmering blanket, spreading to the horizon beneath the low clouds. The wind flowing up the valley brought the fresh salt tang of it. The smaller man came to a halt for a moment, his bag still across his shoulder, as if he had found the place he had been hurrying towards. His companion stood beside him, a puzzled look on his face.

Trevan closed his eyes and breathed in the smell, while the breeze tugged at his pigtail. 'Tell me this ain't as close to paradise as a mortal can come, Able lad,' he said, opening his eyes at last.

Sedgwick looked around him, and became aware that he was being watched from the window of the cottage across the lane. An old bearded man was staring at the new arrivals. He lifted his hat to him, and a curtain was swiftly pulled across.

'Aye, very like,' he said, smiling at his friend's pleasure.

'This one be my house,' said Trevan, indicating a modest, single-storey building of stone walls beneath a roof of thatch. 'I can't wait for you to meet my Molly, and our little Kate.' He went towards the door, but felt a firm hand on his arm.

'I'd like that above all things, Adam, but a man returning to his wife shouldn't have no witnesses,' he said. 'I'll have myself a peek at that little harbour down there first. Then I'll come back.'

'Right you are, Able,' said his companion. 'But don't you be away too long.'

At that moment two young boys came dashing out from one of the alleyways in pursuit of a hoop, with a small girl trailing in their wake. All three of them halted open-mouthed at the sight of Trevan's companion, while their toy bounded on down the lane.

'It be one of them Blackamoors!' exclaimed the larger of the boys.

'Silas Penhaligon, that ain't no way to greet a stranger!' roared Trevan. 'Just you say a proper good morn' to Mr Sedgwick here, afore I box your ears.' The two boys came over reluctantly and shook the sailor's hand, muttering something incomprehensible, before setting off down the street in pursuit of the vanished hoop. The girl was too shy, and instead slid along the cottage wall, bunching her skirts in her little fists, before haring after her brothers.

'Take no notice of them nippers, Able,' urged the Cornishman. 'Folk'll be fine, once they gets used to 'ee.'

'Away off to Molly, now,' said Sedgwick, pushing his friend towards the cottage before setting off down the lane with a cheery wave.

Trevan watched him disappear, and then turned to the low entrance beside him. Every grain and bump in the oak seemed familiar on the old door. It was split in two, like that of a stable, and was studded with iron nails. He paused before knocking, as the memories of a previous return crowded around him. On that occasion the cottage had been cold with grief, his wife up at the church tending a tiny grave. Then he heard the mewing of a baby through the wood, and the gentle sound of a mother singing. He lifted the latch and stepped inside.

The fire was no more than a few glowing embers, but there was enough light from the room's two little windows for him to see Molly, her loose hair a river of copper, as she bent over the crib beside her, gently singing in Cornish. Her eyes lit up at the sight of him, and she rushed across, her excitement tempered with her desire not to wake the baby again.

For a long moment he just held her close, the scent of her hair filling his nose, her warm body pressed close against him.

'You be home, my lover,' she murmured, into his ear. 'I've been awaiting this last month or more, ever since some of the lads from the Channel Fleet started returning.'

'Aye, that I be, Mols,' he replied. 'An' proper home this time, what with the peace an' all.' He felt her grip tighten, and then become loose as she stepped away from his embrace to draw him towards the crib, and the sleeping baby.

'She be as lovely as a spring morn, Molls,' he enthused, 'taking after you, for the most part, of course.'

'She'll be nothing of the sort if you wake her up again,' she scolded. 'Speak soft, lover! You ain't hailing one of them mastheads in a gale, no more!' They both spluttered at this, the need to be quiet making them laugh all the more. Molly led her husband out of the back of the cottage, into the garden, where they could collapse on a bench against the back wall, and let their joy flow.

'Oh, my Adam,' gasped Molly. 'Be you truly back for good this time?'

He drew her close with an arm around her waist. 'I reckon so,' said her husband. 'I come back with Able, that shipmate I told you about. He be as good a man as they come. Proper deep an' all. He ain't got no place to go, being a run slave, so I asked him to come back with me.'

'Be a bit tight in the cottage, lover, what with the babe an' all, but I daresay we'll manage.'

'Don't you go fretting about Able, Mols,' explained Trevan. 'He's got a nice bit of chink laid aside, on account of this book he wrote about being a slave, an' all. Once he finds his feet, he'll get a place of his own. Him an' me, we're going to be partners, an' buy ourselves a Falmouth Lugger. Ain't nothing we don't know about sailing, an' Able, he were a fisher back in Africa, afore he was took.'

'So, where have you left this business partner of yours?' asked Molly.

'He's gone for a walk about the place,' explained Trevan.

'You sent him away for a stroll!' exclaimed Molly. 'What kind of a welcome be that? Half the folk in the village think them from Devon be foreign! What they're going to make of a blooming African, don't bear thinking on! Just you go an' fetch him back, Adam Trevan, while I gets some food prepared.'

*****

Rain again, thought Clay, staring through the small window set in the upholstered door. The shower quickened to a deluge, thundering on the coach's roof, and he felt the horses slow as they shied away from its sudden onslaught. The passing fields and hedgerows blurred into swirling green as water lashed against the glass. The coachman barked angrily, and after a few cracks of his whip the horses sped up once more.

It seemed to have been raining ever since the *Griffin* had rounded the Lizard and come up to Plymouth. It had trickled down from the mass of rigging onto the heads of the crew, as they prepared their ship to be passed across to the dockyard. It had dripped onto his oilskins as he stood by the entry port, shaking the hand of each of his men, as they were paid off to return to their lives ashore. It had thundered down on the deck of the empty frigate, as he had held a last dinner on board with his officers.

That had been a strange meal, he reflected. Had it not been for the absence of the usual pair of eighteen-pounders, he could have imagined that nothing had changed. That beyond his cabin door was the packed, noisy decks of a fully manned warship, instead of the empty, echoing shell that the *Griffin* had become, full of dark shadows and old memories.

The mood around the table had been mixed too. There had been laughter, of course, and the warm companionship that flows from shared battles fought and storms endured. The wine had flowed too, and the conversation with it, but beneath the surface Clay had detected stronger currents running. For some, the peace came with the hope of new opportunities. Like Edward Preston, his face flushed with joy at the prospect of returning to Yorkshire to marry his fiancée. For others peace came with the uncertainty of a life ahead on half pay, stretching away into the future. Most of the younger officers had been little more than children when the war had started. The navy had provided almost all the structure in their lives, from the food on their plates to the clothes they should wear and the duties they must perform. As he had shaken their hands and wished each of them good fortune, he had seen the anxiety in their eyes.

The coach lurched over a rut in the road, throwing him briefly against the padded side, and then steadied once more. The light outside was fading quickly as evening approached, along with the end of his journey. They rattled through a little hamlet of stone cottages. A dog ran alongside for a stretch, barking furiously at the whirling spokes. Two men in smocks and leggings, hooded against the rain, leant on their spades while they watched him pass. Clay stared at both with unseeing eyes, lost in his own thoughts.

Philip K Allan

As a senior post captain, with a generous amount of prize money to his name, half pay should hold no terror for him, even if he had not married well. Yet here he was, with anxiety knotting in the pit of his stomach with each mile he came closer to home. Every moment of my time at sea was full to bursting with the affairs of my ship, he thought. What will I do tomorrow, let alone all the days that follow that? Of course, there were the children. Francis would be over three now, yet he was almost a stranger to his son and his new-born daughter, Elizabeth. And then there was Lydia, beautiful Lydia. He had loved her for years, and yet, thanks to the war, how much time had they actually spent together? He knew the portrait of her from his cabin wall far better than the original.

Then the journey was over. The coach swept up to the front of Rosehill Cottage, and with a final cry from the driver, came to a halt. Clay stepped down from the musty warmth of the interior into the cool dusk. Sometime ago the sun had set, unseen behind the thick cloud, and all around him shadows were lengthening into night. The coach's guard was busy unstrapping his bags and sea chests as he walked towards the house. Rain continued to beat down, splashing up from the flagstones of the path and soaking his shoes and stockings. The door opened as he reached it, and he stepped into the familiar, brightly lit hall.

'Welcome home, sir,' said the maid, dropping a curtesy and taking his hat from him.

'Thank you, Nancy,' he heard himself say. 'Is your mistress home?'

Before she could answer, the drawing-room door was flung open, and there was Lydia. Her hair was a river of glossy night and her eyes sparkled in the candlelight. She ran across the hall and flung herself into his arms, and he wrapped her in folds of wet cloak and warm kisses. With a deep sigh, he felt all the ridiculous doubts that had plagued his journey fade away. Behind his back Nancy was closing the door. Shutting out the rain and, far away beyond a distant shore, the darkening sea.

Epilogue

Jack Broadbent could not quite believe his luck. The trial of the two dozen mutineers who had been apprehended so far had been a brisk, efficient affair. Each man had been brought into a stark room with whitewashed walls and bare floorboards, shuffling in irons between a pair of marines. They had faced a line of stone-faced officers behind a cloth-covered table, as the ghastly details of what had happened aboard the *Peregrine* were read out by the prosecuting officer. After a perfunctory examination of the evidence, each one of them had been questioned and then sentenced to death. Each one, that was, except for him.

Some had taken it badly, weeping and pleading as they were dragged away. Others, like the hulking John Graves, had been defiant, shouting out the justice of what he had done over the drone of the clerk reading out the verdict. Most had accepted their fate calmly, their faces blank, their eyes already far away. But his trial had been different. There had been Clay's testimony, read out by the defending officer. It was a carefully crafted statement, pulling all the best from his time on board the *Griffin*. How he had volunteered to serve, been promoted, settled in well and helped a junior officer in the capture of the *Margaret Harmony*. Then it highlighted his role in the attack on the *Peregrine*, righting the wrong he had helped to do. How he had saved his shipmates from the burning sloop. Finally, it told of how he had been one of the first to board the mighty *Centaure*, and that when he had been accused of the mutiny, he had readily confessed.

The sentences of the others had been agreed in moments by their judges, but his had provoked true debate. He had watched, with a little hope, as Sir George, the court's president, argued forcibly with a red-faced post captain, their exchange one of hissing fury. When all was resolved, he alone had his death penalty commuted to a hundred lashes.

Broadbent had been flogged before. He had witnessed it almost every day on the *Peregrine*, where any offence, imagined or otherwise, was liable to be punished, but he had never been sentenced to more than a dozen. The fiery pain and the dull ache that had spread deep within him was familiar. The seemingly endless nature of the punishment was quite new. After the fiftieth stroke, he had begun to wonder if being hanged might not have been easier. After the sixtieth he had lost count. Shortly after that, he had lost consciousness.

For days afterwards he had lain on his belly in the dockyard hospital, surrounded by the wounded from the fight with the *Centaure*. He had burned with pain, as if gripped by some tropical fever, hovering between life and death. But he was a strong man, in the peak of health, and as the weeks went by, it was life that had won. The ugly, seeping wounds that furrowed his back had become rose-coloured scars, and the agony had lessened to a constant throb.

He could feel it now, as he walked gingerly along a dusty road, keeping to the side shaded by a stand of banana plants. He had set off soon after dawn, shaking the hand of the young surgeon who had treated him and collecting his belongings from the prison guard. It was a scant nine miles across the island to his destination, but already he was regretting his decision to walk. He was surprised by how weak he still felt, and how heavy the bag on his shoulder seemed. The tropical sun beat down on him, making the road ahead shimmer and dance. He pulled his wide-brimmed hat low over his lean, hawk-nosed face, hauled his dunnage sack a little higher on his shoulder, and gritted his teeth against the pain.

A cane field opened up beside him, the green spears of a new crop bursting up through the crumbling earth. A line of slaves, wearing only ragged britches, worked with hoes, scraping around each plant and pausing occasionally to bend down and pull up a weed. Off to one side, the overseer sat on his horse, in the shade of a sandbox tree, his long whip coiled over the pummel of the saddle. A few of the slaves glanced towards the sailor, and one watched his uneasy gait for a moment before nodding in sympathy. When he returned to his work, Broadbent noticed that he too bore the savage scars of a recent flogging, crisscrossing his back and shoulders.

The clop of hooves and the jingle of harness warned him that a horse and trap was approaching from behind. He moved onto the verge to let it rattle past, but it pulled to a halt beside him. The driver was a pleasant-looking young man, in an open shirt and waistcoat.

'You look weary, sailor,' he said. 'Where are you heading?'

'St Johns, sir,' said Broadbent. 'I heard there be a few ships as may be after crews lying in the port.'

'Aye, so there are,' replied the man. 'And I daresay there will be a few of you man-of-war's men looking for an honest trade now. Throw your dunnage in the back, and climb up. I can take you as far as Potters Buff 'Tis just a short step beyond there.'

Broadbent struggled a little reaching the bench behind the horse, and the driver leant across to pull him up. 'You seem a little frail to be returning to the sea so soon,' he commented, once the trap was moving again. 'Were you wounded in the war?'

'Aye, in a manner of speaking, sir,' said Broadbent.

Larcum Mudge

'I don't suppose you were involved in the capture of that huge French vessel?'

'The *Centaure*? That I was, sir,' said the sailor. 'I boarded her from the *Griffin*.'

'Did you, by Jove!' exclaimed his companion. 'And I daresay your wounds came from that handsome victory. Then I shall take you directly to the quayside in St Johns. My aunt can wait for me a little longer.' He snapped the reins against his horse's back, and the trap gathered speed.

After a while the young man turned towards his passenger again. 'Might I know your name?' he asked.

Broadbent considered for a moment before replying. 'Mudge, sir,' he said. 'Larcum Mudge.'

'Larcum Mudge?' queried the driver. 'What manner of name is that?'

'A right good one, I think you'll find, sir.'

The End

Note from the author

Historical fiction blends the truth with the made-up, and *Larcum Mudge* is no exception. These notes are for the benefit of readers who would like to understand where the boundary lies between the two. The only historical character in this novel is Earl St Vincent, who was First Lord of the Admiralty between 1801 and 1804. He brought to the position a zeal for reform not unlike that displayed by Jesus on entering the Temple. All of the ships mentioned in *Larcum Mudge* are fictitious, as are the characters who crew them. As in my previous works, I have done my best to ensure that my descriptions of those ships and the lives of their crews are as accurate as I am able to make them. Any errors I have made are my own.

The mutiny on board the *Peregrine* is fictitious, although students of naval history will notice parallels with the rising that took place on board the frigate *Hermione* against the brutal Captain Pigot in September 1797. That too occurred in the Caribbean, with the crew gathering on the forecastle at night and fortifying their courage with stolen rum. Captain Pigot was hacked down in his cabin, and then tossed over the side while still alive. The slaughter then continued long into that hot night. Just as in the *Peregrine*, it included almost all the officers, the teenage midshipmen, and even Lieutenant McIntosh of the marines, who was dragged from his sickbed despite being in the final stages of Yellow Fever.

The *Hermione* mutineers sold their ship to the Spanish government, in return for twenty-five dollars per man. Once this was done, they swore to change their names, disperse to the four corners of the earth, and never speak of the mutiny again. They were no more successful at this than the crew of the *Peregrine*. Over the following years, one by one, they were brought to justice by the long arm of the Royal Navy. As for the *Hermione*, she was recaptured two years later in a daring attack made by the frigate *Surprise*. It was determined that her name was too stained to be reused. Fittingly, given the fate of the mutineers, she became the *Retribution*.

One of the bolder *Hermione* mutineers, David Forrester, managed to evade capture for nearly five years by hiding in plain sight. He coolly volunteered for the Royal Navy again and served as a bargeman for the captain of the *Bittern*, and there he might have remained had he not been recognised while walking down a Portsmouth street. His story provided me with the kernel of an idea that became the inspiration behind this novel.

The fight with the *Centaure* also has at its root in a historical incident - the defeat and capture of the French eighty-gun ship *Guillaume Tell*. One of the few survivors from the French Mediterranean fleet destroyed by Nelson at the Battle of the Nile, she found herself in a very similar predicament to that in which I placed the *Centaure*. In 1800 the *Guillaume Tell* attempted to escape from the siege of Malta. She was spotted by the blockading British fleet and found herself being pursued by the Royal Navy frigate *Penelope*, backed by two ships of the line. She could outrun the bigger British ships, but not the frigate; and she could outfight the *Penelope*, but only at the cost of permitting the supporting ships to catch her. She chose flight, a strategy that might have worked, since she was a swift ship. Her misfortune was that the *Penelope* was commanded by Henry Blackwood, a shrewd Ulsterman whom Nelson considered one of the ablest captains in the service. After hours of manoeuvre and raking fire, the *Penelope* succeeded in damaging the *Guillaume Tell* sufficiently aloft to slow her to a point that the other two ships could arrive. After long and heroic resistance, the French ship was finally captured.

The Peace of Amiens was signed at the beginning of 1802, but in reality it was no more than a truce in the two decades of struggle between Britain and France. None of the substantive issues between the two powers were resolved, and the fourteen months of breathing space it supplied was probably of most benefit to Napoleon, who was able to fully consolidate himself in power. The two nations resumed hostilities in May 1803.

Writing novels set in the eighteenth century, I am always on the lookout for a good, contemporary name. I found Larcum Mudge inscribed on the wall of the parish church in the delightful village of East Bergholt, Suffolk. The Reverend Mudge was vicar of that parish at the end of the eighteenth century. It appealed to me both in its own right, and because it reminded me of two pioneers of the early Marine Chronometer, Thomas Mudge and Larcum Kendall. I have no evidence of any association between these three upstanding gentlemen and any naval mutinies, brutal or otherwise.

Other books in the Alexander Clay series

The Captain's Nephew

A Sloop of War

On the Lee Shore

A Man of No Country

The Distant Ocean

The Turn of the Tide

In Northern Seas

About the Author

I was a born in Watford in the United Kingdom. I still live in Hertfordshire with my wife, my two teenage daughters, two cats and a chicken. For most of my working life I was a senior manager in the motor industry, but my real passion was always for history and literature. I wrote my first book while I was on a career break between car manufacturers, really just to see if I could. When I went back to work, I sent my manuscript out to a number of literary agents, fully expecting it to be rejected. But it wasn't, and in 2016 my family and I took the decision to give up the certainties of a well-paid job so that I could write fulltime. Four years and eight published works later we are a bit poorer, but very much happier.

My books are set in the 18th century Royal Navy. I could have set them in any one of a number of periods or places, but that was the genre that interested me most. I grew up enjoying the books of C.S. Forester and in particular Patrick O'Brian. They awoke in me a life-long passion for the age of sail. I went on to study the 18th century navy as part of my history degree at London University. When I left, I remained a member of the Society for Nautical Research and also a keen sailor. The 18th century is a period with unrivalled potential for a writer, stretching from the age of piracy, via the voyages of Cook to the battles and campaigns of Nelson. The period also works well from a creative point of view. On the one hand there is the strange, claustrophobic wooden world of the period's ships; and on the other hand, there is the boundless freedom to move them around the globe wherever the narrative takes them.

The eight books I have published so far form a series that follow the adventures of a group of characters, both officers and sailors. They all serve with my main protagonist, Alexander Clay. Each book can be read as a standalone work, as it contains its own complete story; or the series can be read in order to appreciate the progression of the characters. I try and use period language and authentic nautical detail to draw the reader into a different world, although I aim to pitch this at a level where a reader with no knowledge of either will still enjoy my work.

If you want to find out more about me or my books, the links below may be helpful

Website: www.philipkallan.com

Facebook & Twitter: @philipkallan

Instagram: @philipkallanauthor